THE BYRNE BROTHERS

CRAVING
Chaos

Edits by: Editing4Indies
Cover photographer: Daniel Jaems
Cover Model: Chad Hurst

❀ Created with Vellum

Books by Jill Ramsower

The Byrne Brothers Series
Silent Vows
Secret Sin (Novella)
Corrupted Union
Ruthless Salvation
Vicious Seduction
Craving Chaos

The Moretti Men Series
Devil's Thirst

The Five Families Series
Forever Lies
Never Truth
Blood Always
Where Loyalties Lie
Impossible Odds
Absolute Silence
Perfect Enemies

The Savage Pride Duet
Savage Pride
Silent Prejudice

The Of Myth & Man Series
Curse & Craving
Venom & Vice
Blood & Breath
Siege & Seduction

PRONUNCIATION GUIDE

I've made this guide for those who are interested. Keep in mind that I'm not an expert in phonetic spellings and did the best I could.

Amelie— "AH-mel-ee"
Conner Reid— "Cah-nur Reed"
Ettore— "Et-TOH-re"
Fausto— "FOW-stoh"
Gino Revello— "GEE-no Rev-EHL-oh"
Henri Bouchard— "On-REE Boo-SHAR"
Lina— "LEE-nuh"
Mari— "MAR-ee"
Nana Byrne— "NAA-nuh Burn"
Noemi— "Noh-EM-ee"
Oran— "OR-uhn"
Renzo Donati— "REHN-zho Doh-NAH-tee"
Sante Mancini— "SAAN-tay Man-SEE-nee"
Shae Byrne— "Shay Burn"
Tomasso— "Toh-MAA-soh"

Other words

Gandon— (Russian) "ghan-dohn"

L'Ascension— (French) "lah-sen-see-ohn"

Rivière-Rouge— (French) "riv-ee-EHR rhoo-sh"

To all my incredible readers who insisted Shae Byrne get a story of her own, you inspired an adventure as epic as Shae herself. I hope you enjoy every salacious second of it!

CRAVING CHAOS

JILL RAMSOWER

1

Shae

As far as I'm concerned, a ponytail might as well be a leash. People tend to think my short hair is some sort of edgy statement. I love fashion as much as the next girl, but my cut and style are all about strategy. I'm already at a size disadvantage to most anyone who would want to hurt me. Why make it any easier for them?

Judging by the number of young women with long hair, it's clear that not everyone makes their fashion choices anticipating a fight. To each her own. With two older brothers and a family in organized crime, I put more thought into whether a blouse will prevent me from getting out of a headlock than how my cleavage looks.

That's who I am. I wouldn't know how to be anyone different.

In that vein, I've chosen to wear stilettos to my meeting at the docks with the Donatis. Or should I call them the Morettis? I'm never sure with the Italians. Their organization is the Moretti family, but none of them are actually Morettis. At the moment, the Donati family is sitting in leadership.

It makes no sense.

My family business, on the other hand, is exactly that. Blood. My father was one of the three original Byrne brothers who built the business from the ground up. They ensured our name was synonymous with respect, not confusion. Granted, the Italians have numbers on their side, but I'd rather be a Byrne any day of the week and twice on Sundays.

I never gave much thought in the past to the Italians aside from what sort of threat they posed. We've somewhat recently become allies with the Moretti family. In our line of work, *allies* is an amorphous concept. We do business together, but I don't trust them for a second. Showing up to a meeting armed to the teeth, however, might look disrespectful. Therefore, I have to be creative in my weapon selection.

Cue the stilettos.

Guys love to see a woman in heels—all they see is sex. Fine by me. I can do as much damage with a five-inch Jimmy Choo as I can a knife.

See, fashion is all kinds of fun.

Aside from helping me arm myself, fashion is also a useful tool to disguise and mislead. A woman who puts energy into her appearance is often overlooked as nothing more than eye candy. I've worked my ass off to be seen as an equal by the men in my family, but I've found a strategic advantage in allowing a rival to underestimate me.

By the way Renzo Donati's two men are eyeing me with salacious smirks, I know I've hit my mark.

"Shae Byrne," I say by way of introduction. "We're here with a truck to pick up our crates." Crates full of guns. *Lots* of guns.

My cousin Oran had teamed up with the Donatis to take down a powerful man involved in sex trafficking. A part of the intricate plan involved moving a shipment of our guns through the ports controlled by the Moretti Mafia organization. Now that the operation is over, it's time to get our guns back.

A lanky man with hair pulled back in a bun pats the crate beneath him. "Everything's here, but the forklift isn't cooperating. Doubt you want to move all of it by hand."

A machine with more rust than paint sits motionless behind him. Ten crates of guns weighing hundreds of pounds apiece. Guns are a fuck-ton heavier than one might think. That is *not* what I wanted to do with my Friday night.

I look back at my three guys. "Any of you good with machines?"

"Won't do you any good." Renzo Donati appears from beneath the forklift, wiping his hands on a rag as he gets to his feet. "Looks like the fuel regulator is out. Closest working forklift is two piers over, which will take an hour to transport over at the pace these things travel."

If I have learned anything in the past ten years of working in a predominantly male-run industry, it's that men are masters at talking out of their asses. They will assert all kinds of shit as though it's gospel even though there isn't a shred of truth behind it, as if it's better to take a stab in the dark than admit to uncertainty.

Heaven forbid they not know something.

I look back at my guys again, eyebrows raised expectantly.

Sammy lifts his chin. "I can take a look." He rolls up his sleeves and walks to the forklift, ignoring Donati, who narrows his gaze at me.

"You don't trust my judgment?"

"Never hurts to get a second opinion. It's nothing personal." As if a man like Donati can have his opinion questioned and not take it as a personal affront. Unfortunately, I'm not one to tiptoe around a man's fragile ego. "The crates have been sitting here for a month. I'd rather not delay if we don't have to."

Donati prowls toward me, slow as a cat preparing to pounce. He's tall. I'm five-four and wearing five-inch heels, and he's still several inches taller than me. Where my blue eyes are mottled with flecks of gold, his are a pristine blue—crisp and clear as a sunny winter sky. He clearly knows how to use them to his advantage, staring menacingly in a way that might make a normal person need to fidget.

I meet every ounce of his stare head-on and smirk.

You want to play, big guy? Game on.

He doesn't take his eyes off mine except for the briefest glance down at his phone when he places a call, stopping a mere two feet away from me. "Conner, hey. The forklift is acting up. I'd say we could load it up by hand, but your little cousin is here, and she's not exactly dressed for hard labor."

My fingers clench in a fist.

How dare he call my cousin as though I'm not standing right here. And on top of that, he assumes I'm afraid to get dirty like some sort of pretty princess. What I wouldn't give to land him on his pompous ass.

His stare licks down my body, and I debate how much

4

trouble I'd be in if I swept his feet out from under him. Imagining the cracking sound of his back slamming on the concrete teases a twitch from the corner of my lips, but every ounce of my glare spears him with violence. His blue gaze glints with a spark of victory, leading me to believe my reaction is exactly what he was hoping for. He placed the call intentionally to get under my skin.

He clearly has no idea who he's dealing with.

"Yeah, later this week works," he continues. "Should have the damn thing up and running by then … appreciate your understanding. Later."

He ends the call, smugness radiating off every muscular inch of him.

I resist the urge to cross my arms or show any other sign of irritation. "I'm surprised you took the time to handle this matter personally. Figured now that you're running things, you'd have more important matters to deal with, but not everyone adjusts well to leadership." I take a tiny step forward. A challenge.

My blood sings with anticipation and the call to battle.

I refuse to back down from a man like Donati, who slathers on self-importance to hide latent insecurities like cheap foundation over a raging case of acne. That's what happens when Daddy hands you the role of boss without ever making you earn anything. I've scraped and clawed my way to where I am. It builds character. The process also gave me the opportunity to study the men who hold power in the world around me. Disappointing is a massive understatement. And I've had plenty of subjects to analyze since organized crime has been slow to progress out of the Dark Ages where women's rights are concerned.

Renzo shoots me an arctic glare. "You know an awful lot about leadership for someone who's never run anything in her life." He mirrors my step forward, our feet now inches apart.

"At least I've earned where I'm at."

His hand lifts like he's going to touch me, but I never give him the chance. I grab that hand and spin myself under our joined arms until his is bent back behind him. Then I wrap my other arm around his neck until he's in a headlock. The move takes maybe three seconds. Max.

Two seconds in, his guys pull out their guns, leading mine to do the same.

"*Enough,*" Renzo roars hoarsely through my hold on him.

I release him, not wanting to start a bloodbath. He's clearly furious. I expect him to whirl around and unleash his anger on me, but he shocks me by charging toward his men instead.

"Put that *fucking* thing away, and if you ever threaten her again, I'll kill you myself."

The shocked silence after his savage reprimand is deafening.

I give my guys a nod to signal they should put their guns away.

"What they say is true." Renzo turns back to me. "You can hold your own in a fight." His tone shifts so dramatically that he doesn't even sound like the same man. His acidic bark from seconds earlier is now a velvet caress when addressing me. I'm instantly wary.

"I can do a hell of a lot more than hold my own."

"That may be true, but what you can't do is make that hunk of metal work."

We both glance at Sammy standing next to the forklift after jumping to his feet when things got heated. He wipes his hands on the same rag Donati used and cuts his chin to the side. "It's the regulator, like he said."

Hell, I'm gonna have to kick his ass later for not keeping that last tidbit to himself. I don't need him undermining my efforts.

"There you go," Renzo says, palms up in front of him. "Nothing to be done about the matter for now."

I grimace. "Next time, make sure your shit's in order so you don't waste everyone's time." I sound bratty, but it's all I have left. I spin and motion for my guys to follow me out.

His voice drifts behind me, rumbling low like distant thunder. "Not a waste from where I'm standing."

I can't stop from glancing back at him as I continue forward.

He's watching me, and in the time it takes for the wings of a butterfly to flap a single beat, his baby blue stare pierces every layer of armor I have until I feel him knocking on the door to my soul. The intrusion is so sudden and unexpected that it robs me of oxygen. My lungs seize painfully, prompting me to look away and sever the connection.

What the ever-loving hell was that?

Trouble. That's what.

And not the fun kind of trouble.

Renzo Donati is the saucy tattoo you get at eighteen, then spend the rest of your life regretting. No, thank you. As mad as I was a few minutes ago, I'm glad he reached out to Conner. Let the two of them sort out the guns. I wanted no part of it or the man whose stare chases me from the building.

2

Kenzo

RUMORS RUN RAMPANT IN OUR SMALL CIRCLES OF FAMILY AND associates. Who needs social media when the Italian gossip mill can blaze from house to house faster than a California wildfire? I'd heard plenty of stories involving Shae Byrne—our cousins are married to one another—but our paths hadn't crossed until now. Not in such a direct manner. Seeing her at a distance is an entirely different experience than being the sole focus of her charismatic confidence.

I can see why she's developed a reputation. I try not to let whispers color my judgment, but in this case, Shae was everything promised and more. The way she goaded me—few would be so brazen. I would have said it was reckless had she not been able to back up her words with actions, but

8

she can and did. She moved so damn fast that I barely had time to react.

It was beautiful, if I'm honest.

The phrase poetry in motion comes to mind as I watch her leave the warehouse, her athletic frame moving lithely with each confident stride toward the exit. I can't seem to tear my gaze away until the door closes behind her.

I rub my face, probably getting grease all over me, but not caring. I need to shake off whatever spell she cast and get my head on straight. I have too many responsibilities weighing on me to allow in distractions.

I turn to my guys. "I understand you wanted to protect me, and I appreciate that, but no one is to lay a finger on her. Understood?" I demand in a calm but firm tone. I'm not going to explain my outburst any further. It's none of their damn business, and to explain, I'd have to figure it out for myself first. That's not happening. It could only lead to no good.

I meet each man's stare before letting the subject drop. "Let me know as soon as this damn thing is operational." I scowl at the forklift, then head for the back exit where I parked.

Shae wasn't wrong when she pointed out that this meeting today wasn't exactly worthy of my time, but our alliance with the Irish is relatively new, and it was my fault we hadn't returned their guns to them weeks ago. I thought it would be a show of goodwill to handle the matter personally. And I can admit that knowing Shae would be here impacted my decision. I was curious, and rightfully so. Shae Byrne is rather fascinating.

When I get to my car, I check my phone and see a text message from my mom.

Mom: I need to talk to you.

I sigh heavily. It's been one hell of a month taking over the business and dealing with my father's death. Mom has struggled. I feel responsible to help her through, but so many other matters also demand my attention.

Months before Dad died, his own brother-in-law, my uncle Fausto, tried to overthrow him. It seems he'd had his sights set on being boss for years, his fury going back years to when I'd taken over as underboss. I can't say how many others might have the same resentment about a twenty-eight-year-old not only rising to underboss but now boss of the entire Moretti family. The possibilities worry me. If I don't prove myself quickly, I could be facing a violent overthrow and never see it coming.

Our loyalty as a family is unquestionable when it comes to outsiders, but squabbles within the organization are endless. That's how it is with family.

Before Dad died, we'd been discussing a strategic marriage to Ariana de Bellis, daughter of the Giordano family boss. Uniting our families, especially now that the Gallo and Lucciano families have allied, would have been helpful. Christiano de Bellis ended up with a bullet between the eyes before we could solidify anything. The family has a new boss, so I've scratched that plan.

If given time, I'm confident my leadership skills would prove themselves worthy, but time is a luxury I can't afford. I need to find a way to prove myself and soon, especially to the older generation. My ongoing worries about my standing is the reason Shae's goading actually got to me. That sort of petty ploy would normally have rolled right off my shoulders. She managed to stab right where I was most sensitive, and I don't think it was luck. Her ability to read a situation is impressive. That more than anything is why I wasn't truly mad at her. I'm just glad I was able to jab back with equal accuracy.

Shae Byrne would be sitting at the helm of her organization if her cousins would allow it.

Maybe she's content with her current standing. I'd guess she had to work a hell of a lot harder to get there than her cousins did. I respect that. Despite what she and others might think, I've had to face continuous scrutiny to get where I am. It might have been harder for someone else to rise to the top, but that doesn't mean my journey has been easy. There's no such thing as childhood when your father is grooming you for a place at the top.

I grew up in a 1980s mansion that doesn't look much different today as it did then. When I pull up to the house, I feel at home and out of place at the same time. The house is so damn ostentatious. Dad was a big believer in appearances. I think a degree of subtlety can be even more effective in conveying a message. After all, can you actually be all that powerful if you have to tell everyone how powerful you are?

Regardless, Dad loved the place, and I doubt Mom will ever leave it now that he's gone. So many of her best memories took place within those pale salmon-colored walls.

"Hey, Ma. Where are you?" I let myself in and drape my jacket over the back of a chair in the entry.

"In the kitchen." Her voice echoes through the empty rooms. There's furniture and decor and knickknacks, but no real life. My younger brother and cousin technically live with her, but they're rarely home. It's just her in the giant place. I find it depressing.

"Making yourself some dinner?" I smile and place a kiss on her cheek.

"Yeah, you want some? The tuna salad is fresh."

"Nah, it's still early for me."

"You sure? I know how you love this stuff."

"Ma, what's up? You texted that you needed to talk, remember?"

Her eyes flit briefly to mine. Whatever she has to say, she's nervous to say it.

"Don't get upset."

My eyelids drift shut as I blow a deep stream of air through my nose. "Jesus, what did he do now?" I should have known when I saw the tuna salad. She was trying to put me in a good mood.

"Nothing all that awful. You got yourself into a mess here and there, too, don't forget."

I glare at her to continue.

"He's at the station. Got caught joy riding a stolen car," she spits out quickly.

"Fuck, now I have to go down there and smooth things over." We have plenty of contact. I should be able to get the charges dropped, but it's a pain in my ass. I don't have time for this bullshit.

"You know how hard it's been for Sante. We have to be a little understanding. Taking in your cousin didn't just involve giving him food and a bed."

"Don't you think I know that?" When I offered to be his guardian after he was orphaned months ago, I had thought my dad would be around longer so that I wouldn't be parenting a troubled teen while taking over an entire Mafia family. The past month has been fucking brutal.

How do you think it's been for him?

His father killed his mother then tried to overthrow Dad and was killed in an ugly standoff right in front of Sante. And here I am bitching about the inconvenience when I've hardly been around to guide the kid.

"Yeah, okay. I'll go get him out of lockup and talk to him."

Mom's face pinches with worry. "There's one more thing."

Of course, there is. "What is it?"

"He had Tommaso with him," she admits softly.

Just when I was starting to feel bad for the kid. My frustration forms angry knots in my neck and shoulders. I stretch my head from one side to the other.

"This isn't going to end well if he doesn't get his head on right."

"I know, but I hate to give up on him too quickly."

"I'm not giving up on anyone, but it's been six months. Something's gonna have to change."

My younger brother Tommaso is two years older than Sante, but he's not a typical nineteen-year-old. He's crazy smart and impossibly dense at the same time. I don't understand him. Most people don't, which means he hasn't made many friends. When Sante came into the fold, he and Tommaso clicked. They're complete opposites, so I don't get it, but the two are practically inseparable now. That adds another layer of complication to dealing with Sante's behavioral problems. I have to decide whether sending Sante away is better or worse for Tommaso. Fuck if I know.

"I know," Ma says sadly.

I give her another quick kiss. "Don't worry. We'll get it all sorted. I'm going to go get them released."

"Thank you, Renz. If your dad were here…" She trails off. It guts me to see her hurting.

"I really don't mind, Ma. Everything's gonna be fine." I give her the most reassuring smile I can summon before heading to the police station.

🔥

"You are so goddamn lucky it was the 13th precinct that picked you up. Anyone else would have slapped you with a DWI on top of the rest." By the time the three of us get in my car, I'm so pissed I can hardly see straight. Sante fucking reeks of alcohol. Tommaso has shut down and won't say a word. I'm ready to ship both off to fucking boot camp.

"They're not gonna do anything. Those assholes know who we are," Sante mutters from the passenger seat.

"What you don't seem to understand is we don't have an infinite number of get-out-of-jail-free cards," I snap at him. "If we use up our favors on piddly shit like joyriding, we may not have any goodwill left to help when something bigger goes down. It's a give and take. We don't fucking own the entire force."

He looks out the side window and says nothing. Good. I've reached my limit for bullshit.

I drive them back to Ma's house. Even though I'm technically Sante's guardian, he lives with her and Tommaso. I thought it might give him the feel of a more structured home life. At this point, I'm not sure things like that matter. He's got too much shit going on in his head for that to make a difference. I've even tried to send the kid to counseling. He refuses to talk. There's no helping some people. I'm hoping that's not the case with him.

I haven't given up on my young cousin yet, but I've definitely had enough for one day. I park at the curb in front of the house and wait for the boys to get out. As they do, two men exit from the car in front of me, one on either side. They close their doors and stare back at us with scowls on their faces. I don't know them personally, but I'd bet good money they're Russian.

Fuck me, what now?

I turn off the car, discreetly slide my gun back in its holster, and get out. Both boys amble over to stand with me.

"Is there a problem?" I ask, my voice devoid of emotion.

"There is. Seems your Italian brats like to take other people's property."

"That so? You got proof?" I back my blood. Always will. But in my head, I'm strangling the two shitheads standing at my sides.

"Watched the cops take 'em out of Biba's yellow lambo."

Fucking Christ. I never thought to ask about the car. I figured they'd nabbed something random off the street. But no, these two idiots had to target the head of the Russian mob. I can't imagine it's a coincidence, and Biba won't see it that way either. He'll want recompense.

"I don't suppose Biba will be satisfied knowing we'll be doling out our own punishment for their recklessness."

The one who's done the talking slowly turns his head side to side.

Looks like the boys are going to have to learn their lesson the hard way. "Fair enough. Fists only. Three strikes. This is the one who owes you." I nod to Sante. "The other only followed."

"I didn't have to get in that car," Tommaso says flatly.

It takes everything I have not to grimace and scream at him. I'm trying to do him a fucking favor and protect him, but he doesn't get it. He never does.

I give a nod and look over at Sante who rolls his eyes.

"Whatever. It's not like I haven't taken a punch before." He swaggers over with liquid courage still coursing through his veins. Dumbass has no clue that these guys aren't some drunken college punks at a bar. His hands outstretch to the sides. "Do your worst."

The one who's done all the talking pulls his hand from his jacket pocket and I see a flash of gold as his fist barrels into Sante's ribs. Fuck, he's used brass knuckles.

My gun is in my hand and trained on the asshole before I can blink. This is so fucking stupid. We're going to end up starting a war, but I have to do something. Sante will have broken ribs if he's lucky, a ruptured spleen if he's not.

"I said fists only," I growl at them.

He smirks and raises his hands innocently. "It *is* my fist."

"You know damn well brass is a weapon. Sante, you're done. Get back here."

He stumbles back to me, still bent at the waist and wheezing.

"Tommaso, your turn, since you're so keen to get one." This time, I address the Russians. "One hit, no brass, and we're done here, or I play target practice, and I don't give a fuck who I piss off."

The guy shrugs and steps back. Tommaso crosses to the other man, who has remained silent. Both stand and stare stoically at one another.

"Make better choices, *gandon*." He seems totally unbothered, but when his fist collides with my brother's face, it's a savage blow as though he'd been saving up a week's worth of frustration to vent into that one strike.

Tommaso whips around, blood spurting from his mouth, but he doesn't go down. He spits, shakes his head, then slowly stands tall. He gives the man a single look as if to say we're done here, then walks away. He doesn't walk to me or wait for us to be done. He goes to the house and disappears inside as though heading in for dinner rather than escaping the grim reaper. I will never understand him.

"Give Biba my apologies. It won't happen again." I glower

at his thugs, then escort my pissant cousin to the house. I acknowledge as I do that tonight was the last straw. If I don't do something drastic, one or both of them is going to end up dead.

3

Shae

"HEY, COME ON IN." I GIVE MARI A KISS AND LET HER IN, making sure not to touch anything with my right hand because it's covered in egg. I'm cooking chicken piccata, a personal favorite, which I needed after the day I had.

I'm not working at the club tonight, so I decided to invite her over. Mari and I are friends with benefits—that's the best way to describe it. We started hanging out six months ago. She's sweet, and I enjoy being around her, but I don't see any sort of actual relationship in our future. I work nights; she works days. That alone drastically limits the time we can spend together. Between that and needing to keep my work life private, it's easier to keep things simple, which I've been up front about from the beginning.

"How was your day?" she asks, setting down her things and joining me in the kitchen.

"It was a day. I'm glad it's almost over."

"That good, huh?"

"I guess it wasn't all bad. Just a pain dealing with people. At least when you deal with people, they're all smiles and happy for you to order them around." I shoot her a smirk. Mari's a photographer—that's how we met. She was out in the park for a photo shoot while I was on a run. She was too pretty to pass up. With her dark hair and angular features, she could be in front of a camera rather than behind it. But that's not her style.

"Right, and no one is ever fussy when they see the final shots from a shoot. Nope. Always perfectly satisfied." Her brightly sang words are soaking in sarcasm.

"Alright, so you might know a little something about dealing with annoying people," I admit with a wink.

"I took a couple up to my spot for an engagement shoot at sunset a few days ago. They hated it. Had to reschedule the whole thing. I think they're going to end up doing a studio shoot. Can you imagine?" She stares incredulously.

"They didn't like the rooftop?" I know exactly what spot she's talking about. She's taken me up there a couple of times, and I have to agree that it's pretty amazing. Gorgeous views of the river at sunset. I had a little trouble enjoying it, however, because it's awfully romantic. Sometimes I get the sense Mari wants more. She hasn't ever pushed the matter, so I could be wrong. I think more than anything, I project my own concerns about stringing her along. She seems totally content with our sporadic interludes.

"They said the place was dirty and old." She rolls her eyes. "Some people have no vision."

"Gotta trust the professional." I wink at her, then take the last cutlet out of the browning pan and place it on a tray and into the oven. "Dinner will be ready in about fifteen."

"It already smells delish. Anything I can do to help?"

"Don't think so—" I'm washing my hands when my phone rings. It's my cousin Conner. "I have to take this, sorry." I give her a thin smile and lift the phone to my ear. "Hey, what's up?"

"Just checking to see if everything seemed okay today from your end."

"Yeah, looks like it's all there, and I think the delay was legit. That had to be the oldest forklift I've ever seen. Not that I see a ton of them, but still."

"Good. Renzo said he'd let me know when we can come by next week to try again."

"It's all you, cuz. He and I didn't exactly hit it off."

Conner sighs. "Why is it you get on with people I'd rather you didn't and piss off important allies?"

A voice I know well hollers in the background. "Is that my Shae? Got good instincts, that one. You'd do well to follow her lead." It's our grandmother Nana Byrne, my favorite person in our whole family.

"That's right, Conner. You should listen to the woman. She's very wise." I'm grinning because I can already hear him grumbling on the other end of the phone.

"She's something, alright. Told me I had to come out to help with a pest problem. I'm thinking ants or mice, and she tells me to get Paddy out of the house 'cause she's sick of his snoring."

I burst out laughing because that is so Nana.

"Yeah, laugh it up," Conner mutters.

"That's what you get for not being on my side. That guy intentionally pushed my buttons, and I'm not going to let that shit slide. You wouldn't either."

"Whatever, Shae." His exasperation entertains me way more than it should. "I guess I'll handle it from here."

I grin. "Works for me. Give Nana a hug for me."

My cousin only grunts before hanging up.

"That your family?" Mari asks.

"Yeah, one of my cousins."

Mari doesn't know anything about the nature of our family business or the life I lead. I'm particularly careful about what I say when she's around. She thinks I'm a self-defense instructor, and in a way, I am. I help out sometimes at the gym where I train.

I'm tidying up my mess on the counter when Mari hugs me from behind. We're the same height, so her chin rests easily on my shoulder. We sway for a second before she stills and sniffs my neck.

"Is that … cologne?"

Some of Donati's cologne or aftershave rubbed off on me when I put him in that headlock. The scent is fucking incredible, which drove me crazy after we left, and I couldn't escape him. My senses must have adjusted. I don't smell it anymore and forgot all about it.

I shrug. "You know my work involves a lot of physical contact."

"Yeah," she gives me a thin smile. "It just surprised me, that's all."

Her gaze drops to the pendant necklace I wear every day. She doesn't know anything about it, which makes me wonder why she's staring at it now after asking me about cologne. It seems odd, but then again, I could be paranoid. My job lends me to that sort of thinking.

"Well, today was a little unusual, too. That's why Conner called me. He heard that I got a little overzealous today and upset a student when I put him in a headlock. Conner wants to make sure the guy isn't going to sue me." The lies roll off my tongue with such ease that sometimes I scare myself.

"You put a student in a headlock?" She gapes at me.

"He 'accidentally' grazed my tits one too many times. Needed a lesson."

"You're a little crazy, you know that?" She bites her lower lip and peers up at me through a forest of long black lashes. I pull her body against mine and appreciate the way she softens against me.

"I wish I knew how to be a badass like you," she whispers.

No, she doesn't.

Mari is flowy dresses and daisies and picnics under sunny skies. She isn't remotely the type of person who could handle treading the same path as me. We are so incredibly different. And when I think about it too closely, I know that we're too different. That more than anything may be why I've never considered a real relationship with her.

I pull away and smile. "Don't worry. I'll be badass enough for us both."

We have a nice dinner together. I always enjoy spending time with her, but I can't seem to focus on our conversation. My mind is elsewhere, more specifically, imagining endless alternative scenarios of how my afternoon at the docks could have gone down. I can't seem to escape those searing blue eyes.

As the evening draws on, I admit defeat and claim a headache. I tell myself I just need a little time alone when that is the last thing I need because I know all I'm going to do is think of *him*.

I send Mari home. I can tell she's a little disappointed. I am, too. I had hoped having her over would be a perfect distraction. Now I'm starting to wonder if anything but time will effectively drown out thoughts of Renzo Donati. God help me.

♦

"You hear that Oran's engaged?" Conner leans against the welcome desk, where I spend most nights managing security at the Bastion social club. At nine in the evening, our night is only getting started.

"For real this time?" I ask teasingly, knowing he and Lina have resolved their drama.

"For real. Sounds like the wedding will be soon."

"That doesn't surprise me," I mutter. "You people keep getting married, and I'm never going to have a free weekend."

"Maybe you'll be next," he jabs.

"Nope. Not happening. I don't care how fast you Byrne men fall. I'm not like that."

The smug glint in his eyes makes the leather corset top I wore suddenly feel suffocatingly oppressive. "I'm not saying it would be a bad thing to settle down. I just don't see how it would happen when I've never met anyone I've remotely entertained wanting to keep around forever."

"Interesting," he muses. "I had an entirely different take on the situation."

My hand lifts to my necklace without my permission. "What situation?" Playing dumb is always a great defense.

Conner smirks. "It wasn't but a handful of months ago. I doubt you've forgotten."

I shrug. "Considering you know nothing about said *situation*, that's quite an assumption to make." I try to keep my voice light. I don't want him to sense that he's unbalanced me.

It was one week, and I never told anyone. How could he possibly suspect anything, let alone something serious?

"Absolutely." He raises his hands in surrender. "I could have completely misinterpreted things."

I hold my phone out like a reporter, eyes wide as she gets the story of her career. "Can you repeat that, sir, for the record?" I can count the number of times on one hand I'd ever heard one of the Byrne men admit they might not know it all.

He huffs a dry laugh. "Fuck off, Shae."

"Fucking right off, sir." I salute, happy to escape any further scrutiny, and retreat to the back office.

I'm watching feed from our multitude of security cameras when I get a text from an unknown number.

Shae, it's Renzo. Forklift is fixed.

I stare at the screen as if glaring might force it to explain why Renzo has texted me. It's been six days since our hot mess of a meeting at his warehouse, and I hadn't heard anything about the matter since. I assumed Conner had handled it. Renzo didn't even have my number. He would have had to go out of his way to get it. Why?

Me: Thought you were working with Conner on that.

Renzo: You thought wrong.

Me: Well, I'm telling you now. Get with Conner.

Renzo: Either you meet me at the warehouse tomorrow at 1 or we keep the crates. Your choice.

The fuck is he up to?

A strange thudding pounds in my chest. I'm not sure if it's wariness or excitement, or why I'd feel either of them where Renzo Donati is concerned.

Me: You think you can keep our shit?

Renzo: Your family owes me for our part in that arrangement.

Renzo: And if your cousins ask, I'll simply explain that you refused my one simple instruction.

Motherfucker.

It pisses me off that he has me, and he knows it. I don't understand what he's up to, and I like that even less. Why is he demanding to meet with me? Is he trying to intimidate me? Because *hell* no.

Me: No need to get your panties in a twist. I'll be there if it's so important to you.

Dots dance in their bubble, then disappear three separate times before a response finally comes through. God, I love that it's so damn easy to wind up men. The smallest insinuation of emotional dysregulation and they lose their ever-loving minds.

Only, his response isn't what I expect. He ignored my intended condescension and focused on something else entirely.

Renzo: Can't twist what I'm not wearing.

Me: Panties?

I snicker to myself.

Renzo: Anything.

My brain glitches. Renzo is texting me naked?

My eyes squint shut. Damn my vibrant imagination—the unwanted image brands itself on the backs of my eyelids where I can't escape it.

Me: Renzo Donati, are you sexting me?

I try my best to play things off as nonchalantly as possible.

Renzo: You're the one who brought up panties. I was just correcting you.

Renzo: And Shae?

Me: Yeah? If the text could be audible, it would be a whisper. How did he manage to unnerve me every fucking time?

Renzo: You'd know if I was sexting because your fingers would already be buried deep in that pink pussy of yours, desperate for release.

Oh. Shit.

The man has game. Or at least, he talks a good game, and that can be just as important as the rest. Most of the time, when a partner tries to top me, I find it more funny than anything. That shit's innate. Either you have it or you don't. Most don't.

I think Renzo may have been given more than his fair share.

Fuck me. I'm playing with fire.

And while I'm not the type to retreat, I'm not stupid, either. So why is it so damn hard to keep from egging him on? Why do I desperately want to know how far he'd take the conversation? I need to know what he might say next and whether it will cause a surge in my pulse—that delicious feeling of lightheadedness signaling the body's preparation for something *extraordinary*.

It's a sensation I rarely encounter outside the boxing ring. And Renzo Donati seems to summon the reaction at will as though I'm a puppet on strings.

Why is it always the impossible ones that pique my interest?

It's not happening. Not again.

Me: I'm at work, so that's unlikely. I'll be there at one.

I hit send, hoping I don't sound as though I'm presenting a challenge or am affected in any way by his comment. In reality, I wish my panties were in a twist because it might give me the friction I need to soothe my aching clit.

I was right when I decided Renzo was trouble with a capital T.

I need to get those damn guns, then get the hell out of Dodge. I'm just as capable of handling this in a professional manner as any of my cousins.

Warehouse. Guns. Gone.

Easy peasy.

4

Kenzo

I STEPPED OUT OF THE SHOWER TO FIND TWO TEXT MESSAGES—
one from my guys informing me that the forklift was working
and the other from my cousin Noemi giving me Shae's
number. The fact that the two showed up together was too
tempting. I sent the text to Shae before I could overthink it.

Did I ever imagine my lack of clothing would come up?
Not even once.

Did texting about it get my dick hard? Abso-fucking-
lutely.

Hell if I didn't have to get back in and shower again after
our exchange. All it took was the flash of an image—her
smart mouth speechless as I rammed my cock inside her—
and I was too hard to ignore. I had to paint the shower wall

with cum like a fucking teenager before I could think straight again.

That woman does something to me, and I don't like it. My belligerent insistence on seeing her again is evidence enough that she's a dangerous distraction. Like she so graciously pointed out, I have more important matters that require my attention. And yet … when I considered texting Conner or handing off the meeting to one of my men, I couldn't do it. I found myself rationalizing a personal appearance. We've held up the exchange because of my father's death. It would be prudent of me to show respect and appreciation by over-seeing the matter myself.

That crock of shit is what I continue to tell myself as I park outside the warehouse for my second meeting with Shae Byrne. An unmarked box truck pulls into the lot. I expect to see one of her men behind the wheel, but I should have known better. Shae's tiny frame is perched in the driver's seat. She's wearing dark aviator glasses and the unbothered air of a lion with a full belly.

We round our vehicles at same time and pause to assess one another before meeting in the middle.

The stilettos are gone. She's all business in what looks like black Doc Martin boots, jeans that are nothing more than a coat of paint over perfectly toned legs, and a black puffer jacket zipped all the way to her chin, right below vibrant crimson lips. A simple shift in wardrobe took her from busi-ness glam to a goth-girl wet dream. I'm not sure which I like more.

"You didn't bring your men to help load," I note, wondering if they're coming separately.

"Short notice. Everyone was busy." She lifts her sunglasses and squints into the back seat of my car. "Looks like I'm not the only one who came alone."

"I assumed you'd bring your crew."

"You know what they say about assuming…" she says in a singsong voice.

What I would give to fuck that smart-ass smirk off her face. I'd spin her around, press her flush against the hood of my car, and make her pant until she was too cum drunk to give me sass.

Hell, I have to stop thinking like that before I end up with a hard-on and give her more ammunition.

"At least you dressed appropriately this time." My clipped words evidence my irritation.

Shae grins wickedly.

I'd question whether she could be a bit unhinged, but I don't think it would matter. She's like the overturned semi-truck on the side of the highway that you can't look away from.

"Boots are steel-toed. Want to test them?" she asks in a soft, sultry murmur, tapping the toe of one boot against my own leather work boots. No steel tips on mine, but Shae would have to gain another fifty pounds minimum before she had any hope of causing me harm.

She walks two fingers up my chest, hot-pink-tipped nails poking lightly at the fabric of my jacket. "You know my favorite thing in the whole wide world?" Her breathy voice is a tongue licking the length of my cock.

She's toying with me. I know it, but I can't walk away. "What's that?"

"When men like you underestimate me."

Lightning fast, her hand clamps around my balls. She's expecting me to flinch and push her away. I don't. I let her take me in her small fist and feel the stiffness she's already inspired, then I crowd her by moving even closer.

"If that's what you wanted, all you had to do was ask." I

ignore the pinch of pain. She's not actually trying to hurt me. It could be a hell of a lot worse. This is about power. Respect. I have to hold my ground. Trying to outmaneuver her would give her a win the same as if I'd evaded to protect myself.

"If I wanted you, I'd already have you. *This*—" She gives me a slight squeeze. "Does nothing for me."

I raise my hand ever so slowly to circle her neck, my thumb caressing the front of her throat where I can feel her pulse jump. I lean in, pulling her forward at the same time until my lips graze her ear. "Now look who's making assumptions." I pull back, drawing an impenetrable mask of indifference over my features. I give her a cold, hard stare before turning away.

She allows me to go. Amusement brightens her eyes, the only clue as to what she might be thinking. All that damn bravado makes me want to rattle her composure—make her drop her shields and reveal what's underneath. That's the last thing I should want where Shae Byrne is concerned.

"Come on, let's get this over with," I loft dryly over my shoulder.

"I suppose you know how to work a forklift?" Her footsteps crunch on the gravel a few steps behind me.

"I suppose I do. Are you trying to tell me there's something you *can't* do?"

"Never tried, but there's a first time for everything. Happy to give it a go."

"Your guns, sweetheart. You fuck 'em up, you take the blame."

"True, but it seems like a waste if I don't give it a try. When else will I have the opportunity to play with such … *impressive* equipment?"

Jesus, does it ever end? Could she stop herself even if she wanted to? Doubtful.

I shake my head and unlock the door. "Those cousins of yours must really give you hell."

"What's that supposed to mean?" She shuts the door behind us with more force than necessary.

I level her with a glare. "Means you don't have to put on a show all the time. You're a badass, I get it."

A minuscule twitch dances beneath her right eye, so small I would have missed it if I hadn't been primed to analyze her reaction.

She recovers quickly, a Cheshire grin creeping across her face. "Maybe that's just who I am."

"Or maybe you've played the part so long, you don't know the difference."

She inches forward, the first glint of anger sharpening her features. "You're awfully knowledgeable about me, considering you know *nothing* about me. Why is that? Maybe you're projecting. Huh?" She pokes a finger into my chest. "How's it feel to fill Daddy's shoes? A touch of impostor syndrome setting in?"

She has my blood boiling in a handful of seconds. I unclench my fists and open my mouth to respond when reason slams into me. Arguing will get me nowhere. The best way to get under her skin is to rise above her ploys.

I clench my jaw shut and take a deep, cleansing breath before continuing. "Forklift's this way." I push past her, my shoulder bumping against hers.

Way to rise above, asshole.

A humorless laugh dances across the back of my neck as she follows me.

I wait for her retort. There's no way she'll let it end without having the last word. I'm so concentrated on what she might say that I fail to notice half of the crates are gone until I'm right upon them—or where they should have been.

My hands go to my hips as I stare at the remaining crates. Shae stops beside me in a similar fashion. Before either of us can say anything, a searing pain lances through my skull, and darkness threatens my vision.

I'm on my knees.

Hands … pulling me.

A ruckus of sound rings in my ears, but I'm too disoriented to understand what's happening. I do my best to blink away my confusion and realize I hear Shae cursing nearby. That helps clear out the cobwebs more than anything.

Someone is in the warehouse.

They attacked us.

Shae.

If they hurt her, I'll kill them. I'll peel back their fucking ribs and rip out their hearts with my bare hands.

I shake my head, using the pain to focus and take in the scene around me. Four masked men speak rapidly to one another. Foreign. Frantic. Whatever their plan, this wasn't it.

I'm on the floor. My hands are secured behind me to the wide metal beam at my back. I feel Shae before I see her. She's thrashing against her bindings next to me, secured to the side of the beam with our shoulders touching.

"You hurt?" I ask under my breath so as not to draw attention.

"Just my pride. I can't believe I let them get the drop on us," she hisses. "With you bashed over the head, I couldn't take all four."

"They didn't try to knock you out?"

"They tried."

I don't have to see her smile to know it's there.

A grunt of amusement angers the pounding in my head.

"If it's any consolation, I was impressed you never fully

blacked out. Should have known you'd be hard-headed," she adds somewhat wistfully.

It strikes me that she isn't remotely panicked. Pissed, yes. Inconvenienced, sure. But not scared.

The girl has balls of steel.

I'm not particularly worried, but most people would be. From my perspective, these assholes thought they'd slip in without ever being seen. They'll most likely take what they came for and leave us here. Workers are rarely over here. This warehouse isn't used frequently—that's why it was chosen to store the crates. But our families will come looking for us … eventually.

My family knows how busy I've been. I doubt my absence would be questioned immediately. Let's hope Shae's cousins are diligent about keeping tabs on her.

"You have your phone still?" Mine's gone, I know that much. It was in my back pocket, and it's not there now between me and the concrete floor.

"They took everything—phones and weapons."

"Looks like they're taking your crates as well," I point out. Three of the men are still bickering while one drives the forklift in from outside, sliding its prongs under one of the two remaining crates about fifty feet from us. If we hadn't been arguing ourselves, maybe we would have heard the machine, but it's a moot point now.

"So it would seem. Not sure how they knew to come after them."

"You suggesting a leak on our end?"

Her shrugging shoulder rubs against mine. "Just noting there was likely *some* source of information—I doubt a worker happened upon them randomly."

She's right, so I keep quiet. No need to point out the source could have come from her end as easily as mine.

"Any idea what they're speaking?" I ask while the men are too preoccupied to pay us any attention, not to mention the forklift is easily loud enough to drown out our whispers.

"I'm wondering if it's Romanian."

"Sounds almost Greek."

"They don't look Greek. At least, not the one I saw."

"You saw one of their faces?" I crane my neck to look at her, my words taking on a hard edge. If she can identify them, that might make her a target. It's an added complication, and I don't like it.

"Ripped off one of their masks before they got me bound. The short one. Sure didn't look Greek to me, but that doesn't necessarily mean anything. You have beef with the Romanians?"

"Not that I know of. Could also be the Albanians. Their languages sound similar."

"No," she breathes.

"No, what?" A new sliver of tension coils in my muscles.

Before she can explain, a phone chimes. All four men still before one lifts a phone to his ear and answers. His eyes flick our direction as he speaks a string of hushed, wary words. The others watch him with rapt attention.

A call from their superior. And they're having to report a snag. Us.

The call goes on for no more than two minutes, and after, he reports the results to the others.

They immediately launch into an argument, tensions skyrocketing. One man marches over to us and pulls out a gun. It's aimed at her head.

"Wait," she demands. "Don't make a mistake you can't undo. Think about it. If you take us with you, you'll have time to consider your options. Our families will want us back. You could ransom us."

35

The man's hand tremors, and desperation glints in his wide eyes. Two of his buddies seem to try to talk him down. While they are distracted, I murmur to Shae. "You know what you're doing?"

"Isn't that obvious? Buying us time. Can't figure a way out if we're dead."

"True, but don't you think we should at least *try* to convince them to leave us here alive?"

The men start yelling at one another. The one with the gun seems to be running the show. He barks one last time before they begin to get the last crate loaded. Time is running out.

"Shit, *shit!*" Shae's voice is pitched his with urgency. She wasn't concerned before, but something's changed. Something has her spooked, and while I may not have spent much time with her, Shae has made it clear that she doesn't spook easily.

"What the fuck is happening here?" I demand quietly.

"You're right. They're Albanian." The last word is spoken so softly it's nearly inaudible.

"And I take it that's a bad thing?"

"It's complicated. They're not going to want to leave us alive. Not when I can identify them."

Fuck.

The sound of continued bickering announces their return. There's only one reason for them to come back inside, and that's us.

I speak up before they reach us. "The guns are replaceable, we're not. You should know that you'll be making this infinitely worse for yourselves if you kill us. Our families *will* come after you." I inject every ounce of authority I possess into my voice. Their ski masks prevent me from seeing their expressions, but their body language conveys plenty.

Three of the four taper off before reaching us, all of them

tense and fidgeting with nervous energy in various ways. The leader walks all the way over, his steps determined. But when he stands over me and raises his gun, he's close enough that I can see the conflict in his eyes. His back is against a wall. He feels he has no choice.

"Take us with you," Shae demands with absolute confidence. "Why rush this decision when you don't have to? You can always kill us later, but for now, take us with you."

5

Shae

THEY SHOVE US INTO THE BACK OF A GOLD PENSKE TRUCK PARKED on the side of the building. My guess is it's a rental. The crates only take up half the space, so we have plenty of room. Movement is difficult, though, with our hands still bound behind us.

"You guys have security cameras?" I ask once the doors slam shut, and we're engulfed in darkness.

"Depends," Renzo mutters.

"On what?"

"On whether that particular spot was ever monitored. Whether the camera installed still works. Whether footage is being recorded. Monitoring the docks is no small undertaking, and this warehouse isn't a high-volume location."

A sigh slips past my lips. Not the answer I was hoping for, but there's still a chance. So long as we're still breathing, our situation can improve. Making it out of the building alive was the first step.

I'm not completely at ease, though I do feel oddly comforted knowing Renzo is here with me. His presence is zero guarantee of improving my chances. For all I know, having him with me may make things worse, yet the darkness feels less threatening with him in it. Why?

I suppose it's only logical for the brain to hope having a six-foot-something street-smart man at my side will be helpful, but it bugs me. I've spent a long time training myself not to bestow traits such as competence and authority to a man simply because he has a dick between his legs. Renzo is confident. I'll give him that, but I don't know anything beyond what I've seen in our brief encounters.

It's a sign that I still have emotional work to do.

I don't want to accidentally let my guard down in a situation merely because a man is nearby.

"Tell me about the Albanians," Renzo says, drawing me from my brooding thoughts.

I breathe deeply and think of where to begin. "You're aware that my father was gunned down in the summer, right?"

"*Fuuuuck.*" The word is a weary exhalation.

"But wait … there's more," I add in a dry, humorless tone.

"Jesus."

"We figured out that Oran's wife had tipped off the Albanians."

"His *wife*?"

"Yeah, it was an arranged marriage with another Irish family, the Donovans. We had no idea she was harboring a lifetime of resentment. She and her brother also stole a shipment of guns from us. It can't be a coincidence—the guns and the Albanians. We had a tentative truce with them after taking out half their numbers in retaliation."

"I'm surprised you would accept a truce on any level, with or without your retaliation."

"That's why I said it's complicated. They put themselves at risk to help us with a very tricky Russian problem. It was a peace offering. I didn't think they'd shit all over that so quickly." That's why my mind hadn't immediately suspected the Albanians, but now that I've thought about it, I can't imagine we're dealing with anyone else.

"You think Oran's wife is behind this?"

"*Ex*-wife. And that's the thing that doesn't make sense. She can't be behind it. She's dead." I pause and mull things over. "But it seems too coincidental for the Albanians to be taking our guns again. It's not like some greedy Albanian dock workers just happened upon them."

"Considering we haven't had a theft like that since we first took over the docks, I'd say it's unlikely. And I don't think anyone on our end leaked the location of the guns."

I can't help but scoff at his blasé confidence. "I hate to break it to you, but no one is immune to betrayal."

"No, but you guys have seen an awful lot of that lately."

"One demented woman with resentment issues—I'd hardly call that an ongoing problem." Though, she did have a far-reaching ripple effect. It had even caused enough concern from our Dublin associates for them to send a man over. We already had the matter sorted, but that didn't change how impactful her deception had been. "Didn't your uncle recently try to overthrow your father?" Talk about a betrayal. Surely, he hasn't forgotten.

Renzo is quiet for a long minute. "I know we aren't

immune," he finally says in a surprisingly solemn tone. "Trust me, as boss now, the potential for betrayal is a constant concern."

His earnest admission surprises me. Not only that he'd concede to a possible weakness, but that he'd openly admit to it in front of an outsider. That isn't the norm for men in our world.

"Well, however we got to this point," I add cooly, "I plan on getting back home, and then I will hunt down whoever is responsible."

"You and me both." His surly oath draws an amused smirk from me as the truck comes to a stop. The engine turns off.

I can't see Renzo, but I imagine his body is as tense as mine, waiting for whatever comes next. We can hear the cab doors shut, the seconds counting down in my ears with each thudding beat of my heart.

Only ... seconds turn into minutes. Five. Ten. Twenty. And nothing happens.

I'd mentally begun to prepare for possible torture or mistreatment, but I'm suddenly left to wonder if this might be our fate. Stashed in a truck where we can be ignored and disposed of later, once our dehydrated corpses have no fight left.

A shudder wracks my entire body.

I'd rather get the shit beat out of me any day of the week than to sit helplessly while my body fails. I have to force the thought from my mind.

I'm not certain of the time, but I guess it's around a half hour later when the door finally does swing open. The sound startles me, but it's the blinding daylight that causes the greatest shock. My eyes had adjusted to my black surroundings so thoroughly that I'm temporarily blinded by the light and so disoriented that I don't see the man approach with a syringe until it's buried in my neck. I hear a single muttered curse from Renzo before I return to darkness.

6

Shae

I TRY TO SWALLOW, CRINGING AS MY THROAT REVOLTS AT THE lack of moisture. I've had cotton mouth before after a big night out, but this is different. Like my throat is lined in sandpaper.

"Here, have some water."

The deep voice nearby startles me into forcing my eyes open. Renzo Donati sits with his back against a wall across from where I'm lying on a freezing concrete floor. I prop myself up and survey the small room around me. Not a room. A supply closet, by the looks of it.

"Where are we?" I rasp, taking the half-empty bottle of water, noting that our hands are no longer bound. I down the water in one long drink. I swear water has never tasted so damn good.

"Best guess is an airport hangar." His weary tone draws my attention. When I look at him more closely, I see shadows under bloodshot eyes. Alarm bells in my head compete for attention over the dull ache radiating through my skull.

"How long was I out?" Drugged. Fucking Albanians.

"Not sure. They got me too. I haven't been up long, maybe an hour. The bottle of water was here when I woke. No one's been in since, but I've heard voices."

"We were out for quite a while if my aching bladder is any indication." I join him against the wall and take another look around the room. Definitely some kind of storage closet. When a rumbling in the distance grows into a thunderous cacophony that rattles the door on its hinges, I understand the reason for Renzo's airport deduction. The deafening noise retreats into the distance as quickly as it appears until the only thing ringing in my ears is a sense of urgency.

The small room is approximately eight by ten feet in size with rusty metal shelves lining the wall opposite us. A single-bulb light is on above us. I'm glad for the light but a window would have been better. It's unsettling to know you've been drugged but have no idea how much time you've lost or whether it's still night or day.

As the fog lifts in my brain, my sluggish thoughts start to form more quickly. I need to stop worrying about the unknown and focus on what I do know.

Standing slowly, I go to the shelf and assess the contents for anything that might be helpful.

"Most everything on the shelves has French and English on the packaging. I'd say there's a solid chance we're in Canada." Renzo's words settle like melted tar in the pit of my stomach.

My eyes dance from a package of toilet paper to a box of trash bags to a gallon bottle of window cleaner. He's right. All have bits of both languages on the packaging.

"What the fuck?" I breathe.

"Yeah, my thoughts as well. This keeps getting better and better."

When I told them to take us with them, I never imagined they'd go beyond Manhattan, let alone across international borders. This is getting out of hand. It's time to do something.

I crack my neck and sweep my arms in large circles to stretch my shoulders before going to the door and giving it three solid knocks.

"Shit," Renzo mutters. "This should be good."

I consider kicking his booted foot but hold off as footsteps approach.

"What?" a man demands through the door. It's English but heavily accented.

"I need to go to the bathroom, or I'm going to make a mess in here," I call out.

A muffled grunt is my only answer.

I lift my hand to start pounding on the door right as it bursts open. I freeze, fist in midair.

A man with a full beard and shaggy dark hair stares back at me with callous irritation. He grabs my wrist and tugs me across the threshold, his eyes fixed on Renzo behind me, who has launched himself to his feet.

"You use bottle," he orders thickly.

Renzo pays him no mind. Every ounce of his attention bores into me, screaming in warning.

Be fucking careful.

I only have long enough to flash him a quick wink before the foreigner slams the door shut and bolts the lock. A roaring curse bellowing from the closet follows us down the hall away from the main hangar. My escort keeps a firm grip on my wrist until we reach a grimy bathroom.

Sometimes being a woman has its advantages. Even if I didn't need to pee, I would have done the same thing as a ploy to assess the situation. Anything I can do to help us get back home. But as it stands, I'm seconds from wetting myself.

"You're seriously going to watch me?" I scoff at my captor when he leans against the open doorway.

His stare is eerily hollow. "You need to piss. Piss."

I was hoping for privacy—not out of modesty but to give me a chance to search the cabinet under the sink. My waning bladder control prevents me from arguing further. "This is fucking ridiculous," I mutter as I fumble with my jeans. My relief at releasing those clenched muscles is so great, I hardly notice the icy toilet seat beneath me. I also ignore my audience because fuck him. He'd have to do a hell of a lot more than watch me pee to make me uncomfortable.

As I sit, it registers that daylight is pouring in the small window. If we met at the warehouse Thursday afternoon, does that mean it's now Friday? Midday, judging by the height of the sun.

"Where are we? Somewhere in Canada?"

No answer.

"Is it Friday? Surely, it's not already Saturday."

Still no answer. Thank goodness persistence has never been an issue for me.

"What does it hurt for me to know the day of the week? It's not like I can use that to escape."

He sneers. "Finish and get dressed, or I toss you back in the room without pants."

"Well, that's rude," I grumble as I wipe and pull up my jeans. "What exactly is the plan here, chief, because this has gone on long enough. You guys are out of the city. Our families aren't a threat—what good will it do to keep us any longer?"

He steps inside the tiny bathroom, filling up the space with his hulking animosity and the lingering scent of cigarettes. "I hear many things about you, Shae *Byrne*." He overexaggerates my last name as his cold stare drifts lasciviously down my body. "But they must be fairy tales. You are not so tough as they say, I think."

His words bother me infinitely more than his wandering gaze ever could. I'd had my phone and wallet on me when they took us, so it's not surprising that he knows my name. It's the familiarity in his tone that doesn't sit well. I get the sense he wouldn't have needed an ID to know exactly who I was.

"How did you know where the guns were?" I go for the direct approach, hoping to catch him off guard.

He flashes a yellowing grin and pulls me into the hall.

"Jesus." I grimace. "Don't they have toothbrushes in Albania?"

He whips around, intending to backhand me across the face, but I evade, grabbing his arm in the process and swinging him around to press his chest against the wall. I bend his arm back at an angle I know hurts like hell to prevent him from struggling and keep my body close to his. "Who the fuck told you about the guns?" I hiss through clenched teeth.

He yells for help, and I'm quickly yanked away from him and slammed against the opposite wall.

"What the fuck going on out there?" Renzo's voice booms through the closet door.

"Jesus, not the hair," I fuss. I could get out of his hold thanks to my short cut, but there's too many of them now. And besides, I'd prefer not to show them how capable I am until the moment is right. I'm better off de-escalating the situation and trying again later. "Okay, okay. I'm done." I hold up my hands to signal my surrender when Renzo bursts through the closet door, ripping the lock out of its wooden frame.

"Get your fucking hands off her." His words seethe with violence. He's impressively intimidating when he wants to be.

The hand releases my hair and moves to my arm. I'm tugged farther into the main hangar and away from Renzo. The masked foursome who captured us is now a crew of eight men, all surrounding us with disdain carved onto their hardened faces.

Knowing what we're up against is helpful, though I'd hoped for fewer numbers. Even at our best, the two of us would be hard-pressed to take on eight men.

"Now that we have your attention," Renzo slices through the sweltering tension. "You need to know what you're getting into by keeping us captive. You *will* start a war with not only the Irish Byrnes but with the entire Italian Mafia. No one kidnaps a boss without becoming a target of the entire Five Families."

I catch sight of several men exchanging worried glances. They knew who I was, but did they know Renzo? Would it change things if they did, and if so, for better … or worse?

A man lingering in the back casually pushes to the center of our little party. His short brown hair is greasy with a sheen that highlights the evil glint in his black eyes. No one's eyes are truly black, but I swear this man is an exception.

His unrushed movements shift effortlessly into a punch when he levels a mean right hook square into Renzo's jaw. The guy is big, and he knows how to hit, yet Renzo takes the hit as if doled out by a child. He's not even set off balance.

When he brings his malicious blue stare back to the man,

his tongue swipes a tinge of crimson blossoming on his bottom lip as though savoring a drop of ice cream. "One last chance, or I promise this will end *very* badly for you," Renzo says in a tone so calm and even that goose bumps tease the back of my neck.

I don't get the sense threats will work on these men, but I'm not sure Renzo got that memo. He's the type who's used to people withering beneath a simple glare from his direction. I have to fight back tendrils of envy. I could be the deadliest person in a room and never garner the respect Renzo can command simply by virtue of his size and stature. That sort of disparity would normally frustrate me, but in Renzo's case, I think he may actually deserve the respect. He's levelheaded, strategic, confident, brave, and more than a little tough.

Shit. I think I may actually like the guy.

I don't get the chance to ponder my revelation when Mr. Black Eyes barks orders in a foreign tongue. His men shift into action, securing our wrists with a new set of zip ties and scurrying about the room with renewed purpose. Something is about to happen, and I have no goddamn clue what.

7

Kenzo

IRONY IS SUCH A LITTLE BITCH. I'D CHIDED SHAE IN MY MIND FOR banging on the door. It was impulsive and reckless. I'm of the opinion we'd be better served coming up with a calculated plan rather than going off half-cocked. Then I go and bust through the door trying to get to her.

She brought attention to herself, and there's no telling what those assholes might do to her. Sure, she's tougher than most women, but she's not superhuman despite what she might think. It's like she has no interest or awareness of her own safety.

Images of what a group of desperate men could do to a woman started to assault me when I heard Shae get tossed around in the hall. And because life loves to make hypocrites of us all, I ignored my own safety and abandoned all strategy by plowing through the door like a goddamn wrecking ball. Nearly tore the thing from its hinges. I had to get to her. If these guys lay one fucking finger on her … I'll use my last breath making them pay.

What is it about this woman that she makes me lose my fucking mind? I feel like I'm constantly having to react instead of act with her around. Like she's a human tornado—unpredictable and capable of total devastation.

I prefer to maintain a controlled environment, but that's impossible with her around.

And now we're back together, but something's happening around us that has me on edge. It looks like they're packing up—preparing to leave—and I have no idea what that means for us.

We've been ordered to sit against a wall in the main room. A young guy stands watch over us with a gun while the rest of the crew packs up.

"Looks like he's got a huge cock." She eyes the guard above us while I try to keep my head from exploding.

"*Jesus fucking Christ, Shae.*" The growled curse is half disbelief and half reprimand. Is she trying to get herself raped?

"Relax, big guy." Amusement twists her lips with a smirk as her scrutinizing stare finally drops from the guard. "It was a test. Now we know he doesn't speak English—not even the tiniest flinch at what I said."

Fuck, she's going to give me a coronary. "A little heads-up would have been nice."

"And tip him off? That would have made the whole thing pointless."

God, I hate it when she's right.

"What now?" I ask under my breath.

"We know there's eight of them."

"I could probably take three but no more at once."

"Same."

The skepticism I feel must have shown through on my face because Shae shoots me a withering glare.

"Not that any of that matters with these damn zip ties are on." I pull at my bindings, but all it does is bite into my skin.

"Leave that to me," she says almost inaudibly. Her blue eyes meet mine, and though I'm not sure exactly what she has planned, it's clear she has something in mind.

A nauseating cocktail of relief and dread roil in my gut.

"Listen, don't do anything that will get you killed. I don't want to have to explain to your cousins why I came back alive, and you didn't."

"How very chivalrous of you." Despite everything, her murmured words are light and teasing. She's laughing in the face of our circumstances, and I don't know if I should be reassured or terrified.

"As if you'd want chivalry even if it were offered," I shoot back, following her lead.

Her answering grin warms the room a solid five degrees. "Now you're catching on."

I shake my head with a small huff of amusement, though it withers fast. "Listen, Shae. I don't want you doing anything crazy."

Her voice takes on an equally somber tone. "You know as well as I do that the longer this goes on, the worse it is for us. We need to get out of here ASAP. I doubt we'll have more than one chance. We need to use it wisely."

"Agreed." My voice is as grim as our circumstances.

Before we can say any more, the hum of a propellor engine grows louder until a small prop plane comes into view outside the hangar door window.

Shae leans in and speaks softly next to my ear. "I need you to trust me, Renzo. Tell me you'll follow my lead." The pleading in her voice rocks me, but it's the sound of my name on her lips that clamps tight like a vise around my chest. I'm not sure I've heard her use my first name, and I like it far more than I should.

God, help me.

"It's all you."

8

Shae

RENZO WATCHES ME INTENTLY, WONDERING WHY I HAVEN'T made my move. Wishing he knew what the hell I have planned. I can't explain and risk someone hearing. Like I said, we have one shot. I have to make sure the timing is right, and that means waiting until the ratio of men is better.

It's a safe assumption that part of this group is getting on that plane parked outside. It's rather small. I don't think all ten of us will fit. I could be wrong, but I'm hoping this is where our party splits up. It would be ideal if Renzo and I stayed on solid ground. As the universe sees fit to challenge me today, I am not surprised when they usher us onto the plane. It's a cargo transport plane for taking small loads of supplies to remote areas. No seats besides the cockpit, and the metal insides are currently empty.

We're seated against opposite walls of the plane, facing one another. As expected, only four accompany us—two in the cockpit and two in the back with us.

It's fucking freezing in the plane. We're definitely somewhere north. Beyond the tarmac, the trees and ground have a solid blanket of snow. But thanks to the coat I'm still wearing and the anticipation thrumming in my veins, I'm not overwhelmed by the cold.

The engine starts up and makes hearing anything beyond the roaring almost impossible. Renzo's penetrating stare is a cattle prod urging me to action. I want to hiss at him that I'm working on it, but I can't afford to lose focus. Taking the small pocketknife out of my back pocket and getting it open without drawing attention to myself isn't easy.

I was enamored with pickpockets when I was a kid and practiced endlessly until I was an expert. The skill has come in handy innumerable times, like today, when I stole the small tool out of Mr. Black Eyes pocket during our scuffle. Picking his pockets was the whole purpose of riling him up. I hadn't actually expected to escape or get information from the man. I was looking to nab something that might help us, and it worked. I could hardly believe my luck when my fingers wrapped around the familiar object—small enough to go unnoticed but crucial to our escape.

Our captors are a mere five feet away. Any overt movement on my part will easily be seen, so I am extra careful to disguise what I'm doing. When the plane bounces down the runway, the jiggling helps disguise my movements, but they've used two ties, and the little blade is hardly more than a nail file. I don't get free until the plane is well into the air, and we've been coasting for several long minutes.

I hate that we aren't seated next to one another because I have no way to get the knife to Renzo. I'll have to launch my attack on my own and hope for the best.

A small space, uneven footing, and three-to-one odds, possibly four-to-one. Not ideal, but I have the element of surprise, and that can make up for a hell of a lot.

I spear Renzo with a look that screams, *get ready*. The determined set of his jaw tells me he understands. I flick the knife into his lap, then launch myself to my feet fast enough to kick one of the two men in the head, knocking him out with one strike. The other is up in a heartbeat, as is the co-pilot. The cabin isn't large enough for us to stand fully upright, though the men have to hunch more than I do.

Behind me, Renzo curses as he fumbles with the knife.

One of the men yells, then runs at me. I absorb his momentum into a backward roll, taking him with me and tossing him behind me with a kick from my legs. While he's recovering from his unexpected circus trick, I square off with the third man.

The pilot yells at us but stays put in the cockpit.

I use his hollering as a distraction and sweep out the legs of the third guy. He snags my hand on his way down, taking me with him, and we grapple with one another on the floor. What he doesn't know is this is my happy place. I do my best work one-on-one, hand-to-hand.

I maneuver myself until I can get my thighs around his neck, then squeeze like a python. His body stiffens with panic. There is no escape from this hold.

My eyes collide with Renzo's awestruck stare. It only lasts a fraction of a second, but the respect I sense in him makes me feel like I could take on an entire army.

The moment is short lived, however. When my gaze

continues onward to the man I'd thrown to the back of the plane, my blood runs cold.

He roars a single word in his native tongue, then pulls out a small handgun holstered beneath his coat. He has to know guns and planes don't mix, but the fury on his face tells me he doesn't care. He's prepared to fire as he aims the gun directly at me.

9

Kenzo

Fluid grace and exceptional tactical awareness—Shae's fighting prowess is spectacular to witness.

And that's exactly what I get stuck doing. Watching. Sitting with my thumb up my ass while Shae takes on the entire crew. And she's owning these motherfuckers until one has the genius idea to pull out a gun. We're not flying at commercial airline altitude, but it's still a supremely idiotic thing to do.

It's enough to break through my trance and finally give me something I can do to help.

I'm on the ground between them with my legs extended in front of me. I sweep one leg up and around directly at the gunman's knee as hard as I can, a shot ringing out while I'm in mid-motion.

I don't stop to see if he's hit his mark. I'm too blinded by rage.

When he cries out and falls forward, I lift my booted heel and bring it down on his face.

I kick him in the head … over … and over … and over … until his body no longer twitches when I connect with his bloodied flesh. Only then does the red mist part from my vision enough for me to realize the plane is flying erratically.

Shae is tugging a lifeless pilot from his seat in the cockpit.

She's alive. Thank fucking *Christ*.

The tightness in my chest relaxes. "Come get these goddamn ties off my wrists," I call to her, eyeing our motion-less captors—all either dead or unconscious.

She hurries over and scoops up the pocketknife from the ground, then frantically saws the plastic apart. I think I understand her urgency—we're now short a pilot—but the situation doesn't fully hit home until I follow her to the cockpit and see the lifeless instrument panel.

"Shit, shit, *shit*. I don't suppose you know how to land a plane without any instruments?" she asks while flipping switches and pressing buttons seemingly at random.

"Fuck no. I don't know how to land a plane, period. What happened to the pilot?"

"I think the bullet ricocheted off the control panel and into the pilot, taking out both of them."

We're steadily losing altitude, and there's nothing but forest as far as the eye can see. I'm not one to panic, but this is bad. This is real fucking bad.

I reach across Shae and start fumbling with the seat harness behind her, forcing her arms into the straps like I would a fidgeting toddler.

"What are you doing?" she demands, trying to see around me.

"Buckling you in. If we're going down, we'll at least be strapped in. Now, sit still for a second."

She starts pulling on the steering control stick with all her might. I feel so helpless. I don't even know what the fucking thing is called.

"You know about planes?" I ask while strapping myself in.

"I have a cousin with the Playstation flight simulator game and played a few rounds. Does that count?"

"It'll have to because I have nothing better to offer."

"I'm turning off the engines to slow us down. That means we'll also work our way to the ground that much faster."

"You don't think we should keep going until we find somewhere open?"

"We're losing daylight. I don't want to make this any worse by having to land in the dark." She's right. A blind landing sounds terrifying.

Her determined stare meets mine before she turns the key and shuts down the plane. Eerie doesn't begin to cover it. No beeping or warnings. No one screaming or yelling orders. Just wind and clanking and a few moans from the metal frame that has now become a glorified glider.

We shift into a controlled fall, and my heart seems to practice our crash landing by slamming itself against the inside of my ribs. Within seconds, we near the tops of snow-covered trees. Everything after that happens in a stop-motion blur.

The scraping of wood on the belly of the plane.

The moment the front end catches on a particularly large tree and flips us end over end.

Screams—hers and mine.

Splintering plexiglass.

The wailing of bending metal and the monstrous crack of full-grown trees snapping in two.

We're slammed in one direction, then another. A kaleidoscope of pain ricochets through my body while the swirling motion bottoms out my stomach, but I'm too terrified to vomit. Besides, there isn't time. With one final lurching flip, we're slammed back against our seats with enough force that everything goes black.

10

Shae

CALLUM KELLY BROKE TWO OF MY RIBS WHEN I WAS NINETEEN. I thought my brother was going to kill him after it happened even though it wasn't exactly his fault. We'd been sparring, and I specifically told him not to go easy.

Even at that age, I was an excellent fighter.

I didn't start juijitsu training until the following year, but I could box as well as any of my cousins. I made sure of that. In the process, I endured any number of injuries, but I'd never broken a rib until that day. The pain was excruciating. I couldn't do anything without searing pain lancing me from the inside out. Simply *breathing* hurt. The misery was relentless and took forever to heal.

I wouldn't wish that pain on anyone, yet I'm suddenly

glad for those broken ribs. While I feel like my chest has caved in, I know it's probably only bruised because the pain is nothing like I felt when my ribs were actually broken. It may seem like a silly thing to be grateful for, but it's one less thing to worry about, and right now, my worry list is growing by the second.

I take in a slow, shaky breath and open my eyes.

I'm on my back, not quite upside down but at an angle. It's still light out, though dim inside the mangled plane. I look over for Renzo and realize a thick branch has impaled the plane between us.

A flash flood of fear threatens to drown me.

"Renzo? Oh God, Renzo, please be alive." My trembling fingers jab at the harness release, trying to free myself to see to the other side of the cockpit, though I'm terrified of what I might find. When I get both buckles unclasped, I spin around on my back and hold the steering yoke to peer over the branch. Renzo is unconscious but breathing, and best of all, he isn't impaled by anything.

A shuddering exhale wracks my body.

I've seen men beaten to a bloody pulp. I even saw my father's blood-soaked body not long after he'd been killed. I'm no stranger to death, but I can feel in my aching bones that seeing Renzo's eyes wide and lifeless would have wrecked me. It would be a test of strength I would have failed.

"Hey, big guy. Wake up." I lean over and pat his scruffy cheek. "Come on, Ren. I'm gonna need you to wake up now."

I pat him again, this time with more oomph. His brows draw together, creasing his forehead.

"That's it, big guy. Wake up. We need to get out of here."

When his eyes open, I'm struck at how blue they are. We have loads of blue-eyed people in my family, including myself, but I'd swear that somehow Renzo's eyes are more pure blue than any I've ever seen.

His hand lifts to his head, causing him to wince. "Jesus, we're alive."

"For the moment. The sun's going down, though, and it's not going to get any warmer. We need to figure out a plan."

He nods, still a bit dazed, then unbuckles his harness. When he shifts upright, the entire plane creaks and groans. We both go inhumanly still.

"The fuck was that?" he breathes.

"I'm not sure." I look out the windshield at the thick wall of pine branches. Pinpricks of light are all that can be seen. Leaning to the side, I try to peer out the side window. The crack of a breaking branch pierces the quiet a second before one side of the plane lurches downward several inches. The movement gives me the view I need to see that our situation is worse than I imagined, though how that's possible is beyond me.

"*Fuck.*" I hiss. "Okay, so we're not on the ground quite yet."

"What do you mean not on the ground?"

"You remember *Jurassic Park*—the original one with the car in the tree?"

"Are you fucking kidding me?"

"We need to get out of here, fast."

"How?" he barks back at me quietly as if the sound might disturb gravity. "If we move, the whole thing might fall."

"What do you propose we do instead? Sit here and *die?*"

"Maybe. We might be better off," he grumbles. "Jesus *Christ* you are pure chaos, you know that? Never in my goddamn life have I been around someone who attracts trouble like you."

"You wait one fucking minute," I spit back at him, my

eyes narrowing to furious slits. "I could say the same thing about *you*. None of this shit ever happened to me until you stomped into my life. Conner was supposed to be the one dealing with those damn guns but noooo. You threw a hissy fit and demanded *me*. Tell me how that's *my* fault."

"Take us with you—that's how. If it wasn't for *you*, they'd probably have left us in that warehouse, and at least we'd be a hell of a lot warmer."

"No, we wouldn't. You know why? Because we'd be *dead*. Those guys were gonna kill us." I'm so spitting mad I could lean over that branch and strangle the man. How *dare* he blame this all on me?

"You don't know what they were gonna do because you never even gave them a chance. You practically *begged* them to take us."

"And what was your great plan, oh Perfect One? Because I can't recall you contributing a goddamn thing to the situation."

Renzo's jaw muscles clench so tight, I half expect to hear a tooth crack. "Sometimes the best thing to do is *nothing*." He swipes his arm to the side to accentuate his point. The entire plane groans before dropping another few inches.

"Shit. We need to get out of here," he mumbles.

"Sure you don't want to do nothing?" I mutter back while slinking my way past the branch and carefully moving toward the exit. With the plane almost upside down, I have to scale the walls to keep from falling toward the tail end, which would be nasty for so many reasons, including the heap of mangled bodies piled at the bottom. I try to ignore them. No matter how tough you are, dismembered corpses are still unsettling.

The door is to my left and above me. I'm not sure getting it open is possible, even if I could get to it. Down to my right,

I see an opening in the middle of the cabin. The plane bent at some point, cracking open the body on one side.

"We can slip out there. I think that will be better than trying to get the door open." I shift my body to start in that direction, then remember something. "Wait!"

Renzo freezes midway through exiting the cockpit.

"There was a first-aid kit somewhere up there. I saw it when I was moving the pilot. Look around. We might need it."

He stares at me for a second as if weighing his options, then retreats backward. "Got it."

He stashes the canvas bag down his jacket and continues to follow me. Cargo ties along the walls give me the purchase I need to lower myself gently to the gaping hole on one side. I look back to see how Renzo is managing, concerned that he has nearly one hundred pounds on me and might struggle with the maneuver, but he surprises me with his agility.

I poke my head outside. "There's enough branches within reach that I can scale my way over to the tree across from us. Follow me."

I step outside, a gust of frigid air penetrating my jeans as if I wasn't wearing anything. If I thought it was cold in the plane, that was nothing. We both have jackets, mine more insulated than Renzo's, but nothing suited to this weather. I have no idea how we're going to keep from getting hypothermic.

"One disaster at a time, Shae," I whisper to myself.

"What?"

"Nothing," I mutter. The last thing I want to do is give him more things to blame on me.

Once I've made my way to the trunk of the tree, Renzo squeezes himself through the jagged metal opening and onto the branch. It bends with his weight, and we both still.

66

Slowly, my hulking companion eases himself toward me with his hands firmly gripping the branch above him for balance. After I know he's made it out, I take a slow, cleansing breath, then squat down to lower myself to the next set of branches.

We're approximately twenty feet in the air. With a bank of snow beneath us, dropping might not be terrible, but I'd rather not risk a broken leg. I'm standing one level down from Renzo when a distant whooshing fills my ears like a raging river. I peer up at him, unease filling me.

"What the hell is that?"

"I think it's … the wind."

A wall of arctic air sweeps through the trees as if in confirmation. Branches sway all around us, along with a dusting of snow swept up into the sky.

We both cling to the trunk of the tree. The gust isn't strong enough to knock us down, but it's plenty strong to shake lose the dangling plane. A cacophony of cracks and moans announces its sudden descent toward the ground. Like a ball on a Plinko board bouncing off prongs on its way to the bottom, the plane plummets in a jerking motion as it hits branches on its way down. The cockpit touches first with the back of the plane bending in half at the seam, crumpling over itself in a mangled heap of metal.

I watch awestruck as the puff of snow around it settles, then peer up wide-eyed at Renzo. "You think it'll explode?"

"If it hasn't already, I'd say probably not."

I nod, praying he's right.

Wordlessly, we both resume our descent. Once we're both safely on the ground, we walk an arcing circle around the plane.

"We could use it as shelter if we could get inside," I suggest, though I can't see a way in, and I'm still worried the thing could burst into flames at any moment.

"I'm not sure there is an inside left," Renzo adds.

A weary sigh slips past my lips. "Okay, the plane isn't an option. We need to find someplace to escape the cold for the night."

"I suggest we go south toward the border and warmer temps. There's bound to be more towns that way, too." He points to his left.

"How do you know that's south?" The sun sets in the west, but we're far enough north that the sun is behind the horizon and makes shadows hard to read.

"Trees tend to grow thicker and longer branches where they get the most light. That's south up here."

I look around at the trees above me, and I'll be damned if there isn't a subtle pattern of more growth on one side. "How the hell did you know that?"

"My grandmother." His answer surprises me enough to draw my gaze back to him. "She loved plants. Had a greenhouse in the backyard that I loved to play in as a kid."

"She teach you any arctic survival techniques?" I ask with a touch of humor, needing to lighten the mood.

He shakes his head somberly.

"Pity." I shove my hands in my pockets and start our trek through the knee-deep snow.

11

Kenzo

THIS FUCKED-UP SITUATION ISN'T SHAE'S FAULT. I KNOW THAT. She's not the one who kidnapped us at gunpoint. But Jesus Christ have things been insane since the second I met her. I mean, what more could possibly go wrong?

We're probably going to freeze to death in the middle of the goddamn Canadian wilderness, assuming that's where we are. We don't even know that for sure.

I can't think about that crap.

I have to focus on how we're going to survive the night. I consider the options. As far as I can figure, if we walk a little ways and there are no outcroppings or other natural formations that would serve as a shelter, then I suppose we cover ourselves with as many pine branches as possible. A fire would be amazing, but fuck if I know how to start a fire out here. I feel totally helpless, and I fucking hate it.

For the past twenty years of my life, I shadowed my father and absorbed everything I could about what it took to survive in the world—in *our* world. How to detect betrayal and lead a family organization. What business pitfalls to avoid. Who makes the best allies and how to negotiate deals without getting killed. My father exposed me to a wealth of information over the years, but everything I ever learned means jack shit here. This isn't just another world; it's a whole other universe.

Then there's Shae. She may not feel like I'm responsible for keeping her alive, but I do. That's who I am. I feel an enormous pressure to get us out of this, and I have no goddamn idea how. The weight of it keeps me from pushing to catch up with Shae when she starts her march south. I need a few minutes to wrap my head around everything that's happened. I'm so damn preoccupied that I almost miss the fact that Shae is limping.

"You hurt?" I call ahead to her.

"I'm fine," she snaps over her shoulder.

I sigh out a cloud of foggy breath and increase my pace. When I'm close enough, I grab her wrist to stop her. She turns and levels me with a look of indifference so icy it makes the wind out here feel balmy.

"You're limping."

"And? It's fine. Just tweaked my ankle at some point." She tries to turn back around, but I stop her.

"Let's check it out. You can sit on that fallen tree over there." I point at the log on the ground not far from us.

"Seriously? We don't need to waste time on this."

"We'll waste time on what I say we waste time on." *And*

you *are not a waste of time.* "Now, you going to walk over there, or do I have to carry you?"

She glares, then half stomps, half gimps to the log. She undoes the laces to her boot with an aggressive flair to make certain I feel her disdain, then shoves her foot in my direction. I squat and take her foot in my hands, carefully slipping off her sock. A tinge of bruising has formed around the outside of her ankle along with a little swelling, but it's not awful. I slowly give the joint a full rotation, watching her intently for signs of pain. It's nothing too great that she can't mask.

"I suppose you'll survive." I put her sock back on like I would for my little niece and nephew.

"Like I said, I'm fine." She's trying to be petulant, but her tone has lost its bite.

I sit beside her on the log while she laces her boot back up. "We need to make a plan. I doubt anyone knows that plane went down—those guys weren't the type to register a flight."

"We can't be too far from civilization. We were, what … a half hour from the airstrip?"

"That could be a hell of a long trip on foot."

"True," she murmurs defeatedly.

"Let's focus on the plan for tonight and take it one step at a time." One day at a time. "It doesn't seem to be getting darker. I'd thought the sun was setting, but I'm guessing that's just how daylight looks around here." I'm glad we still have light but have no idea how long it will last. "We can keep going a bit farther, but if we don't come across anything soon, we need to work on a shelter."

"Yeah. I'd like to keep walking a little farther. Maybe it's foolish, but I feel like if we keep looking, something will come up."

I note the earnest hope in her eyes—golden flecks that

spark brightly against the blue background of her irises. Even in these dire circumstances, she can't help but be optimistic. That is the foundation of her bold charisma, I suddenly realize. It's not an air of cocky confidence. She's an eternal optimist, and I find that surprisingly admirable. Few people can take life's hits and continue to get back on their feet with a smile.

"At least we're dressed decently." I stand, noting how that optimism has a way of rubbing off.

"Jesus, Donati. Your boot is covered in blood. It's soaked into the leather."

"I had to stop that shooter. Couldn't use my hands, so I had to make do."

Her gaze flicks up to me. "Thanks for that," she says softly. It's the first sign of genuine vulnerability I've seen from her, and it's the most intoxicating thing I've ever experienced. To have her give me that softer side makes me ravenous for more.

"We'd better keep moving." My voice is as ragged as I feel inside, raw with emotions I can't begin to name.

I help her to her feet and follow her lead. We walk for another half an hour. Urgency gnashes its frothing jaws at our heels, keeping us moving at a steady pace. I can't remember the last time I had anything to eat. My stomach tries to complain, but adrenaline is an efficient silencer. We keep going because we have to. Neither of us would have been content to give in without having at least checked out the area. We have to try, but daylight finally dims, and the chill in the wind grows unbearable.

"Shae, stop. It's getting darker. We can't keep up the search anymore tonight."

She lifts her head and peers around as if just noticing the dwindling light. "Fuck," she curses under her breath. "What now?"

"I say we collect as many needle-filled branches as we can, maybe dig out an area next to one of the bigger trees, and make a sort of shelter. Cover ourselves with the branches, essentially. The snow isn't as deep here, which helps."

She nods. "We need water. I'm so damn thirsty."

"We can probably use something in the first-aid kit to hold snow as it melts, but in the meantime, we might have to eat some snow. Just don't let yourself get too cold."

We break apart and start hunting for branches that suit our purpose. Too large, and they're too hard to break off the tree. If they've been on the ground too long, the needles don't stay on. We need as much insulation as we can find.

I go from tree to tree, gathering what I can. I'm about to turn back with an armload of branches when I hear Shae call out my name. She's far enough away that I can't tell if she's in danger or simply looking for me. Fear shoots through my veins. I drop the branches and run in the direction of her voice. When I finally see her, a wide grin on her face, I stop and bend at the waist to catch my breath.

She's okay. Everything's okay.

Except even that short run was utterly exhausting when I'm so low on food and sleep. It's not a good sign.

I stand back up as she approaches.

Shae grabs my hand and pulls me behind her. "Check it out. I think I found something." She retraces her steps through the trees, then stops and points. "Look, it's a cabin, right? Isn't that some sort of shed or cabin?"

The dim light, a forest of tree trunks, and distance make it hard to tell exactly what it is, but it's definitely something. And something is a hell of a lot better than nothing.

"Let's go check it out." Hope gives renewed energy to our steps, and before long, we're in view of a tiny log cabin. While it's not large, the logs used in its construction are thick and sturdy. It's in good condition, though not currently in use from the looks of it. The window is boarded over. No smoke coming from the chimney. I'd guess it's some sort of hunting retreat, which makes me wonder if civilization isn't far.

I look at Shae, who looks back at me with a brilliant grin that could warm the coldest night. I can't help but smile back, and the next thing I know, she's in my arms, and I'm spinning her around as she squeals with relief.

A boulder the size of a city bus lifts from my chest.

We have shelter. We're going to survive the night.

When I set Shae's feet back on the ground, there's a lingering second before she pulls away.

"We should work on getting inside and gather some firewood before it's completely dark." She keeps her eyes averted to the cabin.

I go to the door and knock. "Hey there! Anyone home?" I call plenty loud so anyone in the area can hear, then squat to examine the lock. "You still have that pocketknife by chance?"

"Shit, no. It's buried back in the plane rubble."

"Maybe there's something in the first-aid kit that will be useful." I'd rather not damage the door trying to get in. A cabin isn't nearly as helpful against the cold with the door busted down.

"While you work on that, I'll gather some wood." She gets to work while I open the kit and start searching through its contents. The canvas bag is surprisingly well-equipped. Aside from medical necessities, there's a sewing kit, several glucose pouches, and the basics for a water filter. Among the medical supplies, I find a pair of metal tweezers. I pull them apart like I would a wishbone, then use one of the broken halves to pry at the deadbolt. I figure I have a better chance of sliding the bolt in from the side rather than trying to pick the lock. The wood is relatively young, and after some wiggling, I can feel the end of the tweezer hit metal. I work the tool back and forth while giving the door a little shake until it finally gives way.

Fuck, yes.

I barely get a look inside when I hear Shae call my name again, but this time, there's no question her voice is dripping with fear.

I whirl around and see tiny Shae holding a bundle of sticks with a giant bear not ten feet from her. He's sniffing the ground and shifting his weight from side to side like a fighter waiting for the bell to ring. I don't understand what the fuck a bear is doing out in the middle of winter. Don't they hibernate? At the same time, I should have known something like this would happen right when we thought we were in the clear. Nothing could ever be so simple as a warm, empty cabin where Shae is concerned.

Even in the middle of winter with no food, this thing has to be a solid four hundred pounds. One hit would drop her for good.

"Don't. Move," I tell her calmly, while my insides are screaming.

"Boots," she whispers. "I ... I think he followed ... the blood ... on your boots." She speaks in quick, quiet bursts, and though I told her not to move, she's slowly inching backward. My guess is, she doesn't even realize she's doing it.

The bear's rocking intensifies before he lets out a deafening roar that sends my stomach barreling into my feet.

Jesus Christ, this is bad.

"Shae, I'm gonna count to three. On three, you toss the wood at his face and run for the cabin. Door's open."

"He'll chase me."

"The wood will stop him at first, and I'll meet you

halfway to keep him back. Your turn to trust me, okay?" I urge her gently but firmly.

Shae nods shakily.

I use my shoe to shove the first-aid kit through the door behind me then unzip my jacket.

"One."

"Two."

"Three."

Shae does exactly as I said and tosses the branches at the bear, who rears back in surprise. At the same time, I shove my hands in my pockets, then lift my jacket up like a sail to make myself look as big as possible. I draw deep down to a primal part of me that never quite evolved and roar my fury. I let out all my frustration and anger about the past two days. I tap into the grief of my father's death and release every pent-up emotion held captive since his loss.

I loose a battle cry my ancestors would have been proud of, and it works.

The bear pauses long enough for me to reach Shae. But the second I turn my back to follow her to the cabin, I see the bear lurch forward out of the corner of my eye. I sweep down and grab a branch that Shae had dropped and swing around to slam the thing like a bat across the bear's face just as he swipes at me.

He pulls away and begins a retreat, but not before those monstrous claws rake across my upper arm. I ignore the pain and run as fast as I can for the cabin. Shae waits inside, slamming the door shut behind me the second I'm through.

"Shit, Renzo. You're bleeding."

12

Shae

"HE GRAZED ME—NOTHING SERIOUS." RENZO'S WORDS ARE labored.

It's pitch black inside the cabin, so I feel around for the chair I'd noticed as I ran in. "Here," I pull him toward the chair. "Sit down so I can get a fire going and look at your arm." I crack the door to let in the last bits of daylight enough to see the inside of the cabin long enough to get my bearings. I make a mental map of a few essentials, note a box of matches next to the stove, then close the door again. Feeling around, I take a cup towel from its hook on the wall and wrap it around Renzo's arm. "Keep that pulled tight. I'm going to see if I can grab some of that wood I dropped."

"How do you know Smokey isn't still out there?"

"He ran when you hit him, and I'm not planning to stay out long enough to lure him back. I'm grabbing what I dropped and getting my ass back inside."

He grunts, then drops his head back and closes his eyes. He isn't passed out or anything, but he's not in great shape either now that the adrenaline has abandoned him. I need to hurry.

I do a quick visual sweep of the area, then run like I'm in grade school trying to help my team win a relay race. I collect every stick I can manage and dart back to the cottage. My heart thunders in my chest when I'm done, both from exertion and relief. We did it. We made it to shelter. I lean back against the door and smile.

"Chaos," Renzo says softly as he watches me. "Pure chaos."

I have to bite back a laugh because of the absurdity of it all. The past two days have been absolute insanity. I start snapping twigs to fit in the small iron stove, praying they are sufficient kindling to catch fire. I really, *really* don't want to have to go back out there. "Hey, you can't blame me this time. I wasn't the one pretending to be Uber Eats for the bear. He thought someone had called for takeout when he smelled your yummy shoes."

He huffs out a laugh. "Damn thing should have been hibernating."

I feel for the box of matches I spotted earlier. "You know bears aren't unconscious when they hibernate, right?"

"Why the fuck would I know anything about bears?"

"You knew to make yourself look bigger," I say as I light some pine needles under the pile of sticks then close the door before the smoke bellows into the room.

"That's just common sense. Anyone knows it's best to

look like the biggest, baddest motherfucker out there, even if you aren't."

I watch through the small window and see some of the twigs start to catch fire, helping to light the room in addition to provide heat. The tiniest bit of tension eases from my shoulders. We're much better off in the cabin than outside, but having a fire warm us would be even better.

I take my first real look around our new digs and see a single bed I'm not even sure can be called a twin. There's a bookcase doubling as a table by the chair Renzo occupies, and another cupboard-like set of shelves on the opposite wall. The place is fully stocked. As much as I've cursed our luck, this is a sign that we haven't been totally forsaken. Cooking utensils, tools, almost any supplies we could ask for are either hanging on the walls or tucked away on shelves. There's even a stockpile of canned goods. Mostly fruits and vegetables. Some beans. It won't feed two people for long, but it'll work for now.

I ignore my rumbling stomach and put a few larger bits of wood on the fire before returning to Renzo. Let's get this stuff off and have a look. As I pull his jacket off his muscled shoulders, I have to wonder how he didn't freeze today. He never complained, but his jacket isn't nearly as warm as my coat. Beneath the jacket, he wears a sweatshirt and a simple cotton undershirt. "You okay to lift your arms?"

The flickering light from the fire shines in his eyes. Without answering, he lifts his shirts up and over his head in one clean motion, tossing them on the ground. His stare never leaves mine.

I, on the other hand, have to drop my gaze to the irresistible sight of Renzo Donati's naked chest. I knew he had tattoos. His neck is decorated with a tease of ink that hints at what might be lurking further beneath his collar. I wasn't prepared, however, for the way my body would react to the sight of his.

Need pools deep in my belly at the artfully designed images covering his torso and left arm, bleeding one into the other seamlessly over smooth skin. His right arm is totally bare. I can tell he's disciplined in his workout routine and diet by the definition of his honed muscles. That sort of physique takes dedication. As someone who practically lives at the gym, I respect that.

I lick my parched lips and try to focus.

His arm, dimwit. Check out his arm.

I position myself to get closer but not block the light—there's little enough of that as it is. Renzo has three claw marks across his outer shoulder. Two are manageable and have almost stopped bleeding. "This middle one is pretty nasty. I think it might need stitches," I tell him.

"There's a sewing kit in the first-aid bag." He nods his head toward the floor where the canvas bag and its contents are piled next to the door.

"It's going to hurt like a bitch." I'm sure he knows, but I have to say it. I feel bad causing him that kind of pain after everything we've already been through.

"If you can manage the stitching, I'll manage the pain."

I nod and turn to get the kit, but he grabs my hand to stop me. "Need food and water first. Let's get a bucket of snow melting and put on a can of beans, then you can have at it. Yeah?"

I nod again and help him wrap the towel around his arm. Once it's in place, I give him a playful glare. "You stay put. Don't need you bleeding out. You're too damn big to bury." There's no way he's bleeding out from the wound anytime soon. It needs stitches, but it's not life-threatening. I simply prefer to keep things light, especially when a situation is bleak.

My effort earns me a small smirk that does funny things to my insides. Things I don't want to feel.

I have to remember that this man is the head of one of the Italian Five Families. He's arrogant and bossy. Until we were stuck out here, he frustrated the hell out of me. This man isn't someone to crush over.

I berate myself while collecting a bucket of snow to set by the fire, then open a can of beans and a can of mandarin oranges.

"We need to be judicious with the food," Renzo says gravely. "No telling how long we'll be here."

My gaze locks with his, but it seems neither of us wants to discuss or even think about the matter since we both let it drop. I put the beans in a pan and put them onto the stove, then bring the can of mandarins with a fork to the table. While I get the first-aid supplies off the floor, Renzo helps himself to the oranges, then spears a couple of slices and hands me the fork. I pull over a polished stump that doubles as a stool and slip the fork in my mouth, trying to ignore the feel of his eyes watching my every movement but forget myself and moan when the sweet ambrosia hits my tongue. I haven't eaten in so long that the sugary fruit tastes like heaven.

When I swallow and open my eyes, Renzo has the fork extended toward me with two more slices ready and a heat in his eyes that shouldn't be possible in this arctic hellscape.

This time, I down the oranges without a show and begin diligently organizing the supplies. "You're lucky I can do this sort of thing."

"You couldn't be squeamish if your life depended on it."

"Glad you noticed." I preen with exaggerated pride,

sitting taller as I squirt a line of antibiotic ointment on my finger. I stand and do my best to gingerly spread the cream along the two smaller cuts, then wipe the excess blood from the larger one before adding ointment to it.

Now comes the fun part. I glower at the simple sewing needle and thread, wishing I had real suture tools. It's only about an inch of the top of the cut that is deep enough to need stitches. The tail end isn't so bad. The worst part is where the claw first dug in.

"This isn't going to be the most aesthetic stitching job," I warn him. At least there isn't any ink on that arm. Any design under the cuts would be lost.

"Scars tell a story the same as a tat. I'm good with either. Now get this over with."

See, bossy.

I take a slow, steadying breath and begin my first stitch.

13

Kenzo

"Tell me a story." I have to force the words through tightly clenched teeth.

"A story?"

"Anything, Shae. Just do something to fuckin' distract me." I swear, I'd rather endure a gunshot—a more serious injury in one fell swoop—than deal with the grating torture of something slowly picking me apart. Death by a thousand cuts. That's something you reserve for only your worst enemies.

"Um, okay." She thinks for a second. "When I was six, I was out on a walk with my family. It was spring, so the tree trimmers were out trimming branches from trees on the sidewalk. The trees were huge on that street, branches arching over the street and meeting in the middle. I walked under where the trimmers were working, and a branch fell at the same moment. Landed right on my head."

"That explains so much."

"Don't make me hurt you more than I already am," she quips lightly. "I ran over to my mom, scared but not crying or anything. I didn't even notice the pain until she told me I'd cracked my head open. A family that we knew who lived one house away saw the commotion and came out. They called EMS and brought a towel for all the blood. I was told to hold the towel on my head until EMS could check me out. When they arrived, they told me to move the towel so they could get a look. I refused. Between everyone saying I'd split my head open and the loads of blood, I thought if I let go, my head would fall apart like two halves of a melon."

The amusement in her tone tells me she has a fondness for the memory. I bet it's a story that's been told a million times in her family. I like that she still finds humor in it.

"Did you need stitches?"

"I did. Ten of them."

"I bet you demanded to watch them do it."

Her teeth nip her bottom lip, fighting back a smile. "Two nurses had to hold hand mirrors to get the right view for me."

The image of a feisty little Shae coaxes a weary smile from me.

"It gets better. I normally shied away from anything girly because I wanted to be just like my big brothers."

"Remind me which ones are your brothers."

"Oran and Cael."

"Not sure I know Cael."

"Probably not. He's married with kids and sticks to the accounting side of the business. Anyway," she continues. "I refused to wear dresses and would have cut my hair short like the boys if my mom had let me. Anything to be the same as them. But after the accident, I made my mom put my hair in pigtails for the next six weeks straight to make sure everyone could see my battle scar."

"I bet she loved that."

"She took full advantage, insisting on curling the damn things every morning. I looked like I should have been on a box of Little Debbie cakes, but I didn't care, so long as I could show off my stitches and scar."

"I bet you were a handful."

"I suppose there's a reason my parents didn't have more kids after me," she teases. "Oran was a parent pleaser, and Cael followed his lead. I was stubborn as a mule."

Still are, I think to myself.

"There, last one all tied up. Five stitches. I'd give you a sticker and a lollipop for being such a good boy, but all I have to offer is baked beans."

"Beans sound incredible. Let's eat."

"I'm not sure if they're hot yet." She peers into the pot.

"Don't care. It's time for this day to be over."

"I can't argue there."

"Tomorrow, we'll build a bonfire and hope someone sees. Until then, we both need to sleep."

She first puts a bandage over her handiwork, then helps me back into my shirts. It's still cold inside. The fire hasn't been going long enough to heat the place fully, but it's getting warmer. Once she stokes said fire, she brings over the pan of beans, then pours what water has melted into a cup. We eat straight out of the pan and share the cup.

I'm not a huge fan of beans, especially with maple syrup in them, but these lukewarm beans might as well be filet mignon to my starving tastebuds. It's only enough to whet my appetite. I could eat the entire stock of canned goods I'm so goddamn hungry. But that would be foolish, and I'm not quite delirious enough to go there. Sleep will help, then we can tackle the next set of problems in the morning.

I stand and stare at the small bed. "We'll have to share it. There's no way either of us can sleep on the cold floor." I'm pretty sure I've stated the obvious, but my thoughts are so damn sluggish.

"If you lay on your good side, back to the wall, we should fit—big spoon, little spoon."

I like the sound of that more than I should. It has to be the exhaustion. I assure myself that curling up with a warm body on a soft bed would sound amazing no matter who I was with.

I slide my boots off and pull back the covers, then ease myself onto the mattress. I don't want to break open my stitches and have to go through that torture again. "Get in."

Shae pours a few more dribbles of water out of the snow bucket and has us each take one more drink. Neither of us has gone to the bathroom since the airport hangar. I assume we're both too dehydrated to have anything in our bladders. She adds a few larger branches to the fire, then kicks off her boots and slides in bed next to me. The soft warmth of her body feels amazing. For the first time in two days, tension melts from my aching muscles.

I curl my top arm around her and gingerly tug her back against me, still mindful of my stitches. Shae stiffens, and I get the sense she's going to argue, so I silence her before she starts.

"Arm's gotta go somewhere. Now quit fussing and go to sleep."

"Fine, but you should know you're not exactly my type, so don't get any ideas."

"What's that supposed to mean?" I murmur, already half asleep.

"I prefer more curves and less testosterone."

"Mmm…" I muse, not buying it. I've seen the way she reacts to me.

"If you don't believe me, you can ask the woman I'm dating when we get home."

Dating? That has my attention. How had it not occurred to me that Shae could be involved with someone? Guess I haven't exactly had time to ponder that sort of thing. But now that I have, I take note that she didn't say girlfriend. She may be seeing someone but only casually.

"She's not here. I am." I'm only giving her a hard time, but it makes me realize, as dumbfounding as it may be, that I'm glad I'm here. I'm glad I'm the one stuck in this tiny cabin with Shae Byrne because no other body should be wrapped snugly around hers.

Knowing that must be the final sign of delirium, I give in to sleep and let everything else fall away.

14

Shae

I'M DISORIENTED WHEN I WAKE IN THE NIGHT. NOT BECAUSE I don't know where I am. I'm confused about why I'm awake when I'm still so damn tired. While I don't normally sleep with someone wrapped around me like the stripe on a candy cane, I'm too exhausted for it to have been a problem.

As my grogginess clears, I realize I'm so hot that I'm starting to sweat.

No, that's not right. I'm sweating, but not because I'm hot. Renzo is burning up. The welcome blanket of his warmth has become a raging inferno of blistering heat.

I clasp his limp hand near my stomach to slip from the bed and find it's eerily clammy. I scoot away from him and sit on the edge of the bed. Renzo's forehead is dotted with sweat.

Shit, this is bad.

It isn't nearly warm enough in here for him to be so hot. He's got a raging fever. It's got to be his wound. Infection is the most logical explanation.

I slathered it in antibiotic gel, but who's to say what rancid bacteria could have been growing on those bear claws, and the sewing kit wasn't exactly sterile.

Shit. Okay. What do I do now?

First, the fire. I know he needs to cool down, but I need to be able to see, so I stoke the fire and add the rest of the wood. The snow is completely melted, so I fill our cup, drink half of it, then sit on the bed and try to wake Renzo.

"Hey, big guy. I need you to wake up." I pat his cheek and finally get movement. His eyes squint open and look around, but I get the sense he's not actually present.

"Not yet. I'm still tired," he mutters and lays back down.

"No, no. Not yet. I need you to drink some water." I get him to prop himself on his elbow, then coax him to drink. "You've got a fever, Renzo. I need you to drink as much as you can without getting sick."

He nods and mutters unintelligibly. The second the cup is empty, he plops back down, practically comatose.

I take in a shaky breath and start to work his arm out from his hoodie. I leave the T-shirt on underneath and lift the bandage to examine the wound. It doesn't look terrible, but it's definitely red and puffy.

That's when my damn imagination acts up and decides to whisper that it might not be infected. It could be rabies. Maybe that's why the bear wasn't hibernating.

I'm not sure what's worse—the thought of him slowly dying from infection, or the possibility of me having to kill him to protect myself.

Not helpful, Shae. Stop freaking out.

I put another layer of ointment over the scratches and replace the bandage. Then I slide the hoodie over his head and decide it would be too hard to get it off the arm he's lying on. Reducing the layers will help, but he could use a cool rag, too. I remember my mother doing that when I had a fever as a kid. I fill up our cup one more time, then dig around for another towel. I don't want to have to use the bloody cup towel. I locate a plaid hand towel and dip it in the remaining water in the bucket, then lay it on his forehead while I make a quick trip to fill up the bucket with snow for melting.

I look around helplessly to see if there's anything else I can do, but nothing comes to mind. I've done everything I can for the moment.

The cabin is quiet save for the crackle of the fire, yet there's no way I can go back to sleep. Worry gnaws at my insides like angry termites hollowing out a log. Instead, I sit next to him, my legs crossed, and gently wipe the wet rag over his forehead and cheeks.

"Come on, big guy. I need you to get better. You can't..." Emotions clog my throat, trapping the words behind a sob I refuse to let loose. "You can't leave me here alone."

A fever normally wouldn't worry me, but nothing about our circumstances is normal. He hasn't had nearly enough water for his body to handle a high fever. We don't have much food and no medicines. And our luck is so abysmally low, I hate to test it. Combine all that with my own exhaustion, and I can't hold back the tears that stream down my cheeks.

I'm scared.

No amount of optimism or bullheaded determination can erase the shittiness of this situation.

"You know," I say to the night air. "We met at the warehouse two days ago, as far as I can figure. That was February

12th, which means this is the 14th. Valentine's Day. You can't leave a girl alone on Valentine's." My words thin to a choked whisper.

Renzo starts mumbling in his sleep. His brows knit together, hardening his features. He looks so intense. So commanding. I wish I knew what he was dreaming about, but his words are unintelligible. Delirium. I think there isn't any sense to be made from them until one word rings clear.

Chaos.

I don't know why, but it makes me smile. "That's right, big guy. I'm here."

I wet his forehead one more time, then lie down. I sleep in short intervals, waking every hour to make him drink and make sure he's not hot enough to need the wet rag. By morning, he's sleeping peacefully enough that I eat a can of potatoes, then pass out until midday.

Renzo sleeps peacefully through the afternoon while I familiarize myself with our surroundings. He's cooperative but not fully coherent by the end of the day, and his arm looks better when I clean it before bed. This time, I pass out hard and don't wake until morning when a hand lazily cups my breast.

15

Kenzo

"Um, excuse me." A woman's voice penetrates the sleepy haze fogging my brain. I feel her slipping from the bed and wonder why I have a woman over when I feel so shitty. My body hurts like I was hit by a fucking truck. Twice.

I try to stretch out and find that I can't. What the hell happened to my bed?

I crack open my eyes and take in the tiny cabin around me.

Oh, *fuuuuuck*.

It wasn't a nightmare.

Shae presses the inside of her wrist to my forehead. Seemingly satisfied, she pulls away, and her entire body sags as if with relief.

"What's that all about?" I sit upright and slowly move to the edge of the bed, noting my right shoulder is especially sore. A bandage peeks out from beneath my T-shirt, reminding me of our encounter with the bear.

"You had a fever." She stands and crosses to the fire, keeping me from seeing her face, but I swear I heard a catch in her voice.

"Fever, huh. I suppose that explains the soreness." I cram my feet in my boots but don't bother tying them. When I stand, the world spins. Shae's there in an instant to steady me.

"Hold up, tough guy. You need to take it easy."

"What I need to do is take a piss. I think I can handle that." She's acting like I'm some sort of invalid, and I'm not sure why.

"Good. Maybe you can make it to the trees this time." She opens the door for me with a raised brow.

"This time?" An eerie sense of déjà vu raises the hair on the back of my neck.

"Yeah, I helped you yesterday. Do you remember anything about being sick?"

I avoid her observant stare while slipping on my jacket. "Guess not." I don't remember anything, and I hate it. Blank spots in my memory feel like a violation. I've never liked the way it feels, which is why I rarely get drunk.

She wraps an arm around me and walks with me to the nearest tree like I'm her ninety-year-old grandfather. I want to tell her I don't need her help, but I have a sneaking suspicion that I do. I draw the line, however, when she goes to help me with my pants. "I got it," I snap.

She steps away to give me privacy.

Jesus, tell me she didn't have to take out my limp dick so I could take a piss. It suddenly hits me what she said. "Yesterday? How long was I out?"

"About thirty-six hours," she says in a somber tone that snags in my chest.

Fuck, she had to have been terrified. That means I was out of it a full day and two nights. A long fucking time considering how long I'd been without food and water before that. I take out my dick and unload a full bladder, the relief instantaneous. She must have been diligent in getting me to hydrate. I have a feeling I owe her. Big.

"There's a stream nearby," Shae announces with exaggerated energy. It's almost like she's uncomfortable. There are any number of reasons for someone to feel that way at this moment, but Shae isn't the type to suffer that emotion, which makes me curious.

"That's good news."

"It means water isn't an issue," she continues, "but we need to source some food. There are traps hanging on the back of the house. I got two set up yesterday before the light started to fade. I need to go check them. Wasn't able to work on that bonfire yet, but we can work on that now that you're feeling better."

"How the hell do you know how to set a trap?" I finish and tuck myself back in my pants.

"I didn't." She snickers. "Still don't. No clue if I did it right."

When I look at her laughing despite the epic unfairness of everything that's happened—not freaking out or angry or despondent—I'm struck by how resilient she is. I can't think of a single person I know who would be handling this as well as she is.

"Not sure I know how to rig a trap any better than you, but I'll have a look."

"Are you sure you're up for a trek through the woods?" She leads us back inside the cabin.

"How far did you go?" I don't like the thought of her wandering in the woods alone with that bear out there somewhere. No telling if it'll come back.

"Not that far. You'll probably survive." She flashes me a smile with a wink, and my dick stirs to life.

Incredible.

It doesn't matter that I was delirious with a fever for the past thirty-six hours. Shae Byrne has a way of getting to me like no one else. Frustration, fear, lust, amusement—my body and mind respond to her on every level, whether I want them to or not.

"You can use some of this for washing up." She points at a five-gallon paint bucket half full of water next to the stove. "There's no shower, obviously, but there is an outhouse out back. It's essentially four walls around a hole in the ground, but it's better than nothing."

"You sure I was only out for a day?"

"Yeah, and I even slept the first half of the day yesterday. You'd be amazed what you can get done when there are no distractions."

"I can imagine," I murmur while looking at our tiny stronghold for the first time in the daylight. It takes minimalist living to a new extreme yet appears to have everything we might need at first glance. "This place is pretty incredible."

"I'm glad you think so because … we might be here a while." The hesitancy in her voice draws my attention back to her. She's chewing on the inside of her cheek when she hands me a map.

I unfold the well-worn paper. It's a map of the Quebec province. The cities are primarily clustered along the extensive coastline with the central portion mostly untouched save for a small settlement here and there. A small X has been penciled in a seemingly random location north of Montreal.

"You think this is where the cabin is?"

"It's a safe bet, I'd say. And if you look at the scale, it says we're sixty miles from the closest town."

I let the information sink in. At full strength, I could easily walk fifteen to twenty miles in a day. But I'm not healthy, and we'd be walking in knee-deep snow. That means instead of three days of walking, it could be more like a week. Not to mention, our food situation is sketchy, and the nighttime temperatures would probably kill us.

Getting out of here could be a real problem.

I should be upset with this news. It means we're likely stuck here until the weather is warm enough for us to survive a journey to civilization. I'm not pleased, but I'm not disappointed either. I'm not sure what I feel. Numb, maybe. It's like when you say a word too many times in a row and it begins to lose its meaning. I've been faced with so many intense challenges in such a short amount of time that one more hardly registers.

But what does register is intrigue.

Alone in the wilderness with Shae, possibly for weeks.

I don't hate the prospect. I don't hate it at all.

"Sounds like we need to figure out how to hunt."

16

Shae

It's not often I'm caught off guard. I was fully prepared to defend my actions, expecting Renzo to grumble or yell or find some way to remind me how this was all my fault. Not that *I* think it's my fault, but he certainly seemed to after the plane crash. It was a safe assumption that hearing how stranded we are would piss him off again. But it didn't. He took the news with a grain of salt and moved on.

I'm not sure how to interpret his change of heart, though it has been an eventful few days. It hardly seems real that so much has happened in four short days. Four days that are somehow both the shortest and longest days I've ever experienced. Driving up to the docks in that truck feels like an eternity ago, yet simultaneously like it was only yesterday.

Sitting up with Renzo through the worst of his fever felt like it took a year off my life. I've never been so goddamn scared. Each new disaster we've faced, I've met head-on with determination, in part because of him. Because I know that no matter how sucky the situation, at least I wasn't enduring it alone.

That's why I almost fell apart completely when he finally woke. The relief was an overwhelming tidal wave of emotion. I had to turn away while I fought for composure because I don't want him to see me as some blathering female. I don't personally think crying is a sign of weakness, but I know most men see it that way. That's how our society conditions them.

Don't be a crybaby. Man up.

I know because I've lived my life in a man's world and learned early that it's imperative to speak their language. Normally, that's not an issue. I'm not a particularly emotional person by nature, but those hours with him unconscious were horrifying. Merely watching him move around the cabin gives me new energy.

"We've eaten two of the ten cans of beans—one for each day. I figure that's a reasonable rationing since we haven't had any other protein source yet. Do you want to have our can now or save it for later today?"

"Now. My stomach is currently trying to eat me from the inside out."

"You have your choice of baked beans, baked beans, orrr baked beans with maple."

"Surprise me," he says dryly. "You say there are tools on the back of the cabin?"

"Just a couple of things—the traps and an ax most importantly."

"I'll check that out while you get the beans going."

An hour later, we've had our meager breakfast and are on our way to check the traps I set. They aren't far. My encounter with Smokey was still too fresh in my mind for me to feel comfortable wandering off alone.

I had no idea what I was doing when I "set" the traps. Because of that, I know as we approach that the chances of catching anything are slim, but I'm unexpectedly frustrated to see both traps empty. I would have loved more than anything to bring Renzo out here and present him with something solid for us to eat.

"Not sure how you're supposed to catch anything with a wire," I grumble. "What are the chances something will just happen to walk through the trap?" The whole thing seems impossible.

"These are snare traps, and you're right, they key is knowing where the animal is likely to go. Plus, we need to get every single one of those traps out here. It's about numbers. There are nearly two dozen snares, and we need every one of those rigged."

"I thought you said you didn't know anything about trapping."

"Compared to the sort of person who comes out here intentionally, I don't." His eyes cut to me, and I see a hint of mischief glinting in their depths. "But the city has a lot of rats."

My mouth gapes open. "Why on *earth* would you hunt rats? They make tidy little box traps for that."

"A lot of us boys hung around in the summer with nothing to do. Sometimes we'd make it a competition."

"I will never, *ever* understand men." I shake my head slowly side to side, though I'm amused. I imagine an adolescent Renzo would have been pretty entertaining before the pressures of adulthood sobered him.

The sly grin he flashes me launches a score of butterfly wings flapping in my chest. "Fortunately, you don't have to understand us to appreciate what we have to offer."

"Oh yeah? And what's that? Toxic masculinity and a patriarchy?" I know. I can't help myself. At least my tone is playful.

Renzo glares, matching my teasing energy. "I was thinking catcalls and commitment issues, but you had to go and make it personal."

His comeback is so unexpected, I burst out laughing. "I'm so sorry. You're right. How could I have ignored the obvious?"

He grunts. "Try better next time."

My eyes follow him with no small amount of intrigue as his gaze searches the area.

"You say there's a creek nearby?"

"Yeah, over there about one hundred yards." I point in the direction.

"Let's head that way. We need to look for tracks. Any kind of sign that something is in the area. I figure that's more likely around a water source."

"Makes sense."

He eyes me for an elongated second before starting to walk, and I'd give my favorite left toe to know what he's thinking, but there's no way I'm going to ask. It's probably best I don't know. These next few weeks will be difficult enough as it is. No need to complicate things.

I have to repeat the thought three times to myself before I remotely start to believe it.

We spend the next two hours setting up all the snare traps he brought from the cabin. We stake broken branches into the ground wherever possible to anchor the snare or use low-lying branches suited for rigging a noose.

He's worn down by the time we get back to the cabin. It worries me. I don't want a relapse.

"Why don't you relax a bit—have a can of fruit and some water—while I chop more firewood."

"We need to get that bonfire going, though."

"I have a couple of logs set aside. I'll add any more that I see. Tomorrow, you'll have more strength and can help me finish up."

He gives a single nod and heads inside.

I'm struck by how grateful I am that he didn't try to dissuade me or challenge whether I was capable. Maybe he was simply too tired to bother, but I don't think that's it. I wouldn't go so far as to say I misjudged him. However, I will admit that time together has helped us understand one another better. Possibly even respect one another.

I'm not trying to imply that mutual respect has a deeper meaning. We have no choice but to be a team out here, and respect is crucial when relying on a team member. That's all it is. Nothing to read into and certainly not a reason for me to be smiling while I exhaust myself chopping wood. Therefore, I should probably wipe this stupid grin off my face, but the damn thing's like a virus. I have to let it run its course and hope it doesn't mutate into something worse.

Slinging an ax is a fantastic way to expel unwanted emotions. It's also a great way to end up drenched in sweat. The tiny bit of food we've had isn't remotely enough to support the calories I'm burning. Adrenaline keeps me going, but I can tell I'm worn out way faster than I would be if I wasn't starving.

When exhaustion prevents me from chopping any more wood, I collect an armful of logs and head inside. "What I wouldn't give for a shower and a fresh set of clothes." I plop down on the stool after setting the logs by the stove and pour myself a full cup of water.

"If you want to wash up with what's left in the bucket, I'll go refill it when you're done," Renzo offers.

"I guess I could at least wash my face and rinse my shirt." I take off my coat, then lift my shirt over my head and kneel next to the water bucket. I wet the same towel I swept over Renzo's forehead while he was sick and use it to wipe down my face and upper body. The cold water on my heated skin feels amazing, sending a shiver from head to toe.

As I submerge my shirt in the water, my back suddenly feels warm. The preternatural warm that happens when being watched. I left my bra on, so I'm not naked, but I'm more exposed than I've been in front of him, and I sense his awareness.

His stare rakes over me like a physical touch—the back of my neck, my shoulders, the indentation of my spine. I imagine an intimacy to it, though I shouldn't. We have no choice but to live openly in front of one another.

I chide myself not to read into anything because these aren't normal circumstances. He's not watching me clean up because I invited him to my place. He has no damn choice. And even if he did, enjoying the attention is such a bad idea. What happens when this surreal bubble pops and we return to reality? He goes back to his world, and I go back to mine.

Our cousins may have married one another, but Noemi isn't part of the family business. Her marriage to my cousin Conner didn't create a conflict of loyalties. I'm different. I've worked so hard to be accepted as an equal in the Byrne business. I'd never let that go just to be with a man or anyone for that matter. And if that's the case, it would be idiotic to let myself fantasize about someone like Renzo, even if we're stuck in a place where the rules from back home don't apply.

I squeeze out my shirt and find a place to hang it on the wall, then put my coat on to keep me from catching a chill.

"Not sure what's going on in that head of yours, but I don't think I like it."

"What do you mean?" I finally let my gaze drift to his.

"While you were sitting there—your whole body deflated. Don't like seeing that. We'll find a way back, you know. It may take a while, but we'll get home." He thinks I'm worried and is trying to lift my spirits. It's unexpectedly sweet but reinforces what I've already been thinking.

"Yeah, I know." I can't keep the sadness from my voice because before long, this will all be a distant memory.

17

Kenzo

NIGHT FALLS EARLY OUT HERE IN THE WILDERNESS WHERE THERE'S no electricity to fight back the darkness. It's just as well. Neither of us has had a full belly of food in days, and we're both still recovering from all that's happened. We're both ready to call it a day not long after our meager evening meal of green beans and pineapple chunks.

Despite how tired we are, however, the air in our little fortress grows unquestionably dense with tension as bedtime nears. Our past two nights sharing the tiny bed were inconsequential, seeing as how we were either blind with exhaustion or, in my case, literally comatose.

Tonight is different.

Shae must feel it too because she's acting differently—

fiddling with tidying up and rarely looking in my direction. She continues to fidget once we're in bed. My dick is apparently plenty rested because all it takes is a momentary press of Shae's ass for him to stand at attention.

"Woman, you need to quit your wiggling." My voice is a gravelly growl that I hope she interprets as exhaustion rather than what it truly is—desire.

"I can't help it. I'm a stomach sleeper. Sleeping on my side doesn't feel right."

The image of her sleeping naked on her stomach in my bed back home flashes in my mind. I can see myself align my body with hers and guide her thighs apart before pressing deep inside her. The vision is so detailed, it could be a memory. It's more than enough to make me rock hard. Hell, my dick is a goddamn tree truck sprouted between us.

The next time she wiggles, I clamp my arm tight around her middle and pull her against me. Let her feel the effect she has on me.

Shae freezes on a ragged intake of breath.

"Told you to quit your fidgeting," I murmur, wishing I knew what she was thinking. She has to know I can't help it. His actions aren't exactly voluntary. Of course, I didn't have to pull her against me. That was pure selfishness, and I'm not remotely sorry.

At least now she knows whatever pitiful representation of my manhood she might have seen while I was sick wasn't the whole picture. My pride dusts itself off and sits a little taller, much like my dick.

"I didn't mean to … I was just trying to get comfortable." She's flustered, but I'm not sure if it's a good thing or not. I'll feel like a real asshole if I find out later she was worried I might try to take advantage in the night. I might have fantasized about it, but I wouldn't actually do it. Not really. Not unless I knew she wanted it.

Jesus, I sound like a creep.

I actively force myself to give her as much space as I can, which isn't much, though I leave my top arm draped over her. I can't bring myself to break that connection.

We both lie still. Awkwardly still.

The room is painfully quiet, save for a few pops and crackles coming from the stove. My exhaustion from minutes earlier has pulled a Houdini and disappeared. I wonder how long I'll have to lie here before the tension dissipates. Probably until Shae falls asleep. Next, I wonder how long that might take if we're equally uncomfortable, but all my questions are silenced when Shae slowly, deliberately leans her body back against mine.

Masculine satisfaction swells in my chest. Whatever hit my pride might have taken is now long forgotten as he stands atop a boulder and begins to pound his chest with his fists like fucking Tarzan.

This is a problem.

I want to tell myself it's the circumstances—that it's been one hell of a week, and she's the only person around to find comfort in—but I taste the bitterness in the lie.

This craving in me isn't merely a byproduct of our situation that will fade as soon as we're home. It's Shae. The way her skin is so damn soft under my fingertips. The way her hair still hints at a lingering scent of roses even though we don't have a single bar of soap. It's the knowledge that despite how inexcusably harsh I was with her, she did everything she could to help me when I needed her.

A shit ton of people out there would have seen my illness as a convenient way to conserve supplies. She's plenty capable and didn't particularly *need* me for her survival, but she kept me alive anyway. She's honorable, compassionate, resilient—the list grows every day, making it harder for me to remember why wanting her would be a bad idea.

The fact that I would even consider shrugging my responsibilities as the Moretti family boss is a dangerous sign. A relationship between us wouldn't work.

Not if you were back home. But we're not home.

It's true, and we may never make it back home. Why the fuck shouldn't we do what we want while we can? What happens in the wilderness doesn't have to follow us home.

I'm attempting to rationalize a bad decision. I hear it plain as day, but I don't care. That's the worst part. She's got me so damn wound up that I'd intentionally fuck myself over if it meant keeping her close.

My hand presses flat against her belly as if in acceptance of my fate.

Never thought I'd give in to addiction. I'm not the type. Yet here I lie, happy to know I have at least one more day with my new drug of choice.

Chaos.

MORNING BRINGS another bout of anticipation, equally as consuming, but the source is entirely different. It's time to check our traps. There are no words for how desperately I'm hoping to find that at least one of the snares worked.

I'm so fucking hungry it hurts.

If we didn't eat at all, our stomachs might at least go numb to the hunger, but every tidbit of food we consume seems to enrage my stomach all over again like a child throwing a tantrum over a toy that's been taken away.

"I will never take food for granted again," I say aloud as we start toward the creek where we have our traps.

"No kidding." Shae is especially somber this morning. We're both feeling the weight of reality setting in. If we can't catch our own food, we'll be forced to make our journey to civilization in the dead of winter when the odds of our survival are slim to none.

"What's your least favorite thing to eat?" I ask as a distraction.

"Hmm … maybe sauerkraut. I'm not a fan of anything fermented."

"Would you eat it now?"

"In a heartbeat. I'd lick my plate clean." She shoots me a small smile. "What about you? What's something you usually refuse to eat?"

"Hardboiled eggs," I say immediately. No need to think about it.

"Oh, yeah? Eggs are awfully good for you."

"Sure, and I'll eat them scrambled or over medium, but hardboiled is nasty. One part is Jell-O-like, and the other is all pasty. It's just nasty. Makes me gag."

"So it's a texture thing. Interesting. And right now, if I set a plate of hardboiled eggs in front of you?"

"I'd eat that shit, and I'd be pissed about every damn bite of it," I offer in a playfully petulant tone.

Shae laughs.

Fuck, do I love hearing that sound. It's so uninhibited. So pure.

We grow quiet before cresting the small hill before the valley that houses the creek bed. When the area's in view, we both scan from a distance. Shae's hand suddenly clamps down on my arm.

"Ren, look at the one farthest from the tree. Is that something on the snare?"

I look, though my attention is divided between the snare and noting how much I like hearing her call me Ren. As a kid, I *hated* when people called me that. To this day, no one does because I won't let them. I thought it sounded too feminine, like a cute little bird. On Shae's lips, it sounds completely different. It sounds like *mine*, and I like the sound of that. A lot.

"I think you may be right. Let's go look."

Its white coat made the rabbit hard to see from a distance, but there's no disguising it up close. We caught a goddamn rabbit, and I've never been so fucking elated in my life. The second we see it, Shae leaps into my arms, and we both whoop and holler. Our joy and relief are so effervescent even the sun peeks through the clouds to check out the commotion.

"Oh my God. Your shoulder." Shae suddenly shoves away from me and slaps a hand over her mouth. "I didn't tear the stitches, did I?"

"Wouldn't care if you did."

A brilliant grin spreads wide across her face. "Rabbit's worth the celebration."

Not what I meant, but it's best if that's what she thinks. "Come on, let's get this sucker skinned and cooking."

She whoops one more time and does a little jump that's so fucking adorable, I'm tempted to abandon the rabbit and trap her instead. I'd press her against a tree and fuck her senseless so she knows what it feels like to lose your goddamn mind over someone.

Good thing for me, my stomach staunchly refuses that plan.

I take the dead rabbit from her once she frees it from the

snare, then we fix a few of the snares that need to be readjusted. Our walk back to the cabin is infused with the hum of renewed energy as though we can't get back fast enough.

"You know how to skin an animal?" Shae asks as we walk.

I consider how to answer, not wanting to explain that I've skinned something before, but it wasn't an animal. That's not something a person tends to share—I don't want her looking at me like a savage. I'm still gauging my reply when she continues. "I saw my dad skin the stars off a Russian once, but that hardly seems the same." Her contemplative words are so unexpected that I almost stumble in the snow.

"Your father let you watch that shit?"

"Yeah, my dad was awesome. He always let me be exactly who I wanted to be. It's my cousins and the other dumbass men in the family who made me prove myself. Still do," she adds under her breath.

I think about my two younger sisters and what I would have done if they'd wanted to work alongside me. Bria has only ever wanted to be a mother to her two kids, and Terina spends too much time on social media to have an interest in anything else. I can't even begin to imagine them doing the things I do. But I *can* imagine how hard it would have been for Shae to convince men like me to give her a shot, especially when she was younger. It's in our nature to protect women and children. Allowing her to put herself in danger goes against our DNA, but Shae was made to thrive in our world. She's gritty and clever and so fucking tough.

"Seems like a waste of talent to keep you on the sidelines," I admit.

"Right?" she balks. "Just because I don't have a dick between my legs." She pauses, and her voice is etched in uncertainty when she continues. "You really mean it?"

"I do. Lucky for you, doctors nowadays can fix that whole no-dick problem."

She slugs me in my good arm while shaking her head and laughing. "That's okay. I'm good with my bits exactly as they are."

Fuck, so am I. I'm more than good. I'm fucking obsessed.

♦

I DO my best to skin the rabbit without getting fur on the meat, but we still have to wash it off when I finish.

"Rinse your hands, and I'll take the bucket to get clean water," Shae says once the prep is mostly done.

"No, I'll go. It's not safe for you to be out there alone."

Her spine visibly stiffens. "But it's safe for you? The one with stitches in his arm who's currently covered in blood?"

Fuck, I know this isn't going to go over well, especially after what we just talked about, but I can't help the way I feel. I do my best to collect my thoughts so I don't sound like a total hypocrite. "You're an incredible fighter, Shae. I've seen you in action and know what you're capable of, but there's a four-hundred-pound bear out there somewhere. I probably have nearly a hundred pounds on you."

"You think a measly hundred pounds would make a difference in the outcome?" Her eyes narrow to angry slits. "Because I'm pretty sure you end up dead the same as me if either of us go up against that bear. And in that case, the only reason you don't want me to go is to keep me safely tucked away like a good little girl."

"I'd have a little bit better of a chance," I blurt in frustration before realizing the argument is utter bullshit. That bear would shred me to pieces in a heartbeat.

My teeth ground together until my jaw aches. "Fine." I

shove my hands in the water and start vigorously wiping away the blood with unnecessary vigor. "But you better take the ax."

"So gracious of you, my liege, to allow me outside." She curtsies, then swipes the bucket away from me, leaving me dripping bloody water on the cabin floor. The door slams shut behind her.

Well, shit. That was a clusterfuck.

I wipe my hands on a towel and put the skillet on the stove to distract myself. I've also put bones and other non-edible bits in a pan to stew for broth. We didn't want a single ounce to go to waste. We even set aside the hide, though I have no fucking clue what we plan to do with it. Surely, we won't be here long enough to need it.

I usher out the thought as soon as it forms. I don't want to think about that today. I want to go back to the way it felt when we found the rabbit. For a few timeless minutes, everything was right in the world. Like anything was possible. I need that—*we* need that—if only for a day.

Then you need to find a way out of the hole you dug for yourself.

Seems a little ridiculous that what I said dug a hole, though. Was it so awful to want her safe?

I continue to mull over the question as I watch over the cooking meat. Soon, the savory smell has me feeling ravenous.

"Oh my God. That smells like heaven," Shae says when she returns.

We both stand over the skillet and stare at the meat until it's ready to eat. When that first bit of rabbit settles on my tongue, I have to close my eyes because I'm overwhelmed with how fucking divine it tastes. No spices or flavoring, and it's still more delicious than I could imagine. Hunger has got to be the best seasoning to ever exist.

I don't even care that the meat is still hot enough to scald my tongue. We devour every scrap, and the juices are poured into the broth pot, which we put on the stove to start simmering. The meal isn't huge, but it's so much more substantial than anything else we've had that we both sit back after eating like fat house cats who've licked their plates clean.

"You think we'll get another one tonight?" Shae asks quietly as though she's afraid to ask aloud and jinx our chances.

"God, I hope so. We might do a little more scoping to look for tracks. See if there's any other places we want to set traps."

"Don't you think we should get that bonfire going first? Don't need food if we can get rescued."

"Yeah … I suppose you're right." I'd somehow put the bonfire out of my mind and forgotten about it. "Guess we should get to work while we have energy from the food."

We spend an hour gathering the largest limbs we can. It takes another hour for the thing to get going without any accelerant. Once there's a tower of flames, we stand nearby and watch in silence.

Logically, I know a rescue attempt won't materialize immediately, but it feels odd to set the fire and walk away. Like we need to keep watch just in case. We're so damn exhausted, though, that even standing there feels like a chore. Eventually, we give in and return inside, both of us regularly casting brief glances out the small cabin window. For what, I don't know.

"What the hell do people do out here to kill time besides sleep?" Not that sleep sounds bad. I just don't want to miss anything.

"I found a deck of cards the other night—it's on the shelf. It was good for a few hundred rounds of solitaire." She smirks, making light of the situation, but I'm reminded of what she did for me and how grateful I am.

"You were right," I blurt out of nowhere, making sure to keep my gaze trained on hers. "I was trying to protect you instead of trusting your judgment. It's a hard habit to break, but I'll work on it."

She nods and takes the cards out of their box. "War or crazy eights?" she asks with a soft smile.

I didn't think she'd necessarily rub my apology in my face, but I'm still a bit surprised she lets me off the hook so easily. I remember thinking she always had to have the last word. It's yet another way I misjudged her.

"Crazy eights? What kind of pussy games do you play?" I tease, following her lead back to a worry-free day of celebration.

"Scared you'll lose?"

I crack my knuckles and sit forward on the stool. "Deal the cards and prepare to go down." I hear my word choice after it's already been said. I tell myself that not everyone is tuned in to double entendres, but I know I'm not alone when Shae's blue eyes brighten with a smirk.

"In your dreams, big guy."

As if my fantasies about her are limited to my dreams. If she knew where my imagination takes me lately, she's likely to feed me to the bear.

We play close to a dozen hands of cards—all different games. She wins the majority and proclaims herself champion. For once, I don't mind losing.

When the last glimmers of dusk reflect off the sparkling snow, we go stand by our dwindling bonfire. So far, the only thing to come from our blaze is a pile of ashes.

"Just because no one showed up yet doesn't mean no one

saw it," Shae says aloud, though I have a feeling it's more for her own benefit.

"Absolutely. And we can always try again."

"Yeah," she agrees quickly. "Yeah, that's true."

"I'm beat. Let's get some rest." I bump her shoulder and lead us back to the cabin, a cloud of dense emotions as thick as the smoke from our fire following us inside.

18

Shae

Hope and wariness wage an epic battle in my empty gut from the moment I wake. We need our traps to have caught *something* edible in the night, and a part of me feels like I can will it into reality if I manage to believe with enough conviction. My other half fears the devastation that will engulf me should that not be the case.

I reassure myself that I have good reason to be hopeful with so many more traps in place.

Renzo must be grappling with the same emotions because we're both up and going not long after the first hint of sunrise warms the cabin. We share the broth that cooked overnight, then head out with minimal conversation. Neither of us even glance toward the circle of charred remains that used to be our bonfire.

While anxious thoughts about our traps are a challenge, the uncertainty of a rescue effort is almost too sensitive to touch. It feels safer to focus on the snares, the same as buying into a few scratch-off games rather than hoping to hit the mega ball jackpot.

Flurries fall gently around us, creating a peaceful setting beneath cloudy skies. The possibility of heavy snow or even a storm adds to the existing tension coiling in my shoulders and back. I've been so focused on whether we'd find more game on our snares that I haven't considered the weather. We've been lucky so far, but that won't last forever. A storm will come through at some point—will we still be here when it does?

The uncertainty is the worst part. We can't check the weather on our phones or listen to the forecast on the evening news. All we can do is wait and see.

A tiny fissure of the pressure releases when I see a fat bird at the end of one of our lines. "Look at that! What is it?" I try to think of what birds live on the ground like turkeys. "A pheasant?"

"Couldn't say. When I hunt, it's not birds I'm after."

"Ba-dum psh." I mimic hitting the drum and cymbals. I can't help myself. The line was too much to pass up.

Renzo cuts his eyes over to me, and I think he might be irritated with me, but then he huffs a laugh and shakes his head. "Go check the others while I get this guy unhooked."

Farther down the creek, I find another rabbit on a snare and pump my fist in the air.

Hell, yes!

I take our catch by the ears and display it proudly to Renzo. "Look who's eating good tonight!"

"Nice, though I'd suggest we only eat one today and save the other for tomorrow, just to be safe."

"Probably a good call." I'm surprisingly not disappointed. Knowing we have meat for tomorrow is a relief. "It would be nice to stockpile a little. How exactly does that work? It's plenty cold outside for the meat to keep, but I don't want to attract Old Smokey or any other nasties."

"I'm not really sure. Guess there's the outhouse."

We lock stares, then both shake our heads.

"No shit-flavored meat, no matter how hungry we are."

"Agreed." Renzo nods, leading us back to the cabin. Before we make it all the way, he finds a log to sit on and starts plucking feathers from the bird.

"Grouse," he says out of nowhere. "I think that's what they call these things."

"Sounds familiar. Don't think I've ever eaten it, though. Never plucked anything either."

"I sure as hell haven't. You think there's some sort of system to it?" He holds it up, and we both stare.

"Probably," I say. "You should google it."

When he shoots me a wry stare, I give in to a laugh.

"Sorry, I'm just so relieved. It makes me a little stupid."

"Not stupid." He continues plucking. "I appreciate the way you can stay positive even when things suck."

"It helps that we have food. Things suck a lot less when you're not starving."

"Yeah. I counted twenty-eight cans of food left in the cabin, only three of them beans. The rest are all fruits and vegetables. I figure if we can keep to one can a day and otherwise rely on catching our food, we could make it a month."

"That's essentially one meal a day, and a low-calorie meal at that," I point out.

"Plus, any extra meat we have. If we can catch more than one or two animals a night, that's not so bad."

"True, though catching anything at all isn't a guarantee." A somberness settles over me as reality hits. "You really think we'll be here that long?"

"At least. It's mid-February."

"The seventeenth. I've been keeping track."

"And this far north, we'd likely need to make it to mid-March before nighttime temps aren't totally unbearable. The trip out of here could take a day or a solid week before we run into anyone. We have no way of knowing."

I watch as feathers drift to the ground and begin to form a fluffy pile. "I learned how to fight and count cards," I say distractedly. "I mastered jiujitsu and am comfortable with all sorts of guns and knives. I thought I'd done so well preparing myself to handle anything. Those tools I considered survival skills mean nothing out here."

"I'm in the same boat. No shame in it."

"I suppose you can't prepare for everything."

"Nope. You do your best to get through, and when it's over, you get even."

"No shit," I agree. "When we get back home, I'm finding each and every one of those motherfuckers."

"You'll have to get in line." He lifts the bird and examines its now naked neck and chest.

"I keep thinking about it, and it feels like too much of a coincidence that the guns sat there for that long untouched, and when we finally go to move them, those assholes show up."

"Someone was definitely tipped off," he grumbles.

"Maybe the others will have learned something by the time we get back."

"They probably think we're dead." His tone is morose, but

I'm oddly entertained by the thought. Renzo sees my smirk and cocks his head. "That funny?"

I shrug. "Can't say I won't enjoy seeing my cousins' faces when I stroll back into town."

"You say that like they might be glad to be rid of you."

"Nah, but we've always pulled little pranks to piss off one another. This wasn't a prank, but it'll still shock them. I'll enjoy the big reveal." The part that worries me comes after. I've worked so hard to gain their trust and respect. Will the guys try to stash me away in a glass case after having to face the possibility that I've died?

It's been five days since we met at the warehouse. They won't have written me off yet, but after another month, they'd be foolish not to assume the worst. The prospect of regression is frustrating, but I can't exactly blame them for wanting to avoid losing me again.

My gaze drifts to Renzo as he works, and I think about how he tried to keep me in the cabin for protection. He may not be family, but I shouldn't discount his worries about my safety. I was terrified when I thought he might die and leave me out here alone. Is it so ridiculous to think he might feel the same? And what did I do? I bit his head off for wanting to keep me alive.

Hell, I might have overreacted.

I have so much baggage about men not taking me seriously or being overprotective. But I'm woman enough to understand that there is honor in protecting the people you care about, and sometimes, I may have to let myself be the protected rather than the protector.

An hour later, the bird is plucked, rinsed, and ready for the skillet. I watch Renzo intently as he cleans his hands in the water bucket. It'll need to be rinsed out. If I did overreact yesterday, this would be a great opportunity for a do-over.

I shove my hands in my jeans pockets and rock back on my heels. "You want me to swap out the water, or would you rather do it?" The hesitation in my voice sounds foreign to me. I rarely ask for other's opinions on my actions. Renzo is an exception.

I try to tell myself it's because of our circumstances, but I know I'm full of shit.

He dries his hands and stands opposite me, and I swear his penetrating stare reaches deep enough inside me to examine the rough-hewn patchwork pieces of my soul. Eventually, he gives a single nod. "You're not back in ten, I *will* come looking for you."

"You better." I offer him a shy smile before grabbing the bucket and bolting from the cabin to escape the sweltering tension.

The number of unspoken words that fill the air when we're together could compete in length with a Tolkien manuscript, should they ever be put on paper. I don't even know what words would be spoken on my end. Maybe that's what makes them feel so heavy. The uncertainty. A part of me is fascinated by Renzo Donati, and the rest is sure any interest in him is a terrible, *awful* idea.

Unfortunately, that's never stopped me before.

🔥

AGAIN, the meat is incredible. We savor every bite, then sit back and relish the feeling of being full.

"We still have half the day left," Renzo comments. "I'm thinking of trying to construct some sort of storage container on the side of the cabin in case we can catch enough meat to store some for our trip to town."

"Will that small box of nails with the tools be enough?" I

raise my hands and run my fingers through my hair, letting the nails scratch at my filthy scalp.

God, what I wouldn't give for a shower.

"It's worth a try. Guess it'll depend on what wood I can round up. We'll have to either chop down a tree soon or start gathering wood from farther out as it is. I hate to use good firewood for the box, but it's just as important to our survival."

"Agreed. You need any help?"

"Don't think so at the moment." He watches me go to the water bucket and stand over it.

Those five-gallon paint buckets are tall. I bend at the waist and consider how I might get my head down into the water to wash my hair. The bucket gets heavy with too much water. I only filled it with enough to get us by without straining myself on the walk back.

"What the hell are you doing?" Renzo finally asks.

"Trying to figure out how to wash my hair," I answer absently.

He stands and closes the distance between us, hitting me with that devastating stare again. "Go lie on the bed." His words are soft yet frayed at the edges.

I have to swallow twice before I can summon my voice. "That fever coming back? You seem to be a little confused."

His hands lift to cup either side of my neck, his thumbs sliding along my jaw. His presence suddenly feels immense, like he fills every square inch of space, leaving no room for oxygen. And when he brings his face an inch away from mine, I forget how to breathe.

"I know exactly what I'm doing. You—" His thumb sweeps across my cheek. "Just need to trust me, Chaos. Now, lie on your back on the bed. I'm going to wash your hair."

My entire body sways when he releases me. Or maybe I'm floating. I could be floating.

He called me chaos again, and I swear it sounded even better this time than the last.

"Um, yeah. Okay." I do as I'm told because, Jesus Christ, I'm only human, and Renzo is obviously not. Be it deity or wizard or voodoo shaman, I'm not sure, but he's definitely not playing fair.

He sets the bucket and the stool at the end of the bed while I get situated, lying on my back with my head hanging over the edge. My insides riot when his hands move with deft confidence through my short hair. Electric bolts of pleasure shoot from my scalp to my nipples and lower. It takes all my control to keep from arching with need.

Am I simply horny, or is Renzo that adept with his hands? I'm scared to know the answer because if he's truly that gifted, a girl could become addicted.

The first cup of water poured into my hair is a shock to the system. It's cold as a witch's tit, but each round is more tolerable than the one before. He continues until my hair is fully soaked, my scalp tingling, and I'm feeling pleasantly relaxed. Then he begins to massage my head.

If I were a cat, I'd purr.

"You're better with your hands than I would expect."

"Why wouldn't I be good with my hands?"

"Seems like most men aren't very intuitive about touch."

He stills. "Sounds like you're talking from experience." When his hands resume their circular motion, my eyes drift shut in ecstasy, preventing me from seeing him lean in toward me. I almost gasp when he continues from an inch away. With so little distance between us, the deep timbre of his voice vibrates a path from my ear directly to my clit. "I thought you said you have a girlfriend."

"I do." It's the breathiest two words I've ever spoken. I have to get a grip on myself.

"But you've been with men?"

"I'm attracted to all kinds of people, but I prefer to be with people I respect, and that doesn't seem to happen as frequently with men as it does with women."

"And the men you *have* been with." His words sound oddly strained. "They didn't know how to touch you?"

His hands feel so incredible. If I wasn't on my back, I'd be drooling.

"Not really," I say dazedly.

Renzo lifts the cup and pours more water over my hair. When a drip strays to my temple, his finger catches it, then drifts along my cheek to my jaw and down the side of my throat. This time, I can't resist the urge to press my chest upward. I'm so hyper sensitized by him that I don't miss the hitch in his breath.

"Let me prove not all of us are worthless in bed." Each word is a physical caress, flaming the already raging fire inside me.

"I don't think that's a good idea, Ren."

"Why?"

"You're you, and I'm me. Our families. Our loyalties."

"There are no loyalties out here." He continues slowly in a soft but urgent voice. "No families. Just you ... and me."

That's true. What happens in the wilderness could stay in the wilderness.

I could scratch that itch. It's tempting. I've never made Mari any sort of commitment, and the fact that I've hardly thought about her since I've been gone speaks volumes. What I need to remember, however, is just because I can doesn't mean I should. This is Renzo Donati, boss of the Moretti Mafia family, not some schmuck off the street.

He must sense my indecision when he takes another angle.

"How about we make a bet?"

Oh, *fuck*. I do love a bet.

There's a reason my family's primary source of income is gambling—we *live* for a game of chance.

"What sort of bet?" I ask hesitantly.

"How about this … if I can catch a fish from the creek, you let me show you how good I am with my hands?"

A desperate voice buried deep in my psyche begs for me to let him show me now. Logic clears her throat until I'm forced to pay attention. Any sort of sex with this man is a bad idea. *However*, what are the chances he can catch a fish?

"How would you do it? A spear or something?"

"There's some fishing line in the cabinet. I'll make a rod." He sounds so confident that it's easy to fall in step with his words, but I know better. The city boy using a homemade fishing rod with no reel to catch a fish from a half-frozen creek in the middle of winter—that's got to be the best odds I've ever been offered.

"And if I win?"

"I'll jump in that creek naked, fully submerged."

He'll never win, but even if lightning strikes, and he not only catches a fish but also manages to make me come, it's still a win for me. What kind of Byrne would I be if I didn't take those odds?

I steel myself and say the one word that may be the best or worst thing to ever happen to me.

"Deal."

19

Kenzo

I'VE NEVER FISHED A DAY IN MY LIFE, BUT PEOPLE DO IT ALL THE time. How hard can it be? I'd already been thinking about giving it a go—this is simply an added incentive.

Whether I win the bet or not, however, I will get Shae naked beneath me.

The way she's responding to my touch has sealed her fate. I don't care who she was dating or what her family name is. Her body responds to mine as intensely as mine does hers, and that's all I need to know. If the bet is the fastest way to get her to drop her guard, then so be it. I'll do whatever it takes.

Is that manipulative? Probably.

Should I respect her hesitations? Definitely. A woman's right to say no is absolute.

Is that going to deter me from my mission? Fuck, no.

I *should* be an upstanding citizen who never breaks the law, but we all know that isn't me. It isn't Shae either. If she truly didn't want me touching her, she'd kick my ass. Instead, she's trying her hardest to keep from writhing on the bed while I rinse her hair.

Hair as black and soft as a raven's wing.

Yet another reason this incessant craving for her has infected my bloodstream. Fighting it feels more pointless with each passing day. Life is short—maybe even shorter than we expect. Who are we to set aside what could be the greatest sex of our lives because we might get home to families who may not want us together? Seems like an awfully pathetic excuse to me.

And besides, it's my duty as a man to prove we aren't all shitty in bed.

"Let me grab a towel." I hand her our cleanest one, which isn't saying much. "No fancy shampoo, but hopefully, you feel better now."

"Yeah, definitely. I can already tell the difference." She pauses, then looks up at me hesitantly. "You … want me to wash yours?"

Shit. I should have been ready for that question, but it's hard to think straight when every ounce of blood has detoured to my dick. As much as I want to say yes, it'll only be worse when her lithe fingers rub sultry circles against my scalp. I'm not one to torture myself. If her fingers clench in my hair, it better be because my cock is buried deep inside her.

"Nah, I'll dunk my head in the creek."

"Oh, okay. Seems like it'd be awfully cold that way, but it's your call."

Good. Maybe the cold will tame this never-ending hard-on she's created. "I'll survive," I mutter like a grumpy old geezer. The frustration of wanting what I can't have is wearing on my nerves. I need to relieve some of the mounting tension. Now.

"I'm going to see what wood I can gather for the meat locker." But first, a trip to the outhouse to tend to a different kind of wood. I head for the door, making sure to keep my back to her.

"Sounds good. I'm going to stay inside while my hair dries, but let me know if you need any help."

"Yeah," I grunt, then escape outside and around back. The flurries have stopped falling. A solid blanket of light gray clouds set a mellow tone for the day. They don't look overly ominous, but our situation is precarious enough that any hint of possible bad weather is unwelcome. Even more reason to get some sort of storage device constructed. As soon as I'm done in here.

I step inside the outhouse and close the door behind me. It's dark in the tiny cubicle except for slivers of light that slip in through the cracks. Where the cabin is built with solid tree trunks carefully aligned to keep out the weather, the outhouse is constructed of standard one-by-six boards brought in from a building supply store. They've warped with time. The place serves its purpose, though. And right now, it's exactly what I need. Privacy.

When I grip myself, my cock goes impossibly hard with the knowledge that relief is in sight. I can't believe I'm out here in the frigid cold choking my cock as if I can't go a few weeks without shooting my load, but the woman drives me insane.

It only takes a momentary vision of her for my balls to pull tight in preparation. She's lying on the bed on her back like she was moments ago, but instead of washing her hair, I'm shoving my cock deep down to the back of her throat. I fight back the tingles that try to radiate out from the base of my spine. I'm not ready for the fantasy to end, but when I picture her spreading wide and touching herself while moaning around my cock in her mouth, my orgasm catches me by surprise. I miss the first jet of cum before it rockets to the back wall. I don't even fucking care. Pleasure washes over me like a spring rain shower. It cools my blood almost instantly, my strokes growing leisurely as I draw out every last wave of release.

Fuck, I needed that.

As I clean up, I study the toilet contraption for the first time. It's more complicated than a hole in the ground but not sophisticated enough to be a septic tank. Whoever built the place must have had help or brought out machinery because the hole is too deep and narrow to have been dug by hand. A hole for a toilet gets me thinking about how a hole would probably be a great way to store our meat. I would only need to construct a lid.

I go out and scan the back wall of the cabin where a few outdoor tools are stored. There's a pickax but no shovel. Not ideal but doable. Maybe even necessary, considering how frozen the ground is.

Hell, yeah. Why didn't I think of this before?

After an orgasm and a great idea, I'm feeling energized—the best I've felt since our kidnapper's plane fell out of the sky and left us stranded. We have food, shelter, and I'm one fish away from burying my face between Shae's thighs.

I'm feeling so optimistic that I'm starting to view our time here as an enticing challenge. A return to life at its most basic form.

If I'm honest, it's been refreshing to focus solely on survival.

No politics or strategizing. No worries about who might reject my role as boss. No dealing with other people's catastrophes. I've hardly thought about what might have happened in my absence back home—who took leadership in my absence and the trouble Sante and Tommaso might have gotten into. Both concerns should have been looming in the back of my mind, but we've had more critical problems that took precedence. Out here in the wilderness, life is oddly simple. Ensure we have food, water, and warmth. Every day that we achieve that is a success.

Back home, I'd have to sort out what judges and politicians need to be bribed or how to keep the peace with another organization. The big question of the day here is whether we should eat the rabbit or the bird first. And when I finish constructing our freezer, I will have used my own two hands to create a solution that will help keep us alive.

I never knew something so simple could be so satisfying. Technically, I don't know it yet, but I'm about to find out because I'm going to build the best damn in-ground freezer known to man.

20

Shae

RENZO SPENDS THE REST OF THE AFTERNOON OUTSIDE WORKING on his storage contraption. I probably should have joined him at some point to help at least look for suitable wood, but I need a little space. If I'm not going to help, then I ought to at least consider what's happening between us and how I feel about it. Him touching me. Our bet. But no, I lean full-tilt into avoidance and play no less than one hundred rounds of solitaire.

At the end of the day, Renzo returns to the cabin with a wet head. He actually dunked his head in the creek like he said he would and washed his hair. Once he towels his hair somewhat dry, he shows me the creative in-ground container he's constructed. We store our spare rabbit inside but have to eat it the next day when every single trap is empty come morning. The disappointment does nothing to lighten our equally pensive moods. Neither of us seems interested in conversation.

We spend our afternoon post-rabbit energy on building another bonfire. The quiet continues. At least our silence is companionable while we work. Once the fire gets going, he disappears to the creek to fish. I stick around the cabin and watch the fire. The wind is unusually calm, making it pleasantly warm if I sit at the right distance. Smoke billows into the overcast sky. Birds caw and flit about in nearby trees. I sit and try not to think about how no one is coming.

I do my best to avoid thinking, but there's so much damn time. I find myself reflecting on him washing my hair and wonder why he refused to let me wash his. He made it clear he wants me physically. Why avoid an opportunity that might lead to something more? In fact, I've been surprised he hasn't tried anything since making our bet. No accidental groping in the morning or innocently misplaced hand at night.

Renzo isn't the type to let chance determine his fate.

When I consider how contemplative I've been, however, it seems silly to think he wouldn't be going through the same. To keep myself from overthinking it all, I busy myself playing botanist. I discover one of the handful of books stored at the bottom of the bookshelf is an encyclopedia of edible plants. The information could be highly useful, and I have nothing better to do, so I dive in.

I learn what I can, but most plants are dormant for the winter. I'd love to go around and see what I could identify from the book. Hopefully, we'll be long gone by the time the local vegetation resurfaces.

On the eighth day after being captured, we find a record three catches on our snares. The discovery gives us both an enormous boost in spirits. We grin from ear to ear, and I realize that's what's been missing. Yes, we've been quiet, but it's been more than that. We've been a bit somber. It feels great to smile again.

"The animals were busy last night," I say cheerily as I watch Renzo free another dead grouse from a snare.

"Sure looks that way. If only we could make it a nightly occurrence."

"No kidding. I wish we had some feed we could throw out to lure them or find a way to predict where they'll be. Were the traps set any differently last night than the night before?"

Before he can answer, a flash of lightning strobes across the sky, followed by the most ominous rumble of thunder I've ever heard.

My gaze locks with Renzo's. "You think it's coming here?"

We've enjoyed relatively nice weather since arriving. I'd like to think the disturbance will pass us by, but something tells me our luck has ended, at least where the weather is concerned.

Renzo looks down at the three dead animals on the ground between us. "I think that's exactly what's happening, and these guys knew it."

"They were preparing," I continue his thought, my heart thudding higher and higher into my throat. "I'll gather the traps; you get us water. You can carry more than me."

He nods. "And once we've done that, I think we should move our wood pile to the side of the cabin."

We break apart into our tasks, no arguing today for either of us.

We could be totally overreacting. We simply don't know,

which is why we have to prepare for the worst. As the clouds darken and the lightning intensifies, certainty sets in.

A storm is coming.

The arrival of winter's wrath blots out the early afternoon sun to a preternatural twilight. I work as long as I can moving our wood supply closer. I'd felt like we had so much firewood stockpiled, but with the threat of being snowed in, I'm now questioning if we shouldn't have gathered more. Renzo continues to work a bit longer after a bone-breaking chill forces me inside.

The thick walls of the cabin generally hold in the heat well, but the wind whipping with such unrelenting fury challenges our stove's heating capacity. I don't know where the cold is seeping in—it's not an obvious draft—but it's finding a way somewhere.

When Renzo finally joins me inside, I'm wrapped in the bed quilt and sitting on the floor by the stove.

"I hung our catches on the eave outside the door. Nothing will be out in this weather to steal them. That way, we don't have to unearth the freezer to get to the food." He dusts the snow off his jacket and rubs his hands together. "Guess an in-ground freezer has its drawbacks."

"Hey, you got it sorted. That's what counts." My jaw chatters when I speak. It's not overly cold in the cabin, but I'm having trouble getting my core temperature up after being outside in that deadly windchill. My condition doesn't escape Renzo's notice. Without asking, he takes the blanket from me, then sits me between his legs so his chest can press close to my back. Once he's situated, he wraps the blanket around us both.

"You don't have to do this. I'll warm up eventually." I don't know why I say it. I should let the man warm me if he wants to, but denying weakness is too ingrained in my being. It's second nature to put on a strong front.

Renzo must know this because he ignores me. "You ever gone camping?"

"I'd like to think I'd be at least a tiny bit more adept at this survivalist crap if I had."

"Me either. I haven't ever spent much time outside of cities. I've traveled but to Chicago and LA and even Rome. Never thought to go to a national park or something like that. Always seemed boring, I guess."

I huff out a laugh. "Think we've proven that theory wrong. Nothing boring about trying to stay alive."

He doesn't respond as long seconds pass. I must be learning how to read him better because I get the distinct sense he wants to say something but is holding back.

"What is it?" I prod him.

"You'll think I'm batshit crazy."

"You already think I'm crazy. That way we'll be even." I press one shoulder back to nudge him playfully. The wind is still whistling all around us, but I'm finally warming up. Hard not to with my own personal heater wrapped around me.

"I never thought I'd say this," he continues hesitantly, "but it's more than not boring here."

I slowly peer over my shoulder at him, eyes wide. "Are you trying to tell me you *like* being stuck in the wilderness?"

He grimaces before jumping to his feet. "Just forget it," he mutters as he wrenches his hoodie and undershirt off in one go, giving me my first unhindered view of his tattooed back before he puts the hoodie back on without the undershirt. I'm entranced by the giant serpent tattoo encompassing most of the available skin. I have to force my attention back to our conversation.

"Don't be like that." I wrap the blanket back around my shoulders. "You surprised me is all."

He sits in the chair at our makeshift table, arms crossed over his chest. "Not something I expected either. Doing shit like catching dinner and chopping wood is a hell of a lot more satisfying than I would have thought, that's all."

"I get that."

His eyes finally cut to mine briefly, but he doesn't say anything, so I continue. "Providing for yourself without relying on others is incredibly satisfying." I don't want to outright point out the similarity to my situation back home because this isn't about me, but I'm still hoping he catches on.

"I always thought of my father as a powerful man because he commanded so many people and his decisions were so far-reaching. I get that there's power in that, but that sort of power only exists with the cooperation of others."

"There are no others here."

"Exactly. And I'm realizing there's an entirely different sort of power in self-sufficiency. A power in knowing you don't need anyone else to survive. The simplicity appeals to me. Everything is so straightforward here. Eat. Sleep. Survive."

I study him but find his stoic features inscrutable. "You're not saying … you want to *stay* here, are you?"

"No," he answers immediately. "Definitely not. But it's changed my perspective about a lot of things." He begins to shuffle the deck of cards, not elaborating.

Since he seems to be done with the topic, I indulge in my curiosity about his tattoos. "What's the snake about?"

"It's sort of our family symbol. Not like we put it on shirts or anything, but it's representative of our role. We control the unions in the city. Workers are the scales of the snake—small and fragile on their own—but together, they can become a deadly beast."

Interesting. I can see why he never thought much about independence. His entire world is based on a cooperative existence.

"Do you have to deal with politicians much? Seems like unions go hand-in-hand with politics. My brother Oran handles most of the schmoozing with city officials. I'm glad it's him and not me. I'd piss off too many people to be given that responsibility." I strive to be a valuable asset to my family, but we all have to acknowledge our strengths and weaknesses. I don't exactly excel at stroking egos. As the head of the Moretti family, I wonder how much of that sort of thing Renzo has to do.

"Politics can be a big part of our world, though the Giordano family is ensconced in city government, so they control most bureaucratic functions. We keep to the blue-collar side of things. But the two families rely on one another in many ways. That's why my father had talked to me about an alliance with them before he died."

"An alliance? When someone throws that word around in my circles, it means a marriage." It's a simple observation and not technically any of my business, but I have to know.

"Her name's Arianna De Bellis. Her father was the boss of the Giordano family."

My stomach turns itself inside out. I don't know what she looks like, but her name is fucking gorgeous. She sounds like an Italian princess. I've never thought much about my name, but it suddenly sounds abrasive and unsophisticated. And Irish.

"Was?" I prompt.

"He was killed back in June."

I wonder if he hadn't been killed if Renzo would currently be engaged or even married. Again, my stomach contorts itself angrily.

God, Shae. What idiotic fantasies have you been entertaining in that head of yours?

Admiring the man's mouthwatering body is one thing, but being jealous of the women he dates is entirely different. It makes me realize my interest in him is getting away from me. My attraction to him has become intertwined with emotions like respect and admiration. That is a fucking dangerous combination. I have to put an end to it.

First and foremost, I need to tell him the bet is off. I can't even chance the remote possibility that he wins because it wouldn't just mean a delicious orgasm. I would be laying the groundwork for my heart to be shredded to pieces.

My hand goes inadvertently to the pendant at my neck.

Renzo Donati is *not* an option. He is not, nor will he ever be mine. Letting myself pretend otherwise would be unforgivable. That slippery slope will lead to devastation, and considering I've already started to fall, I need to catch myself immediately.

I tell myself to say the words—to back out of the bet—but my mouth won't cooperate. A voice in my head whispers that it probably won't be an issue. The chances are so slim. And if it should happen, I can back out then.

And in the meantime? Am I going to let things linger or be up front with him?

I should tell him. Woman up and be honest with him.

"I need to pee." Not the words I had in mind.

I inwardly grimace but note that it was at least an effective end to the conversation. Sometimes I can't even believe the crap that comes out of my own mouth.

"You can try to brave the wind, but I figured while it's at

its worst, we'd use one of the empty Mason jars." He grabs one of the three jars and sets it on the table. He's not grossed out or even fazed for that matter. Peeing is natural enough, but in my experience, men tend to get squeamish about bodily functions beyond an orgasm.

I suppose peeing in a jar with him in the same room is one way of cockblocking myself without having to say the words. Just one of the guys—that's me. Always have been, and I suppose I always will be.

"Sure, sounds like a plan." I get up and take the jar from him. "Turn around. I don't need an audience."

I take exactly two squares of toilet paper—we only have two rolls, so we've been careful to ration them—and I pee in the damn jar. It's awkward, and I hate that. I have a perfectly good reason to be doing what I'm doing. I shouldn't be ashamed, but no matter how many times I tell myself that, it doesn't stop my cheeks from flushing what I can only assume is a bright crimson.

When I'm done, I set the jar down and pull up my pants. "What now? Put on the lid and ignore it?" There's not all that much in it. Probably because I didn't need to pee so much as I needed a distraction.

"Yeah, I'll pour it out when I go out to pee."

"You're going to go out in that?" I gape at him. Some of my reaction is surprise and the rest is frustration that I look like a ninny for not braving the weather, if that's what he's going to do.

"I only have to take a step outside the door. If I was in your shoes, I'd use the jar, too. No reason for you to have to squat in this storm or trudge all the way to the outhouse."

His answer is sufficient to quell my indignity.

I appreciate how he handles himself. He could have easily

laughed at my insecurity, but that's not Renzo. He's surprisingly empathetic for a man in his line of work.

Aaaand, there I go again.

"Food," I blurt. "You ready to eat?"

I'm stranded in the wilderness, and my greatest concern has nothing to do with survival. Who would have guessed?

21

Kenzo

THE STORM PUMMELS THE WALLS OF OUR TINY FORTRESS FOR TWO solid days. And when the winds finally subside, we spend another two days dealing with the aftermath. The snowfall totals wouldn't be an issue if the incessant wind hadn't formed giant snowbanks. We're lucky the front door wasn't covered, but a wall of snow formed on one side of the cabin all the way to the roof—the side we'd used for our wood pile and the storage locker.

We don't have a shovel, but it turns out the bucket is an excellent alternative. Once we clear our access to the outhouse, wood pile, and the storage locker, we re-rig all our traps down by the creek. The two days of energy stored while we were stuck inside helps make up for the extra activity.

141

We work companionably and return to some semblance of normal, but I can't escape the feeling that Shae seems distant. She's been awfully quiet for days now. If it were anyone else, I'd say a little moodiness along the way was normal. We've had to endure a hell of a lot in the past ten days. Shae isn't like most people, though. A wellspring of energy flows within her. She vibrates with optimism and ideas and purpose. The Shae I've been living with for the past few days is a deflated version of the woman I know. She's withdrawn, and I don't know why. Something's weighing on her. It could be a simple case of homesickness, though she's not exactly the type to get depressed over that sort of thing.

As I sit at the table and watch her re-organize a cabinet that doesn't have enough crap in it to need reorganizing, something dawns on me.

"Is your period coming soon?" I feel like a dumbass for not considering it sooner. If I was a woman, having to deal with that sort of thing out here would stress me the fuck out, too. And she could easily be uncomfortable mentioning it to ask for help.

My mind is instantly brainstorming solutions when her reply lashes me like a whip.

"*Excuse* me?"

I raise my hands placatingly. "Now, don't get sharp with me. I was only trying to figure out what might be bothering you."

"And you figured I must be hormonal?" She's almost begging for a fight.

My jaw muscles flex and strain. "No, but now I am."

"Because if a woman is upset about something, she must be hormonal." Her hands go to her hips, and I feel the quicksand pulling me further underground.

"Quit putting words in my mouth." I stand and give her a menacing glare.

She shoots back one of her own. "And how else am I supposed to take that? You decide I'm acting funny so you figure my period is coming? Sounds like man math to me."

I close the distance between us and lean so I'm towering over her. "I thought you might be worried about how to manage without any supplies here. I wanted to help you figure out a plan and not be an insensitive prick, but since you'd rather jump to conclusions than hear me out, I'll leave you to it." I whirl around and storm from the cabin, making sure to grab my jacket on the way out.

Time to do some fishing but not because I want my prize. Right now, I need for Shae to lose. It pisses me off that she occupies so much of my thoughts, and when I try to be considerate, she throws it back in my face.

I ought to tie her up and force her to tell me what the hell is wrong. Instead, I imagine all the things I want to do and say to her while I cast my fishing line into the creek. My pine branch rod with the line tied at the end is laughable. I don't know why I'm still trying. I've spent a number of hours casting without the slightest nibble.

Thickheaded determination won't allow me to quit.

Plus, what the fuck else do I have to do?

I can't even find peace when I sleep because she's there, her supple body pressed against mine. It's getting harder and harder to keep my hands from roaming. Maybe we both just need to get laid.

No, she's pulling away from me. I can feel it, but I don't understand why.

I know her body responds to me. If that's the case, what's the hangup? Surely not her girlfriend. She hasn't said a word about the woman since we arrived.

I know I can't always have my way, but being denied what I want for no good reason feels pointlessly infuriating. Maybe tonight, I return the favor. Let her know how it feels to be cast off without explanation.

22

Shae

RENZO TURNED HIS BACK ON ME. LITERALLY.

We slept back-to-back last night, and I *hated* it. The bed wasn't any more or less comfortable in our new arrangement. We were pressed as close to one another as always, so I was plenty warm. Nothing was physically wrong, yet I was miserable.

The emotional isolation penetrated so much deeper than I could have imagined.

The truth is, I think my period would start soon if I wasn't stressed and starving. I wouldn't be surprised if I skip this cycle, all things considered, but hormones could still be amplifying my emotions. It would explain why I snapped at Renzo. I've thought about it all morning and have decided six different times that I should apologize and explain, only to circle back and insist the distance between us is for the best. Renzo may be able to keep his emotions separate from sex, but I can't. Not where he's concerned. And if we have no chance of a relationship, I refuse to let myself be hurt for nothing.

I will not fall for another person I can't be with, nor will I sacrifice who I am for the sake of a relationship.

I don't like hurting him, but I have to protect myself. I have to be smart. Every time I tell myself that, another voice asks if keeping him at a distance is the best thing for me, then why does it feel so yucky? Not only do I miss feeling connected to him, I feel guilty about hurting him and anger over the hand we've been dealt. And frustration. So much fucking frustration.

The negativity of it all is so much that I do some shadow-boxing in front of the cabin. I should conserve my energy. We're not eating enough calories to justify exercise, but I need it to clear my head.

Renzo follows me outside. I expect him to grab his fishing pole and head to the creek, but he surprised me by joining me instead.

"You interested in a sparring partner, or you prefer to practice alone?" His gruff tone is intentionally indifferent. I've done that. He's put up barriers to match my own, and the guilt is more than I can bear.

"Sure, training's always better with a partner."

He lifts his hands in front of him to serve as targets and spreads his feet to steady himself. "Jab, jab, cross," he calls out, instructing me of my next moves. I'll have to keep my touches extra light since we don't have pads for his hands. The point of the exercise is more about quick thinking and reflexes than brute force, so hitting hard isn't all that crucial.

I perform the trio of moves in rapid succession. He calls out another combination, this time tossing in a mock swipe of his hand so that I have to add a dip to evade him. We do about a dozen rounds. He's no stranger to this sort of training, calling out creative combinations and truly challenging my reaction times. We're both competitive and with all the unspoken tension mounting between us, each set seems to grow in intensity. It's invigorating—physically and intellectually.

Pretty soon, I have a devious smile teasing at my lips and a burning desire to one-up him. "Come on, is that all you've got?"

His menacing smirk tells me he's more than ready to put me in my place. He calls out a long combination that I launch into, but I only get halfway through when he grabs my fist in the middle of a jab. He yanks my back toward his chest and starts to wrap his arms around me. I instantly drop to my knees, which throws off his hold on me. I quickly transition to a forward roll away from him, leaping right back to my feet and into my ready stance.

We're both breathing heavily as we circle one another. I can only imagine my eyes spark with the same excitement I see in his because I'm buzzing with energy. My bloodstream is spiked with intoxicating endorphins. The rush makes me want more—more of the thrill. More of him.

I'm planning my attack when he catches me off guard by swiping his hand through a snowdrift against a tree, sending a wave of glittering powder right at my face.

I cry out with mock indignation and try to keep my eyes open, knowing his next move is coming. The second he's close enough, I drop and swipe his legs out from under him, sending him tumbling to the snowy ground. I immediately launch myself on him to pin his hands.

I'm straddling his middle, laughing as I grab his hands and press them into the snow. Once I have him secure, my eyes finally find his. The heat radiating from those Caribbean blues could melt every bit of snow beneath us.

"*Mercy*," he breathes.

A word has never been spoken with such ardent reverence.

I'm stunned speechless. Breathless. I don't know what to think, but I know how my body wants to respond. It's screaming for me to give in. To give myself to this indomitable man who will undoubtedly ruin me for anyone else when he returns to his Mafia throne. You don't fall for a man like Renzo and simply shake off a broken heart when the ride ends. When he leaves you broken, the pieces never fully fit back together again.

And he will leave. He's duty bound, the same as me.

I leap off him so quickly that I surprise us both. "I, uh … I need to go to the bathroom. Sorry." I shake the melted snow from my hands as he slowly rises to his feet.

When I peer up at him, I inwardly wince. He's scraped away every hint of emotion as he walks past me like I never existed. He calmly lifts his fishing pole from where it leans against the cabin and walks away without saying a word.

And just like that, we're right back where we started.

I feel like I've been forced into an impossible situation, and it makes me want to scream. Why can't I stop wanting him? If I know I'll only end up hurt, why would I still want to be with him?

Maybe I'm already broken.

Are we serving cake at this pity party?

Ugh. Of course, I'm not broken. Any woman would be nuts not to find Renzo irresistible. My problem is, I'm resisting. To protect myself, granted. But maybe if I let my intuition guide me rather than my logic, I'd find I'm worrying for nothing. I could be completely wrong about how hard I'd fall for him. Maybe he drives like an old lady or sleeps with the TV on in the bedroom.

And maybe, you're just horny and not nearly as desperate for him as you are for an orgasm.

I want to smack my head against one of the nearby trees. Why hadn't I already considered that? That could absolutely be the answer, or at least help take the edge off until we get back home.

And this is the perfect time. Renzo won't be back for at least an hour.

I go back inside and take off my jacket and boots, then add a log to the dwindling fire. Once my jeans are off, I lie back on the bed. I don't even remember the last time I used my fingers on myself. Not since I was a teenager, probably. After I discovered the delights of a vibrator, there was no reason to ever go back where self-pleasuring was concerned. Why take a horse and buggy when a car can do the job better in every way?

I lie with my knees bent and listing outward while my feet are planted on the bed not far from my ass. It's been long enough that my body is starving for touch. The thought of masturbating in the bed we share doesn't hurt, either. It feels so naughty, like a dirty little secret, and I'm here for it.

I imagine Renzo at the window watching me. The bed is situated perfectly across the room so that he'd have an unobstructed view of my fingers diving in and out of my core, then circling madly over the clit's delicious bundle of nerves. In no time at all, the divine cascade of tingles begins to build in my center. It feels so incredible that I arch, pressing my head back into the pillow. My eyes squeeze shut, and my lips part.

So close. I'm so fucking close.

I need that one last spark to send me over the edge. I open my eyes to bring back the image of him there at the window, only I don't have to imagine anything because he's really there, eyes devouring every inch of me.

I don't fall off that cliff; I'm launched like a rocket into orbit. I'm suspended in time by sheer ecstasy, and the only things tethering me to this world are twin pools of liquid blue desire that threaten to latch on and never let me go.

23

Kenzo

I'VE NEVER BEEN SO CLOSE TO COMING IN MY OWN GODDAMN pants as I am while I watch Shae finger fuck herself on our bed. I came back to the cabin after realizing I forgot to grab my bait. When I walked past the cabin and caught sight of Shae through the window, I reversed my steps. I'd only seen a glimpse of her on the bed out of the corner of my eye, so I thought maybe she'd lain down to rest.

I was so fucking wrong.

My heart ground to a lurching halt in my chest. I couldn't look away. I still can't. I want to memorize every detail of her spread wide for me. Inviting me to watch.

Her eyes are closed, lips parted. She doesn't know I'm here, but I know she's thinking of me. She'd been so turned on after our sparring that she hadn't waited five minutes to touch herself. I'd felt the same, which is why I was so damn pissed that she refuses to acknowledge what is so obviously happening between us.

There's no denying this.

I consider taking my dick out when her eyes open, and our stares collide.

In a fraction of a second, I wonder what she'll do. Will she cover herself or panic? Will seeing me trigger embarrassment or anger? I haven't been able to figure out what's going on in her head, so I can't predict how she'll react, which makes it all the more rewarding when seeing me is what pushes her over the edge.

She isn't shocked or repulsed. My eyes on her are exactly what she needed. What she wanted, whether she acknowledges it or not.

At that moment, I know two things with absolute certainty. One, if I walk into that cabin, Shae's vulnerability will cause her to be more defensive than ever. She has to willingly submit. And two, I cannot accept failure. Shae is mine. If she needs to lose our bet to justify giving in, then so be it.

I will catch a goddamn fish if it kills me.

I tear myself away from the window and grab my bait baggie out of the storage locker. Then my raging hard-on and I charge back to the creek.

We call it a creek, but it could be a river. Hell if I know what the size cutoff is between the two. Our creek is about fifteen feet across and varies in depth from a few inches to several feet where the larger boulders cluster together. The water is crystal clear and flows steadily. You can see to the bottom where ice chunks don't cover the surface, and I've seen fish. Not many, and they're small, but I've seen them. I know they're in there.

I use small bits of tendon and other less appetizing tissue from our kills to bait my hooks. The flow of ice bumping my line makes it hard to tell if something is nibbling at my bait. Then again, maybe I have no fucking clue what I'm doing. After sitting for an hour with nothing to show for my time, I'm definitely questioning my abilities.

I know I could do it if I had the right equipment. It's so goddamn frustrating.

I set down my pole and toss a rock into the water. The splash is satisfying, so I do it a few more times. I'm wondering if I might have more luck catching something like this than with the line. I could whittle a spear and try to fish that way. The fish are awfully small, though, and hard to spot in the moving water.

The more I think about it, the more frustrated I get.

The damn things are right there in front of me. All I have to do is catch one. How the fuck can I make that happen? If I knew I could grab one with my hands, I'd jump in without a thought to the cold. But I know I'd probably just freeze to death for nothing.

I pick up another rock to toss at the water when a large hawk swoops down out of nowhere, pulls up short of the water's surface, and plucks out a fish in its curved talons. Majestic and effortless.

If I didn't know better, I'd say Mother Nature was laughing in my face.

The rock in my hand is flying through the air before I even realize what I've done. It hits the bird square in the chest, and though it isn't large enough to do any real damage, it's enough to shock the hawk into dropping its catch with an angry screech.

I race up the stream to where the fish's scales shimmer in

the sun as it flops back toward the water. "Sorry, little fella, but this is *not* your lucky day."

I snatch him up, then whack its head against the rocks to end its fight. It's only about six inches, and I technically didn't catch the thing on a line, but neither of those stipulations were a part of our deal. I caught a motherfucking fish, and now it's time for my reward.

24

Shae

I'M NOT EMBARRASSED. I'M A CONFIDENT, SELF-ASSURED WOMAN comfortable in her own skin. Everyone masturbates. I have nothing to fear.

The statements have played on an endless loop in my head for the past hour. I believe them. I swear, I do. So why won't this crippling anxiety go away? If anything, it's only gotten worse because the later it gets, the less time I have until Renzo returns.

He's coming, and he knows what I did and why. The part that has my stomach in knots is wondering what he's going to do about it. I saw that look in his eyes. Something in him snapped, and the waiting is killing me. Solitaire isn't even an effective distraction anymore, which means I'm sitting at the table, staring vacantly at the fire when the door bursts open.

My eyes snap to his.

Renzo's broad frame fills the doorway for three elongated heartbeats before he steps inside and slams his hand down on the table in front of me. And when it retreats, a small silver fish remains.

I can hardly believe my eyes. I stare dumbfounded at the silver-scaled creature the entire time Renzo washes his hands in the water bucket.

He did it. The bastard caught a damn fish.

My mouth hangs open like the fish's—we're equally shocked.

"You … you can't…"

"I can't what, Shae?" He returns to my side, his thick fingers wrapping around my neck and coaxing me to my feet. "Tell me what I can't." His lips are so close to mine. I can't breathe. I can't think.

"You can't … be serious. That was a joke."

His lips quirk upward in the corners with more vicious delight than I would have thought him capable of. "You knew exactly what you were signing up for. A bet is a bet—there's no backing out."

"But … but I'm all sweaty, and I haven't shaved in ages. You seriously don't want to go there." I could fight him off if I needed to, but that's not the problem. What worries me is how intensely I want to feel his body touching mine in the most intimate, primal way possible. If I let this happen, I'm not sure I'll be the same after. I know I won't. I won't be Shae anymore.

I'll be his.

"Oh, I'm going there. And if I need to, I'll lick you clean myself." He takes the hem of my shirt and sweeps it up and over my head so that I'm left standing in my bra and jeans. Then he's in my space again, his hands threading into my hair as he brings his cheek to mine. "What's the matter, Chaos? Scared you'll like it?" He bites my earlobe with the perfect amount of pain and pleasure before kissing his way down my neck.

The way he touches me lights every nerve ending on fire. His body somehow speaks to mine on a molecular level, and I'm powerless against it.

"Just this once," I breathe, my head tipping back. "Because I'm a woman of my word." I don't even know what I'm saying because I'm so lost in sensation.

His hands unclasp my jeans. I breathe in shallow, shaky breaths as he walks me backward to the bed, then yanks my pants down to my ankles. His hand flattens on my belly to lay me back on the bed before he pulls my jeans the rest of the way off.

It all happens so fast that my head is spinning. I'm not used to a partner taking control. I'm usually the one in the lead, but Renzo is a man possessed. He's done playing, and he's certainly not asking for permission.

That doesn't mean I have to let him.

I wonder if taking control is what I need to neutralize the situation. To keep from being swept away.

Yes, that's it. And besides, if he's going to wreck me, he should have to work for it.

I get up quickly, spinning us so that his back is to the bed. I make him sit, then climb on his lap, my legs straddling his. His cock is so impossibly hard, it feels incredible pressed against my core. My pelvis grinds with the need for more. I move in to press my lips to his when his head twists to the side just enough to prevent me from achieving my goal.

Dark amusement deepens the azure of his eyes. "Nice try,

but that's not how this is going to happen." He grips my wrists in one of his hands while the other keeps my body connected with his while he stands long enough to spin me around and place me on my back again. This time, his body follows mine and holds me in place. "This is *my* prize, and I'll take my winnings on *my* terms."

His natural dominance has the alpha female in me purring so loudly I can't hear myself think.

"Just remember the deal—you can touch me, not fuck me. You're not getting me knocked up out here." I glare at him, and I'd swear something primal and untamed stares back at me.

"We wouldn't want that, would we?" I find the eerie dissonance to his words unsettling yet captivating. I've never been the focus of such intense desire.

He holds my hands above my head, resting his body to the side with his back against the wall. He uses his free hand to part my thighs. I wonder if he's going right for the main attraction—so many men do—but he surprises me when his hand slowly glides up my body, feeling, testing, learning. When he reaches my bra, he hooks his finger in the middle, his eyes connecting with mine as he achingly slowly tugs it low enough for my breasts to pop free.

I'd been anticipating this moment to the point of obsession, and now that it's here, it's even better than I imagined. Renzo's chest expands on a shocked inhale.

"Oh, Chaos, baby. You've been keeping secrets." Each gravelly word scrapes across my skin with exquisite pleasure.

At this rate, he won't even have to touch me to make me come. I'm so damn turned on I could light the night sky.

Renzo leans forward and runs his tongue around one of my pierced nipples, then sucks it into his mouth and releases me with a pop. I practically levitate off the bed.

My padded bra prevented him from being able to tell I was pierced. I thought he'd appreciate the discovery, but I was wrong. Judging from the way he rises to straddle my body and lavish each taut peak with adoration, he's well past appreciation.

His hands snake beneath my back and unclasp my bra, then tosses it over his shoulder. His stare devours me. I love the way it feels but still have to fight back insecurities about my current appearance. I've never in my life let another person see me so natural. Even if I'm not dating anyone, I don't let myself get this overgrown.

I hate that this is how he's seeing me for the first time, though I don't detect any repugnance coming from Renzo in the slightest. Quite the opposite. He's acting as though I'm the tastiest dessert he's had in years.

And when he moves down my body and lowers my panties down below my hips, Renzo proves my impending mortification is unnecessary when he runs the bridge of his nose along my slit and moans his approval with a guttural sound that brings a flush to my skin. It's the most primitively masculine sound I've ever heard. And the most possessive.

My thighs part as if on command.

"Fuck, you're so responsive." He spreads my labia and lavishes a slow swipe of his tongue against my clit. "You were made for fucking."

"Jesus, Ren. I need more. You want to prove you can make me come, then do it. Show me what you've got."

He's already got me halfway there, but I'm not telling him that. I'm so desperate for the finish line that goading him into proving himself is more to my advantage.

"You can't help but try to top from the bottom, can you?" He gives my inner thigh a warning nip. "I may let you take the reins when it comes to daily life around here, but when your body is naked beneath mine, you *will* do as I say."

"I told you, only this once." I don't miss his implication that this interlude is only the beginning.

"I won't even dignify that with a response." His tongue swirls around my clit as he buries a finger deep inside me. I grind against him, moaning with delight.

Renzo brings me to orgasm like his life depends upon it. No teasing or dallying. He works my body as well as I do, giving me a release that has me screaming in pleasure.

"Now that I've proven not every man is a worthless prick, it's time to play."

"Wait, Renzo. That's two already for me today. I can't do more."

I'm flipped onto my belly, and his hand slaps my backside faster than I can comprehend what's happened. "What did I say about giving orders?"

"That's not an order!"

Smack.

Fuuuuck, there's something about a man who can give a good spanking. It's not about the pain. It's about the confidence. The control.

My spine arches, pressing my ass farther into the air.

"Jesus, you're perfect." His hand caresses the sting on my cheek before he lifts my hips in the air. I'm on my knees, but he presses a hand on my upper back to keep my chest down against the bed.

"Keep your hands over your head." That wolfish bite is back in his voice. His need has taken over again.

He starts to lick my center again, lazy strokes that reignite that spark of desire. When my body starts to undulate into his touch, he pulls away. I hear him spit, then feel warmth drip onto the pucker of my backside. My breathing hitches. I'm no stranger to anal play, but I consider lube to be a must. That sort of thing has to be done right, or it can hurt like a bitch.

He sees me tense. "Easy, girl. I'm not going to do anything you won't love." He caresses my ass cheek. While his tongue returns to working my clit, his finger gently tests the puckered ring of muscle. I try to relax and open for him, making him moan. The sound drives me wild with need.

When his hand reaches forward to toy with my piercing, the storm inside me ramps up with a frenzy. He uses the opportunity to ease his thumb inside my ass. Just the tip. He teases and caresses the entrance in a way that feels deliciously naughty, more so than full-on penetration. Like he's secretly doing something he's not supposed to do. The taboo nature of his teasing touch is more arousing than any I've experienced in that realm.

He is unlike anything I've experienced—his unwavering dominance, his expert touch, and especially his unquestionable desire for me. It all combines in a cacophony of sensation —a perfect orgasmic storm. My body feels like it might lose control of all bodily functions in a mass meltdown.

"Shit, Ren. I'm gonna come again. It's too much. I can't."

"You can, and you will. Give me that chaos. Give me every bit of it."

I'm helpless to deny him.

My body bows to his command, hurdling me into a new dimension of existence where there is no awareness save for pleasure. The orgasm doesn't merely barrel through me. It incinerates my insides until I'm nothing but ash. The panting, mindless remnants of a woman.

I lay with my ass in the air and soak in the endorphins. I'm so blissed out that I don't notice the bed shaking until Renzo growls behind me. Warm jets of cum decorate the cooling skin of my ass cheeks.

My initial reaction is twofold: delighted at the look of victorious satisfaction on his face and simultaneously disappointed I didn't get to feel him thicken inside me in that initial moment of release. I desperately want to be irritated or insulted. He came all over me without any warning, after all. We don't even have a way to bathe here.

I can't summon a single ounce of outrage.

And any fight I could have theoretically summoned would have been decimated when he tenderly kisses my hip.

"Stay there. I'll clean you up."

I lay flat and wait as he diligently wipes off all traces of himself with a wet towel. When I flip over, he hands me my panties, and I slide them back on.

Now comes the tricky part.

We've crossed that line and have to figure out what it means going forward.

"This doesn't have to change anything," I say quietly. It's my one last-ditch effort to protect myself from the inevitable crash landing I see coming my way because I'm not simply falling for the man. I dove in headfirst.

Renzo leans over and gently sweeps a strand of hair off my forehead. "You're right. Nothing has to change if we don't want it to." His touch and words seem like they're supposed to be reassuring, but his stare is so frigid it burns. A stab of pain lances through the center of my heart.

And so it begins.

25

Kenzo

JUST THIS ONCE. NOTHING HAS TO CHANGE.

How the fuck am I supposed to act like nothing's changed when my entire world has been turned inside out? Some events are too monumental not to leave an indelible mark on your soul.

When a hurricane decimates a coastal town, the buildings may be rebuilt, but that community will never be the same. Having Shae Byrne—the most independent, headstrong woman I've ever met—give herself to me and submit to my command was like no other high on earth. I can't simply forget it ever happened. I'll crave that feeling for the rest of my goddamn life.

The fact that she's still resisting makes me want to kill someone.

Why? Why won't she give in? Our families complicate things, but they aren't here. And even if they were, I'm the fucking boss of my family. I'll do what I damn well please. So what if she's not Italian. It's not the 1970s anymore, and we aren't dogs needing to be AKC registered.

What matters is loyalty and character. Not bloodlines.

And even if someone disagrees, there's always the alliance exception. My father had no qualms marrying off his niece to Shae's cousin in the name of an alliance. Why should my role as boss preclude me from a similar relationship? If I say it's not a problem, then it's not a fucking problem.

She wants to refuse to accept me?

Well, I refuse to accept her refusal.

I can't go back home and pretend I'm okay with her sharing that side of herself with anyone else. I'll go fucking insane. That untamed spirit of hers is *mine*. I know it. Her body knows it. I have to find a way to convince her mind.

I need to know what's holding her back so I can bury that reason six feet under.

Is it her independence she's worried about? The opinions of her family? My family? Whatever the source, I have to convince her I'm not a threat. That being with me is worth the risk.

I spend the rest of the afternoon thinking over my options. After we've eaten and the last of twilight's glow has faded from our small window, I decide to do some digging. If I can get her talking, maybe I can get to the root of the problem.

"Tell me more about your family." It's such an obvious question. I'm suddenly kicking myself for not pushing to know more about her sooner.

"Like what?"

"I don't know. I guess you can start with your role in the business. What do you do most days?"

"I oversee security at Bastion, so I usually work at night."

"That's one of your social clubs?"

"We only have the one social club, though I suppose some people might call Moxy a social club." Her lips twist into a wry smirk.

"I'm sure there's enough regulars at a strip club to justify the moniker."

She raises her cup of water in agreement. "I would imagine you're right, though I don't spend much time over there, so I wouldn't know the particulars."

"Conner works at Bastion as well, right?" I helped gather information on Conner for Dad when he was deciding whether to approve my cousin's marriage to him. It's my understanding the social club is a front for a high-roller gambling setup. All pretty uppity—no losers using rent money to bet on ponies or anything like that.

"Yeah, he runs the club. Because we work together at Bastion, I tend to help him with other things."

"Like meetups for retrieving gun shipments?" I raise a brow.

"Precisely."

"You enjoy working with him?"

"Sometimes he gets a stick up his ass, but I'm pretty good at keeping him humble. He likes to pretend I make him crazy." She smirks. "It works for us."

I can picture her giving him hell, and it makes me smile.

"What about your brother Oran? Any reason you don't work with him instead?"

"He's entirely too overprotective. If he had his way, my role would be limited to bookkeeping or something equally mundane to keep me out of danger."

"Conner isn't like that?"

Her eyes lift as though her thoughts have taken her back to another time and place. "You know, there's something different about Conner. I don't know if it's because he's adopted or just his personality, or something entirely unrelated, but he's always been more open about giving someone a shot. He manages to be a surly bastard while also being open-minded and fair."

"What about the older generation? I can't imagine they made it easy for you to join the ranks."

Her gaze drops to her hands, and I can almost sense her walls trying to rebuild.

"My dad was never an issue. He accepted me just as I was, but my uncles were harder to convince. They refused to let me in the fold for quite a while." She's somber, but when her eyes flick up to mine, a mischievous spark melts those barriers. "That is, until my nana got ahold of them. She got fed up with their ridiculous misogyny and put them in their place. After that, no one stood in my way of being a part of the family business."

"Really?" I'm intrigued. I had no idea the family was matriarchal. "Did she run things when she was younger?"

"Depends on who you ask. Never officially, but if there is a head of our family, it's Nana Byrne. She keeps everyone in line and never takes shit from anyone."

"My mother and grandmothers always took a more supporting role than leadership. I think that's why it's been so hard on Mom since Dad passed. She's lost without him."

Shae's smile falls. "Yeah, my mom's the same. Losing Dad destroyed her. Oran and Cael have been looking after her, though."

"You two not have a good relationship?"

The smile that now tugs on her lips is a sad, paltry

shadow of the joy that overtook her talking about her grandmother. "She's never understood me. I know she doesn't mean to make me feel like a disappointment, but it's there in the fine print. She'd hoped to have a mini-me to do girly stuff with, and I've never come close to being that person."

"I saw those stilettos you wore the first time we met. You can't tell me you don't enjoy any feminine pursuits."

"You noticed." She bites back a grin.

"There's very little I don't notice about you."

She sucks her lips between her teeth and drops her gaze. "Well, what isn't as easy to discern is that my interest in clothes and hair and accessories is all about functionality. When I look for heels, I select them based on how well they'd double as a weapon, not whether they're runway-worthy. If I went dress shopping with Mom, I'd get excited to find something that hid my thigh holster well."

"You were still out shopping together. Was that not enough for her?"

"Not her. She'd get so frustrated about why I couldn't buy things that were pretty but impractical. Time together hurt our relationship more than it helped. I found it's best to keep things superficial and brief."

"Her loss," I say as I lift my hand and trail a fingertip along the neckline of her shirt. The pulse point at the base of her neck doubles its fluttering motion. As my hand pulls away, I detour to the pendant on her necklace, lifting it for a better look.

"This from your family?" The inlaid woven border is obviously Celtic. She could have bought it herself, but a gift seems more likely.

"Um, no. It's not." The odd hitch in her voice draws my gaze from the pendant back to her face. Her eyes stay averted, and her spine stiff. "Guess it's probably time to call it a night. I'm pretty wiped out."

She couldn't have shut down faster if she'd had an off switch.

What the hell is up with that?

The pendant clearly has meaning to her—a sentimentality that she's not comfortable discussing. Why? I consider who might have given it to her but realize its importance could come from a million different reasons. Grasping at straws is pointless and will only rile me up for no reason. I reluctantly let it go and get ready for bed.

Once we're both under the covers, the awkwardness intensifies. It's strange to have been intimate with someone and then return to platonic bedmates. Am I supposed to forget that my fingers have been inside her? That I know how she tastes when she comes?

Her body curves into mine like the two were made for one another, yet the invisible barriers between us keep her beyond my reach. I don't understand it, but I don't want to force the issue. I want her to come to me willingly. To give me her body and her secrets.

Seeing progress helps me be patient. And so long as we're out here in the wilderness, she can only run so far.

♦

THE NEXT DAY starts like any other. She's holding fast to her stance that nothing has changed between us. I didn't necessarily think she would have changed her mind overnight, but a part of me had hoped she'd at least show signs of softening to the idea.

When I notice her scratching at her scalp come afternoon, I

recognize an opportunity. "Let me grab some fresh water, and I'll wash your hair. It's been nearly a week since the last time." She couldn't hide how much she enjoyed my hands in her hair. It's a perfect excuse to touch her and hopefully remind her how good I can make her feel. Anything to wear down her resistance.

"Thanks for the offer, but I think I'll just dunk my head down at the creek. No reason to haul the water all the way up here for that." The way she says it, you'd think I offered to help with a chore rather than suggest an intimate act shared between two people. Like she's doing me a favor by handling it herself.

"If I minded hauling the water, I wouldn't have offered." I can't keep the irritation from my voice.

"I get it. Some time outside sounds nice, though. The creek is gorgeous. I don't spend enough time down there." She's smiling and keeping her tone light, but she's too intuitive not to grasp the deeper meaning of my offer and her rejection.

Come on, Donati. Patience isn't your finest virtue, but it's only been a day. Calm the fuck down.

Someone as headstrong as Shae probably struggles to accept an unexpected curve in the road like sleeping with a rival. She's more apt to drive straight through the trees in pursuit of her original objective than to pivot.

She needs time to adjust. I can give her that. For now.

♦

THREE DAYS. Three fucking days and not the slightest indication that Shae is even a little bit tempted to open up to me. I'm starting to think I know what it feels like to be gaslit. If I were to ask how she can pretend we never did anything, I wouldn't be surprised if she cocked her head in confusion and asked me what on earth I was talking about.

Only it did happen. And I'd put my whole goddamn fortune on a bet that she's just as affected by it as I am despite her impressive show to the contrary.

"Can you believe we've been gone for two weeks?" She sounds so forlorn as she sits looking out the cabin window. Snow has kept us inside most of the day.

I understand the frustration of cabin fever. I also understand missing home. Therefore, I should empathize with her statement, but I'm incensed instead. She can't get out of here fast enough. Get away from *me* fast enough. Instead of hoping for a rescue, I see the dwindling cans of food as a fucked up advent calendar counting down our days together. Once we're back in the city, I have a feeling she'll slip through my fingers like glitter in the wind.

I have to do something. Find a way to get through to her.

Giving her space hasn't done jack shit. Maybe it's time to change tactics.

I rise from the bed and cross the room. Once I'm next to her, she drags her gaze from the window and peers up at me. A flash of surprise widens her eyes a fraction when she sees the intensity in mine.

"You know what I can't believe? I can't believe I've yet to feel that sharp tongue of yours licking my cock." My thumb drags across her lower lip.

I'm not sure what led me to this route except instinct. If the only way she'll submit is when I force the issue, then I suppose she leaves me no choice. She's proven repeatedly now that it's the only way to get through to her. When it comes down to it, I don't care about the method of transportation, so long as I get where I want to go.

"Why's that so hard to believe?" Her voice is husky, reinforcing my decision. And not only that. She's proving to me that she likes her partner to take control. She wants her choices taken away.

"Because I know you want to. I've seen the way your eyes drift my way when you lick the food off your fingers. And because there's no reason not to—not when we're out here alone with no guarantee of survival."

"I like to be optimistic and think we'll be home soon."

"I'm all for optimism. That's why I've tried to be patient, but I'm done waiting. Now ..." I curl my fingers in her hair gently but firmly and angle her head back. "Get on your knees and suck my cock like a good girl."

26

Shae

I prayed he wouldn't do this. Not because he's forcing me to do something I don't want to. It's the opposite. My resolve to keep our relationship platonic has been hanging by a thread. I knew I could never withstand the temptation if he pushed the issue. His ability to take control is too alluring. Too thorough.

A commanding energy seethes inside him beneath the surface. He doesn't wield it unnecessarily, but when he does choose to exercise his dominance, his confidence is absolute.

The mark of a true alpha.

My knees crash to the floor. I have to swallow to draw moisture back into my mouth. No question where it's all gone. My panties are suddenly soaked.

I free his swollen cock from his pants. It falls heavily into my trembling hand. I saw a brief glimpse of him before, but up close is another story. He's thick. My fingers won't go all the way around. So thick and heavy and *hard*. Bulging veins. And so velvety soft.

I have to run my hand slowly up and down his shaft to memorize the feel.

His hand cups my jaw, pinching my cheeks to coax my mouth open. "I appreciate your admiration, but I want your tongue more." He brings his cock to my lips. "Show me how talented that pretty mouth can be."

God, I love what his words do to me.

I flatten my tongue and lean forward, taking him in my mouth and circling my tongue around his head.

"*Fuck*, that's it." His guttural moan makes my heart soar. I want to make him feel good, especially after causing so much frustration. I'm not sorry for trying to protect myself these past few days, but I haven't enjoyed pushing him away either.

Each lick I lavish upon him is an attempt to soothe the hurt. And when I take him into the back of my throat until tears burn my eyes, I'm trying to tell him how desperately I want him. How he gives me the freedom to let go without worrying about the consequences.

He gives me no choice but to simply be his.

No proving myself or worrying about how I'll be perceived. I know Renzo respects me. I know he wants me. And if our circumstances were different, I'd throw myself wholeheartedly into making him mine.

Instead, I'll have to settle for the time we have here within these cabin walls and worry about the fallout later.

I take him deep and moan my delight.

Renzo hisses. "I should tan your ass for making me wait for this."

In response, I take his balls in my hand and give them a tug.

"That's it. I'm not going to last long. When I come, I want you to swallow every bit of it. Understood?"

I nod and flex my hips, desperately needing to alleviate the pressure in my aching clit. If I could even put a pillow between my thighs—something to rub against and give me the friction I need.

God, I need it. I need *him*.

I grip the base of his shaft and pump in tandem with my sucking, making sure to pop my lips over the rim of his head with each movement. His abs clench tight while he fists his hand in my hair. When the moment comes, he holds my head in place with his cock in the back of my throat, bellowing a curse as he shoots warm cum into my throat. I swallow repeatedly, making him flinch and moan with pleasure before releasing his grip on me so I can breathe easier.

I sit back on my heels and wipe my face as I watch him watch me. He eases his cock back in his pants, then holds his hand out to help me up. Once I'm on my feet, he sits in the chair I was previously occupying.

"Unzip your pants and drop them to your knees."

I do as he says, far too entranced by his spell to question him. Not to mention, I'm desperately hoping he'll make me come. My need is crippling at this point.

He cups my sex, and the relief of his touch has my eyes rolling back in my head. Only, his presence is fleeting. My eyes pop open in dismay.

"Look at this." He holds his middle finger up for me to see. It's coated in my milky cream and glossy arousal. "Don't even try to pretend you didn't love every second of that."

He commands my attention with his gaze locked on mine while he sticks the entire finger in his mouth and sucks it clean.

My lungs empty of air in one fell whoosh.

Renzo stands, his face inches from mine. "I don't know what you've got going on in that head of yours, but you're wrong. We can play it this way if you want, or you can decide to grow up and talk about it. Your call." He grabs his coat and disappears outside into the falling snow.

I'm left standing with my pants around my knees and my pride scattered across the floor.

How dare he be so fucking presumptive? How dare he judge me when he can't possibly understand. He's not in a position to lose anything. It's not like he has to decide whether loving someone is worth losing everything he's worked toward in his life. No one would ever expect him to step down as Mafia boss so I could keep working for my family. And if he's still boss, where would that leave us? With me making all the sacrifices.

If I could screw around with him and not catch feelings, that would be great, but it's not possible. Not with Renzo. I'm already inching down that slippery slope faster than I care to admit. If I make it all the way to the bottom, there will be nothing but heartbreak waiting for me because I'll have to either walk away from my entire identity or give up the man I love. I can't see any other outcomes from continuing down that path. And if I want to avoid finding myself in that unenviable situation, I have to change courses.

These thoughts have haunted me for days.

I know Renzo is frustrated. I know none of this is easy, especially out here, but he hasn't even tried to see things from my perspective. Just because I want to be with him doesn't mean it's as simple as that. How could he possibly be oblivious to the impacts of such an obvious roadblock? It's either that or all he wants is a physical relationship and doesn't understand why something like that wouldn't work for me. Either way, his impatience and failure to empathize burns through any guilt I might feel otherwise.

He's not a mind reader, but I don't think I'm under an obligation to explain my hesitancy.

I should explain. I should give in. I should, should, *should.*

What about him? Why shouldn't the *shoulds* fall on his shoulders for once?

The roller coaster of emotions I'm riding has tears burning the backs of my eyes, and that pisses me off even more.

I knew he'd do this to me—carve out my insides and leave me a broken mess. I'm not there yet, but I see it happening like an out-of-body experience. I see myself careening toward a brick wall, and I'm powerless to stop myself.

The only thing I can think to do to mitigate damages is an abrupt about-face. I have to jump tracks and get myself going in a new direction. The opposite direction as Renzo.

If I pretend he doesn't exist, I can't fall in love with him … any more than I already have.

I have to shut him out and get control of my heart again.

The thought alone sends a searing stab of pain through my chest. I collapse into the chair and let the sobs take over. Silent heaving sobs of loss and frustration built up from years of intense discipline. The funny thing is, I'm not entirely sure if the loss of Renzo or myself shakes me the most. Either way, I'm adrift.

I give myself a handful of minutes to bleed the emotions dry before wiping the salt from my cheeks and securing an impenetrable barrier around me. Not only between me and the outside world. I erect a reinforced barrier separating me from my emotions. If I can't trust that part of me, I'll have to lock it away until the threat is no longer present.

I don't like the emptiness. It feels foreign and cold, but I know it's the best way to protect myself.

When Renzo finally returns, I can sense his scrutiny.

I feel his wary gaze following my movements. Studying. Calculating. I sense him, and I don't care. His curiosity or concern is irrelevant to me. His existence is inconsequential aside from his role in aiding my survival.

The numbness would be a relief if I was open to feeling anything. But I'm not.

All I feel are facts.

His body against mine while we sleep. I am warm.

His presence on a walk to the creek. I am not alone.

My emotions are not part of the equation, and I don't allow myself to waste energy dwelling on his thoughts and feelings because they are as irrelevant as he is.

27

Kenzo

SHAE HAS HARDLY SPOKEN IN THE TWO DAYS SINCE THE BLOW JOB. It wouldn't bother me if she were simply giving me the silent treatment. I have two younger sisters who are experts in the art of passive aggression. I know the silent treatment when I see it.

This is different.

At first, I played into her silence and was equally distant. I realized as the day went by that something was off. The emptiness in Shae's eyes sends an eerie chill down my spine.

She's not merely silent; she's gone.

The profound shift throws me completely. I can't stop worrying what I did has resurfaced a past trauma, triggering her to shut down. Guilt drips from a leaky faucet I usually keep welded shut.

Even if that isn't the case, something has caused her to withdraw into herself. Something about what we did. I don't get it. She was unquestionably willing. I know she got off on it. So why have such an adverse reaction after the fact?

I didn't want to hurt her. I just didn't know of any other way to get through but to speak to that side of her that hears me. I want to ask her what's wrong, but I know she won't tell me. She won't even fucking say a word, let alone explain herself. Do I force it out of her? Would that finally push her to break through to the other side of this mental block, or would I do irreparable damage?

I spend two days crippled with indecision. That is not something I'm used to experiencing, and I hate the feeling. I'm a fixer. A leader. Flailing about in a sea of uncertainty only leads to drowning. I know I need to decide on a course and follow through, but hell if I can figure out what that course is.

On the third day, when I return from a walk, I find Shae working out. She's using a tree as a stand-in for a sparring partner. She's been at it long enough that the pink in her cheeks is no longer from the cold. It's the most animated I've seen her since she gave me the most incredible blow job I've ever had.

My gut tells me this might be my chance.

It's the first inkling of intuition I've had in two days, so I'm quick to pay attention. I join her by the tree. I don't say anything. Instead, I take a fighter's stance and hope she'll engage like she did the last time we sparred.

When her stance shifts in my direction, her stare spears me through a millisecond before her hips swivel and send her shin flying at my kidneys in a perfectly performed sidekick. I manage to block the brunt of the kick with my forearm and breathe a sigh of relief when she doesn't launch into an immediate follow-up attack. Instead, we circle one another.

Electric energy surges in my veins both in preparation for a fight and because there's a spark in her eyes—a flash of life that wasn't there before.

Shae—my *Shae*—is close. I have to find a way to lure her out.

I haven't trained to fight like she can. She's beyond incredible. But you don't grow up in a Mafia family as the eldest son and not pick up a few things over the years.

I throw out a jab followed by a quick left hook. I don't hold back. I want her to know that I take her and whatever is going on between us seriously. She blocks both strikes and connects to my gut on a well-timed uppercut. She's not holding back either. My abs flex to absorb the hit, so I'm not winded, but it still hurts like a bitch. I breathe through it, and we resume circling one another.

"That's it, Chaos. Give me all your anger."

Her blue eyes flare. "Don't call me that." Her tone is still flat but transparent, giving me a perfect view of the raging emotions lurking close to the surface.

"You can't hide from me, Chaos." I jab, then evade her return strike. "I know you're there, and I won't quit until I have you."

This time, I charge her and use my size to its best advantage, trying to put her in a bear hug hold.

Shae rears back and slams the top of her head into my face, then lifts her legs to become dead weight. The two maneuvers are highly effective, and she's quickly free from my grasp as I hold my now bleeding nose.

"If I'm so chaotic, why would you even want me?" She spreads her arms wide, her voice demanding. "Let it go, Donati. I'm not worth the trouble."

"That's for me to fucking decide," I growl back. Ignoring my nose, I return to a fighting stance and instigate a new round of circling. This is happening, here and now. Whatever the outcome.

She mirrors my stance, a scowl marring her beautiful features. "And what about me? Don't I get a say?"

"I'm all ears, Shae. I'd love to hear every last reason for the walls you've erected between us."

"Why do you think?" The words are an angry hiss through clenched teeth. "Why do people usually build walls?" She drops and whips around, swiping my legs out from under me. I immediately roll and get back on my feet.

"To keep people out. To protect themselves."

"Ding, ding, ding! Give the man a fucking prize." Desperation and anguish claw at her words.

"What have I done to hurt you?" My bellowed words send nearby birds cawing into the sky. "If you don't tell me, I can't stop doing it."

"You make me want you. If you want to stop hurting me, then quit making me fall for you." The last words are so jagged and raw that they tear my heart wide open.

"Not that," I breathe. "Don't ask that of me because it's the one thing I can't do." I close the distance between us and clasp her upper arms. "Why is this so bad? Why do you keep pushing me away?" I have to force myself not to shake her in my desperation to understand.

The pleading in her glassy-eyed stare threatens to shred me. "It's not you; it's *us*. Our families. The oaths we've sworn. They may not be an issue here, but it will be back home. And maybe all you're wanting is temporary relief while we're here. Normally, I'd be all for that, but you're different. I can't … I can't seem to control the emotions."

"You're not a temporary anything, Shae. I don't like not

having you for a day, let alone walk away from you once we're back in the city."

Her chin quivers before she yanks out of my grasp. "But don't you understand what that means? Don't you see what you're asking?" A tear tumbles over her lashes and down her cheek. "I've spent my entire life fighting to be seen as an equal. To earn my place in the family business. If I want you, I have to give up all of it. I lose *everything* that I am."

"Why? If I don't ask you to leave your family, why can't you keep doing what you love?" My question reeks of naivete. I know it the second the words are out and have no explanation for how foolishly I've been simplifying things in my head.

"You truly believe my family won't have concerns about my loyalties? I love them. They love me. But if I'm put between you and them, how do I choose who takes priority? It's an impossible choice. I know it, and so will they."

"Then work for me." I cross over to her and cup her tearstained cheeks in my hands. "You can do whatever you want—I'm the boss, and I make the rules." I *will* find a way to make this work, goddammit.

Her eyes drift shut as more tears trickle down to her achingly sad smile. "That's sweet of you." She fixes me with an earnest stare. "I can tell how much you want this—the fact that your blind to reality proves how much you care—but it's impossible. Not only would I have to start fresh proving my worth as a woman, but your men will never trust me to work beside them."

"What about Conner and Noemi? The families had no issue with their relationship."

"Because Noemi isn't the same as me. I'm the problem. Always have been." Her voice catches on words that make me want to kidnap her and leave both our families behind. Because *fuck* them.

"Not a goddamn thing is wrong with you." For the first time, I bring my lips to hers.

The kiss is tender but urgent. A plea. Because I understand now, and it changes nothing. No matter how much I hate myself for continuing to hurt her, I can't walk away.

28

Shae

His lips move against mine with such possessive demand, I feel certain he's branding them. I know he's left his mark on my heart if nothing else. With each caress of his tongue against mine, my fears and frustrations blur into the background like a faded photo. Renzo makes it hard to see anything beyond him.

He's all-consuming. World-ending.

I only wish I knew whether I'm capable of rising up from the ashes because I'm tired of fighting off the inevitable.

"You need to stop saying shit like that, or people will think you've gone soft," I say when we drift apart, an unexpected sense of acceptance settling over me.

"Fuck what other people think."

"Ideally, yeah. But that doesn't cut it in reality. You *are* the boss of your family, and it matters what the men under your leadership think."

His lips thin, knowing I'm right.

I place my hand on his chest, avoiding meeting his gaze. "I'll think about it, okay? But I need a bit of time." I finally peer up at him through my lashes and am relieved to see resigned acceptance etched on his face. I offer a small smile. "Besides, we have nothing but time out here, right?"

His gaze darts to the side before he nods. I get the sense something shifts in his demeanor, but it's so amorphous that I'm not sure what it is or what might have caused it. Considering the state of my heightened emotions, I'm not even sure I didn't simply imagine it.

"I'm going to fill the bucket with fresh water," Renzo informs me. "You go in and wait for me—I'm washing your hair, and don't even try to stop me."

My heart is officially a puddle at my feet. I lift my hands in surrender. "No arguments here."

Renzo washes my hair, then agrees to let me wash his. I could run my fingers through his thick hair all day, every day. He seemed to enjoy it as well. His cock is so visibly aroused that I feel a little bad. I don't want to be a tease, but I can't be reckless with my heart when our situation is so precarious. I need to think through how this would work. What I'd be willing to give up to have him.

Renzo is amazing all evening. He doesn't push to be physically intimate beyond making sure I'm clean and fed. And when it comes time for bed, I find myself turning over for the first time, bringing us chest-to-chest. Even fully dressed, lying like this with Renzo feels more intimate than almost any other sexual encounter I've ever had.

He shifts to his back, guiding my head onto his chest and

my body half draped over his. We don't talk. The room is free of awkward tension. It's just he and I in a bubble of comfort and warmth. I fall asleep almost instantly.

29

Kenzo

"A squirrel. That's hardly enough to feed a kid, let alone two grown adults." Shae stares at our meager catch for the day.

"We still have a rabbit and a bird in the freezer," I remind her.

"Yeah, but if we keep eating our reserves, we'll never save up enough for the trip out of here."

The worry in her voice gets to me, especially after everything that was said last night. She finally trusted me with her fears. I was so incredibly relieved and also humbled at how self-centered I've been. I couldn't understand why she'd be so resistant to being with me, but that was because I hadn't taken an earnest look at the situation from her perspective. I'm embarrassed at how easily I overlooked the sacrifices she'd have to make.

And now, not only is she torn about her desire for me, but she's worried about starvation and how we're getting home on top of it. I hate that I'm making a difficult time even harder for her. That was never my intention. I just wanted her to give me a chance. To give us a chance.

The tap holding back my guilt gives a little more, allowing the acidic substance to fill me more quickly.

"Let's take it one day at a time, okay?" I start back toward the cabin, mired in my dark thoughts.

Doubt is a mental tar pit that will suffocate you from the inside. I've always tried not to succumb to the sticky death sentence. Gather information. Make informed decisions. Accept your mistakes and move on. Doubt and regret serve no purpose. Yet I'm questioning my choices. If I wasn't seeing the whole picture where Shae was concerned, what else might I be missing?

I can't deny that if my priorities were what they should be, I wouldn't even be here now. And if Shae has become my top priority, what does that mean for me? Can I be the boss of the Moretti family, knowing the organization will never come first?

"Did something upset you?" Shae asks when the cabin is within view.

"Just thinking about things back home."

"Like what?"

"Like who's been running things in my absence. And what trouble my brother and Sante have been getting into." Technically, I was thinking about how little thought I'd put into the situation back home. Po-tay-to, po-tah-to.

"Who was most likely to step in?"

"My uncle Gino. He's a good guy. Never wanted the role of boss, but he's the most obvious person to step up without me there. I think a lot of people were expecting him to become boss when Dad died. He's older with more experience."

She listens, nodding silently.

"You know my other uncle was pissed when I became underboss. I can only imagine he's not the only one. This would be a perfect opportunity to shake up leadership if someone wanted to do that." I feel oddly removed from the situation when I explain it, as though I'm talking about a television program rather than my life.

"I haven't seen you in a business setting, but from what I know now, I have no doubt about your leadership abilities. That sort of thing isn't something you can fake. It's innate, and you have it. Anyone with two brain cells will know that."

"Oh yeah?" My eyes cut to hers. "What about me handling trivial matters and not taking to leadership?" I tease, reminding her of the slight she threw at me back when we first met.

Shae grins. "I only meant to rile you up. Everyone knows a good boss, whether running the Mafia or a Taco Bell, is willing to get in the trenches on occasion. To do what needs to be done and promote loyalty."

Fuck, this woman is incredible.

I can't imagine the idiots who came before me and didn't lock her down instantly. Not that Shae could be claimed by any old schmo. The circumstances would have to be exceptional for her to justify upending her world for a relationship, which is why I can't shake the feeling that we need to sort out how this works between us before we leave here. Find a way to be together that doesn't entail her sacrificing who she is.

I want her, but not at that price.

Some things are too valuable to give up, no matter how painful it might be.

30

Shae

RENZO AND I HAVEN'T SEEN HOME IN TWENTY DAYS, ALMOST three weeks. It's hard to fathom.

I've probably lost ten pounds. We're both looking quite a bit leaner than when we arrived. And I had no idea someone could get used to being this filthy so quickly. That's not true. We're not filthy so much as au naturel. No soap or deodorant. No razor. No toothpaste or mouthwash. I can't imagine how badly we'd stink if it were summer and heat was added to the mix.

As it is, I hardly notice the smell and even find comfort in Renzo's natural musk when I curl up with him at night. Now that we've found a sort of peace between us, everything seems a little less burdensome. I even have faith that we'll find a way home despite having no idea how that will happen. Being a team gives me confidence. Maybe a little less so in regard to what happens after we're home, but that's a work in progress.

I can't imagine what my family has gone through. The fear and uncertainty. Have they given up yet, or are they still holding out hope? Mari, on the other hand, may not have even noticed my absence. I'm surprised to realize that something about being here with Renzo makes my time with Mari seem so pointless and empty. Why have I let myself be content with such a shallow connection?

Because it was easier. Less risk.

It worked for a while, but I don't think I'll feel the same when we get back. If we get back, regardless of how things work with Renzo, it's time to end things with Mari.

No ifs, Shae. You will *get back.*

Today is by far the warmest day we've seen. It's only March third, so any warm-up is likely to be brief. Not knowing is the hardest part.

"Pretty day for fishing. You going to get back at it now that you've had success?" I ask Renzo while we sit at the table after eating. He hasn't fished since bringing me his catch over a week ago.

He considers my question before answering. "No, I don't think I will."

"But that would another food source for the trip home." I'm surprised he doesn't at least want to try. It's not like we have anything better to do.

"Chances are awfully slim that I'll catch another."

"You don't know that. Maybe you're just getting the hang of it."

He stares at me with challenge darkening his eyes.

"Unless I happen by another hawk, we won't be eating fish anytime soon."

My head cocks to the side. "A hawk? What does that have to do with anything?"

"Because that's how I caught that fish. I stole it. From a hawk."

I stare blankly back at him as I envision how that might have played out, then burst into laughter from the visual. I doubt he actually wrestled the fish out of the hawk's mouth, but that's the scene in my head, and it's hilarious.

"Oh my God. You did not, you cheater," I say with a laughing grin.

His lips widen in a devious smile. "I won that bet fair and square. We never stipulated how I had to catch the fish."

I can't be mad. It's flattering to know he was willing to do whatever it took to win. Whatever it took to be with me.

"Touché." I raise my water cup in salute. "I'll be more specific next time."

Those last two words hang in the air around us. *Next time.*

We haven't been intimate since the blow job. I told him I needed time, and he's been incredibly patient. I haven't felt the slightest pressure from him to go beyond my comfort zone. That doesn't mean the intense chemistry between us died. It's still every bit as intoxicating. And each day that passes chips away at my resolve to keep things platonic while I sort my feelings. The mention of *next time* has my brain replaying the thrill of that day he won the bet, bringing a flush to my cheeks.

If Renzo's now hooded eyes are any indication, I'd say he's doing the same.

The pull is too strong—it drowns out everything else and coaxes me to my feet. I straddle Renzo's legs and sit on his lap, my chest straining forward instinctively for his touch.

"This isn't me making a decision." I drape my arms over his shoulders and roll my hips.

His hands squeeze my thighs and pull me against his thickening cock. "Oh, no? What is it, then?"

"Important research. What if the last time you made me come was a fluke?"

"Twice," he corrects in a slow, sultry tone. "I made you come twice, but I agree. You should do your due diligence."

"Exactly. I'm glad you understand."

He stands, holding me in his arms with my legs clasped around his middle, and transfers us to the bed.

His body feels so incredible over mine. The weight of him. The controlled flex of mature muscle, hinting at the power within. He could easily fit in here as a hardened lumberjack with his new beard and scraggly hair as well as he could back home in a finely tailored suit running the city. I love how either suits him equally well. With his commanding air of confidence, I can't imagine him being out of place anywhere.

He works his way down my body, kissing and nipping until I'm writhing with anticipation. When his tongue first touches my slit, all my inner muscles clench hungrily. I want more. I want him inside me.

I can tell myself all day long that I'm simply horny, but I know it's so much more than that. It's Renzo. He stirs up this maddening need inside me. It doesn't matter how many times I get off; I'll always want more of him.

Renzo gives me a spectacular orgasm that leaves my head spinning. I feel so incredible that my inner voice forgets her warnings and starts spouting reasons not to give up hope that we can make this work. I let myself float on a river of optimism and dopamine. After all I've been through, I deserve the moment of happiness.

My blissed-out state amuses Renzo, who kisses my belly button with a chuckle and stands.

"Where are you going? It's your turn," I say lazily.

He leans back down, scooping the back of my neck in his rough palm. "The next time I come, it'll be inside you. Until then, I'll wait." He seals his proclamation with a kiss, which is good because I have no idea what to say in return.

"I'm going to replenish the firewood pile. Holler if you need anything." His husky words wrap me in a blanket of warmth that stays with me even after he heads outside. I'm so comfortable and content that I wrap up in the quilt and drift to sleep, wrenched awake sometime later by a horrifying roar.

The bear. He's back.

31

Kenzo

I HEAR HIS HUFFING BREATHS BEFORE I SEE HIM. THE BEAR IS somewhere behind me, though I'm not sure how far. I'm also not sure he's seen me.

We've had to move farther away from the cabin in our search for wood to avoid having to chop down an entire full-grown tree. We have an ax, but it's small, and chopping anything stout would be a huge effort. I chose to wander in a new direction today and came across a fallen tree that wasn't too rotted out and had decent-sized branches I could chop. Once I had a small pile, I took what I could carry back to the cabin and was dropping off a second load when I stopped to pee.

Now, I'm standing with my dick out, wondering if this is seriously how I die.

Slowly, I tuck myself back in my pants and turn around. The bear has his eyes trained on me like a pit boss watching a card counter.

Adrenaline surges in my veins.

I have no weapons. I had to leave the ax at the tree so I could carry the wood back. I'm not too far from the cabin but far enough that I'll never make it. The bear is thirty yards away. He can build up one hell of a head of steam in that distance.

The best thing I can think to do is to go up. Some bears climb trees, and this could be one of them, but there's no better option, especially when the tree right next to me has a branch low enough for me to reach.

I slowly move around to the back side and pull myself up. The bear makes an irritated grunt and lops closer. It takes all my strength to pull myself as high as I can go. I can only hope he decides I'm not worth the effort.

When he reaches the bottom of my tree, he sniffs at the trunk and starts rocking back and forth. He's angry, and he lets me know by releasing a furious roar.

Fear rockets through me because I know what happens next.

I squint through the trees at the cabin, my ears still trained below me. Seconds tick by, and I start to convince myself that maybe she's smart enough to stay inside. That's when the door eases open.

My eyes pinch tightly shut.

"Shae, get the fuck back inside," I yell with every ounce of authority I can summon.

She stills, then looks up, scanning the trees. "I'm not leaving you out here alone."

The bear barks at her as though in challenge. I maneuver so that I can see him below me. He's looking toward the cabin, then back up at me, trying to decide on the easiest target. When I look back to see what Shae's doing, she's gone. My fingers tighten around the tree branch I've been holding, wishing it were her neck I was throttling instead. She's going to get herself killed.

"I swear to *Christ*, Shae. Get the fuck back inside," I roar.

The bear roars.

Shae ignores both of us.

She scurries into the open from the side of the building with our pickax in one hand and all three of our extra kills in the other.

"Here, bear," she calls, waving the carcasses in the air. "You're hungry? I have food here."

The bear lifts his snout and sniffs the air.

Shit.

He's interested. I'm guessing it's for the same reason he hasn't come up here for me. He's hungry and tired and doesn't have the energy for much of a fight. Would he have come up after me if Shae hadn't appeared? I can't say, but given the option, he's clearly open to something easier.

"Come on. You want a snack? Here you go." She tosses the animals in the opposite direction of my tree.

My heart thunders in my ears as I watch helplessly.

The bear sniffs the air again, then stalks warily toward the kills. With each step he takes away from me, I grow more anxious. I want to fuss at Shae to go inside now that she's done her part, but I don't want to distract him in any way, nor do I want her fleeing to trigger his predatorial instinct to chase. I have to sit quietly in place and pray that the giant beast takes the food and leaves us long enough that we can both get safely back inside.

When he finally reaches the bait after what feels like a goddamn eternity, he prods one with his snout. He's closer to me than he is Shae, but she's on the ground.

Come on, you bastard. Take it and run.

I hate this.

I hate this so fucking much, and if something happens to Shae, I'll never forgive myself.

The first twinge of panic I've ever experienced in my life starts to constrict around my throat when the bear scoops up the kills in his mouth. He barks as if announcing that the meat is his now then sways as if shifting his weight to run. Except he doesn't. He drops his head, shifts his weight again, then charges right at Shae.

32

Shae

THE BEAR IS SO DAMN FAST IT'S UNREAL.

I can hear Renzo screaming. Or maybe that's me. All I know is that I've defaulted to pure survival mode. My hands grip the pickax as I ready myself. There's no time to run. I have to face him.

When the bear is seconds from reaching me, I swing with all my strength and fling the ax at the bear's neck while using the momentum to carry me into a flip evasion move. I go flying to the side.

The bear wails in unexpected pain. I'm up and in a ready stance as fast as I can manage. My chances against the bear unarmed are abysmal, but I'm not going to simply lie down and let him have me. I'll fight with every goddamn ounce of strength I have. Only the attack doesn't come.

The bear is bolting away from me. At the same time, I see Renzo jumping down from the tree. I'm terrified the bear will go after him again, but the animal scoops up all three of our kills and lumbers away into the distance. I'm so keyed into watching for another attack that I don't see Renzo until he's tugging me back toward the cabin.

It's hard for me to focus on his words. Between the ringing in my ears and my heart pounding like a drum, I can hardly hear.

"Jesus, Shae. You're bleeding. Did he get you?" Renzo says frantically once we're in the cabin.

"What? I don't…" I look down, unsure what he's talking about until I see the ragged red edges of a rip in my jeans. Only once I see the blood coming from my hip does the pain register.

Renzo has the first-aid kit out in a heartbeat and gingerly slides my pants down over the wound. "It's not bad, but I don't like it. We hardly have any antibiotic ointment left. I don't want you getting sick like I did. Or worse." His face is all hard edges as he begins to clean the wound.

My entire body sways with the sudden drop in adrenaline. "I think I may need to sit," I mumble, darkness threatening the edges of my vision.

"Fuck, hold on." He sweeps me into his arms and sets me on the side of the bed. "I'll get you a can of pears. You need to get your blood sugar back up."

"I know what it is," I say dazedly, not wanting him to think I'm clueless. I drink straight from the can when he hands it to me, going for the immediate sugar in the juice before I eat the pears themselves.

The relief is almost instant. Within minutes, I don't feel

quite so weak, but my hands and body continue to shake as the adrenaline runs its course. I close my eyes and take a deep breath.

Renzo places his hands on my face and kisses my forehead. "You scared the shit outta me, Shae." A tremor ravages his already hoarse voice. "Don't ever fucking do that again."

"Not how it works, big guy. You don't get to be the only hero in the room."

He huffs a laugh, then stands. "Lie on your side, and let me finish cleaning that up."

I let him do his thing.

Exhaustion tugs at my limbs and eyelids as if weighted by tiny anchors. I might have to sleep for a week after this to recover. Then again, I might need to sleep anyway since the bear snagged our entire food stores.

Emotion lodges in my throat.

How much more can we take? I'm so tired and so sick of being hungry.

I want to go home.

A sob hitches in my chest.

"Shit, did I hurt you?" He stops righting my pants.

I shake my head. "That all of our meat. Everything we'd managed to save."

I fight back the tears to no avail. The onslaught of emotions is too brutal to withstand. Relief that we're both alive. Guilt and frustration that I couldn't come up with a better way to stop the bear without handing over our hard-earned food.

"Shit, baby girl. Don't cry. Not my Shae." He's on his knees beside the bed, his forehead resting against mine while ragged sobs claw their way out from deep inside me.

I wrap my arms around him to keep him close. "He almost got you," I choke between the sobs. "When I came out and saw you up that tree, I was so fucking scared. I just did the first thing that came to mind."

"You were incredible, baby."

"But our food…"

Renzo sighs deeply, then pulls back to look at me with an unexpectedly grave expression. Confusion quiets my tears. I thought he was going to reassure me, but that's not what's happening. Whatever he's about to say, it isn't good.

"I have to tell you something. Something you're not going to like." His entire body is rigid with tension.

I sit up and scoot to the edge of the bed. A part of me wants to tell him no. To refuse to hear whatever he has to say if it's going to upset me enough to warrant the brutal intensity radiating off him. But I stay silent for the same reasons. If it's that bad, I need to know.

Renzo stands, turning his back to me. "There's a man who lives five miles from here. He can get us to safety."

33

Kenzo

"How? Who? How?" She's so stunned she can't even form a clear thought. It's understandable. What I've done is more selfish than I thought myself capable of. If I wasn't so worried about her getting sick, I never would have admitted to such a betrayal.

I still won't admit the worst part—that I don't regret my choice.

I'm glad I had two extra weeks out here with her. It's been hard as hell, and I wouldn't give it up for all the money in the world. I wanted that time with her. I wanted her to have the time to give me a chance. I made the decision because of a fixation, but since that time, my feelings have evolved more than even I realized. My entire being screamed in horror when that bear charged at her. If needed, I would have given my life to save her without hesitation.

I'm irrevocably in love with Shae Byrne.

I love her so deeply that I'd rather destroy her trust in me to get her home safely than preserve my secret. It's the most unselfish thing I've ever done.

I cross to the table and chair and sit down wearily. "The day after our first bonfire, I walked out a ways, searching for branches straight enough to build the lid for our storage locker. I encountered a man on a snowmobile who'd come our way to check on the fire. He lives five miles up the creek and knows the owner of the cabin. I told him about the bear encounter and that we were hunting when it happened. I said we were doing fine but had stayed at the cabin until I was feeling well enough to make the trip back. He said the owner would be glad we found it and, should we need anything, to come by his place. I didn't make a conscientious decision not to tell you. I knew I would if things took a turn, but each day I told myself that I needed one more day here. One more day with you."

My eyes lift for a quick glimpse of Shae. I don't regret what I did, but I hate seeing her so upset with me. She sits perfectly still, her eyes closed, and enough pain etched on her face to carve my heart wide open.

I have to clear my throat before I can continue. "I never meant to hurt you."

"Hurt me?" She opens her eyes, venom swirling in their depths. "Was the hunger and fear and filth not a constant form of pain?"

"Maybe for any other woman. You thrive in adversity," I try to explain.

She rockets to her feet and jabs a finger in my direction. "That doesn't give you the right to make me suffer."

I rise to my feet as well, my eyes narrowing. "I'll apologize for a lot of shit, but if you want to hear me say I'm sorry for keeping you here, you'll be disappointed. As far as I'm concerned, every minute of discomfort was worth it to be with you. If we'd gone back to the city right away, you *never* would have given me a chance."

"You don't know that," she yells, her hurt and anger boiling over. "And even if you never told me what you did, we still may not have stayed together in the city."

"No, but at least I would have had a fighting chance this way," I shoot back.

I'm dangling from a cliff's edge. My nails scratch and claw to hang on, but there's not a single root or rock to cling to. All I can do is accept my fate, whatever it may be.

I let go of my anger, my posture softening, and give her the truth. "I thought that if there was anyone who would know what it's like to fight for something—to risk it all in pursuit of your calling—it would be you."

Her middle bows inward, and her mouth parts on a silent gasp. She slowly closes her eyes. When they open, the fiery gold embers have all burned out, leaving only frigid ice and shards of blue glass.

"We should leave while there's still plenty of daylight." Her voice sounds as hollow as my heart feels. "Why don't you go collect the traps while I get things ready here."

I watch helplessly as she begins to straighten up the cabin.

With nothing left to be said, I let myself outside and start for the creek. I feel the bond between us stretch thinner with every step I take. That connection sank its barbed hooks deep into my heart, and the tension now straining the connection shreds me until I have to double over from the pain. It hurts so badly that I almost forget the crucial lessons I learned from my father's hard-fought battle with cancer.

One, I will survive the pain of loss, no matter how crippling.

And two, I cannot ever give up, no matter how bleak the odds.

This challenge won't be easy to overcome, but that doesn't mean it's impossible. I still believe with all my being that Shae is meant for me. If that's the case, I continue to fight. This is not the end.

34

Shae

WE WALK FOR CLOSE TO TWO HOURS ALONG THE CREEK UNTIL WE see a cabin on a hill. It has solar panels on the roof and lights shining through the windows. It looks more like a home and is at least twice the size of our cabin, though that's not saying much.

Our cabin.

The yawning crevasse in my chest creaks open another degree.

It was never our cabin. There is no *our*. No *us*.

It boggles my mind that Renzo knew this was here and kept it from me. I can't imagine keeping such an enormous secret, especially from someone I care about. That's what he claims—that he was so desperate to be near me he couldn't bear to leave. I thought about everything he'd said while we walked in silence—whether his motivations changed anything. Motives are undoubtedly important. I can't deny that. But he kept me here for two whole weeks after learning about a way home.

Not a day.

Not three days.

Two *weeks*.

I don't know how to look past that. It's egregiously selfish behavior that could have gotten one or both of us killed. And we weren't the only two impacted by his actions. The first week of our fiasco couldn't be helped, but he added two extra weeks of worry and fear that our families endured for nothing.

No. I can't overlook such willful disregard for others. He made a conscientious choice, and I have to hold him accountable.

"I take it you haven't made it to town yet?" A slender man with a thick gray beard greets Renzo with a smile and a hand-shake when we knock on the cabin door. His French accent catches me by surprise, though it shouldn't since we suspected we were in Quebec.

"We ran into a few more issues. Henri, this is my wife, Shae. Shae, Henri Bouchard."

Henri reaches out to shake my hand. It takes me a second to catch on because my brain is still skipping like a record over the word *wife*. "It's good to meet you," I finally say in a daze.

"If your troubles mean I get to see a lovely lady up here in the hills, then I can't say I'm disappointed. Please, come in and tell me what I can do to help." He seems pleasant enough, though his drooping eyelids cover keenly observant eyes that have picked us apart from the second he opened the door. This man is suspicious of people. He's chosen a solitary life for a reason.

The cabin consists of a main room combining kitchen, dining, and living. Two open doors lead to a bedroom and a bathroom, with a third door closed, though I suspect it's a closet. The faucet over the kitchen sink and the toilet in the bathroom indicate he has indoor plumbing. Never in a million years did I think I'd be so damn excited to see indoor plumbing.

Henri takes a seat in a well-worn leather recliner while Renzo and I claim the two dining chairs. He has a small sofa, but we're entirely too filthy for that.

"We appreciate your hospitality," Renzo tells him. "What we'd really love, though, is a lift into town."

"Weren't able to get the ATV going?"

ATV? Wife? What exactly did Renzo tell this guy?

"No, I'm not sure what's wrong with it."

Henri nods slowly. Sagely. "Should we swing by and get your gear on the way? We can even tow the ATV with us. I suspect you are ready to get home."

"That's kind of you, but we've had another encounter with our furry friend." Renzo nods at me, an indication to show Henri my hip. "I'd like to get her to the hospital to prevent infection."

I stand and display the bloodstained rip in my jeans.

"Mon dieu! You two have been very lucky to have survived not one but two encounters with a bear. I will have to mention the activity to the rangers. Something may be wrong with the animal for him to be out so early in the season."

"I don't know what to tell you about that part, but yes, we've been very fortunate." His eyes cut to me.

I'm ashamed to admit how much I want to know what

he's thinking behind his now guarded gaze. One thing I can tell is that he's being sincere when he says we've been lucky. I can still hear him in my head when I think back to that first day when we crash-landed here—the day he accused me of being pure chaos. He didn't think we were so lucky back then.

What shifted his perspective? Surely, he doesn't count himself lucky based purely on my presence. That's absurd … isn't it? We've faced so many adversities. Spending time with me couldn't possibly outweigh such a harrowing series of events.

"We should get going, then. It will take a couple of hours to get to town, and most of that on a snow-covered dirt road."

"It'll be getting dark by that time," I point out. "Will it be dangerous for you to drive back then?"

"Oui, I'll stay the night with a friend. No need to worry about me, belle." He pushes to his feet. "Do either of you need to freshen up before we go?"

Renzo and I glance at one another. I'm equally as filthy as he is, which makes it almost comical when we both shake our heads.

"I think we'd just prefer to get going," Renzo explains.

I could spend hours in a bathroom completing all the bathing and grooming I'd like to do, but not until I'm safely in town. I don't even want to take advantage of his toilet. I just want to get out of here.

Ten minutes later, we're loaded up in Henri's small 4x4 truck and one step closer to home.

35

Kenzo

SHAE INSISTS ON SITTING BY HERSELF IN THE TRUCK'S COMPACT second row. Sitting apart from her wouldn't be of consequence if it wasn't for the yawning emotional distance between us. The chasm makes even a few feet feel like miles. I refuse to think about how little I may see her when we get home.

I can't blame her, though. She has every right to be upset. I get that.

And all things considered, she's handled the situation with incredible decorum. She could have lashed out at me much more vehemently, if not violently, when I told her what I'd done. Not to mention the way she played along when I introduced her as my wife. I had to. I'd already told the old man I was on a hunting excursion with my wife. It rolled off my tongue at the time, shocking me at how natural it felt.

Most of our trip into town is made in silence. We pass through patches of dense trees, pockets of open field, and even skirt by a large lake. The landscape is breathtaking in its beauty. Especially when we sit in a heated truck with the promise of food to come.

We turn onto a paved and plowed road over an hour and a half into the trip. Within minutes of the turn, we see signs of civilization. Other cars. A stop sign. A restaurant billboard.

Relief that I'm finally headed home takes up arms against my reluctance to part from Shae, launching a bloody war in my chest. I have to focus on my breathing to keep my lungs from seizing tight.

Henri drops us at the local hospital, which isn't much more sophisticated than an urgent care clinic back home. That's fine. We don't need anything fancy.

When they call Shae's name, she gives me a look to indicate I'm not welcome back with her. I briefly consider ignoring her but decide I can use the time to get ahold of my family. I go back to the reception counter and plaster on the most charming smile I can muster.

"Ladies, my friend and I had an encounter with a bear and lost our phones in the process. Is there any way we can use the phone here to get ahold of our families?"

"Oh! How terrible," one of them says in a heavy French accent. "Of course, chérie. Call your family." She hands me her cell phone in a red glitter case, turning to speak French to her coworker, whom I assume doesn't speak English.

"Thank you very much." I nod and return to my lime-green vinyl waiting room chair.

Now, who to call? I decide to go with my uncle Gino. Thank God he's had the same phone number since the dawn of time, or I never would have remembered it. I only know his and two others—neither of the other two options would have been helpful in this situation. I knew my dad's, but … yeah. Even less helpful.

I have to call three times before he answers the unfamiliar number.

"Yeah?"

"Uncle Gino, it's me, Renzo."

"Fuckin', Christ," he breathes, then yells, "Etta! Get in here, it's Renzo. He's alive."

"Alive but now I'm deaf. Thanks for that," I tease with a smile. The ringing in my ears is worth hearing his voice.

"Where the fuck have you been, kid? Whose number is this? Are you hurt?"

I chuckle, comforted by the concern in his voice. I knew my family would be worried, but it still feels nice to hear how much they care. "One at a time. First, it's a long fucking story, so you'll have to wait until I get back. The key points are Shae Byrne and I were kidnapped and ended up stranded in a shack up in the middle of nowhere Quebec. We just managed to make it to the nearest town."

"The fuck you say? You fucking serious?"

I can hear my aunt in the background fussing at him to explain or put the phone on speaker.

"I know, it sounds crazy, but it's even more insane than that. I'll tell you everything, but I need help first."

"Anything. Tell me what I can do."

"We're in a small town called L'Ascension. I need you to get us a couple of hotel rooms." I pause as he gives my aunt her marching orders.

"What else?"

"I need credit card info to pay for some stuff until I can get back."

"Done. I'll read it off before we're done with the call."

"The other thing I need might take a bit more finesse. We need to get back in the States without passports, and I don't want to wait for legal channels."

"Of course not. That would take fucking forever."

"Exactly."

"Don't worry about a thing. I'll make it happen."

"Thanks, Gino. It's been pretty rough going these past three weeks."

"I can't imagine. You both alright?"

"Aside from losing some weight and a couple of run-ins with a bear, we're good." Physically. I can't say the same for our emotional status.

"Fuck, a *bear*?"

I can practically see his eyes bulging through the phone.

"Christ, I can't wait to hear this," he says almost to himself. "Etta, babe. They got attacked by a bear—you believe that? I don't know. I don't know, I tell ya. He can tell us when he gets back … yah, okay. I'll tell him. Your aunt says there's a hotel a few minutes down the main road in a place called … what is it? Oh yeah. Rivière-Rouge. She's got you two rooms for the night."

"She works fast."

"Four kids. The woman can move mountains when she wants to."

"Give her a big kiss for me. I'm gonna get a burner phone on the way to the hotel. I'll get you the number once I have it so you can keep me informed on how we're getting home."

"Good deal. Fuck, I can't believe it's you. I mean, we hadn't given up hope, but there's a part of you…" His voice catches, and he has to clear his throat.

"I get it, Gino. There were times we weren't so sure we were going to make it back." It's true for that first week, but hearing his torment amps up my guilt. I'd been so focused on Shae that everything else had been out of sight, out of mind. Now, I have to face the consequences.

Uncle Gino goes quiet. When he speaks again, his voice drips with malice. This version of Gino is all business. "You know who did this?"

"Not exactly, but you better believe I'm going to find out."

He grunts his agreement. "Get some paper, I'll give you that card number."

We wrap up the call not long before Shae returns.

I know she's pissed at me, but it's so fucking good to see her that I wrap my arms around her and press my lips to her head. "They got you squared away?"

She nods, not hugging me back but not pulling away either. I'll take every inch she'll give me.

I pay the hospital bill with the card info and get the number for a cab company in the area, which apparently consists of a man named Jean hauling people around in his wife's minivan. Again, you won't hear complaints from me.

It takes him a half hour to show up, but he's all smiles and nods when he does. He doesn't speak a word of English. I'm still able to communicate we need a drug store, then our hotel. When I see a fast food place by the hotel, I have Jean make a quick run through the drive-through.

Food, toiletries, a phone, and minutes away from clean beds and a shower. I should be floating on cloud nine, but instead, all I can think is this is where we part ways, and all the creature comforts quickly lose their luster. White linens and a pillow-top mattress mean nothing if I don't have Shae.

36

Shae

My hotel room is next to Renzo's. One thin wall lined with floral wallpaper from the nineties separates us. One wall and a heartbreaking betrayal. If only one were as easily overcome as the other.

I'm relieved to finally be alone, though I also feel oddly out of sorts. Everything is so quiet and clean and spacious. The old me would have scoffed and called the place outdated, but it's positively regal compared to where I've lived for the past three weeks. I'm almost overwhelmed with my options. I desperately want to shower, but the food we picked up is getting cold. I used the toilet at the hospital, so I've already basked in that particular delight.

I'm standing in the middle of the room debating what I

should do when there's a knock on the door. I jump a foot in the air, then chide myself. It's so unlike me to be jittery. I don't like it, nor do I understand it. I feel like I've been dropped in someone else's body—someone else's life—and nothing feels quite right.

My heart skips sporadically when I see Renzo on the other side of the door.

"I forgot. You'll want to call your family." He hands over the disposable phone we picked up at the drugstore.

For a second, I thought … I don't know what I thought he'd come for, but that wasn't it. And whatever *it* was, *it* not happening leaves me feeling empty inside. I choose not to examine my reactions. I simply don't have the capacity.

"Thanks. I'll bring it back when I'm done."

He nods, pausing awkwardly before returning to his room. I put the odd interaction out of my mind along with my growling stomach because, for once today, I know exactly what I want to do.

My hand starts to shake as I dial my brother's number. I may be close to my cousin Conner, but Oran would never forgive me if I didn't call him first. True to form, he answers after a single ring.

"Yes?"

"Hey, big brother. Remember me?" I joke when I'm emotional—it's what I do—and I'm suddenly engulfed in more emotion than I can process.

Oran is the opposite of me. He can be charming, but I wouldn't call him playful. And when he's upset, his intensity level goes through the roof.

All I hear over the line is a swift intake of air.

"Shae? Is it really you?" he finally says in a voice so heart-wrenchingly childlike, all attempts at composure fall to the floor.

The tears hit me so fast and hard that I can't breathe. I'm nodding, and I know I need to say something, so I force in a gulp of air and squeak a single word past the vise around my throat. "Yeah."

"Jesus Christ … *Shae*." My name, so often spoken in a tone of frustration, is pure exaltation from my brother's lips. "Shae butter, where are you?"

His childhood nickname for me brings a shaky smile to my lips and a bonus round of tears to my eyes. I hated it when he started to call me that after learning there was such a thing as shea butter. He thought it was hilarious. Me, not so much. I'll happily take the reminder now of those innocent days in our lives.

"I'm in Quebec. A little town called L'Ascension."

"Canada?" he says in surprise. "How the hell did you end up in Canada?"

"It's too long of a story to tell you over the phone. I assume you guys figured out that Renzo and I were taken?"

"We did, but we didn't know much else. None of it made sense. If they had killed you, why hide it? And why hadn't we received a ransom request if they'd taken you?"

"Again, it's a long story that led us to a remote cabin in the middle of nowhere. It's taken Renzo and I this long to get to safety." Two weeks longer than necessary. I don't tell him that part because it's not any of his business. I'm not sure how I feel about what Renzo did, but I do know that I don't want my family to judge him for it.

"Jesus," Oran breathes across the line.

"Oh, it gets much more interesting, trust me. We're safe now, though, and Renzo said he's got his family working on getting us back across the border. We don't have our passports and don't want to get stuck waiting on red tape."

"Definitely not. I'll get with the Morettis and offer our

help. We've already been in regular contact while looking for you guys."

"Thanks, O," I say softly.

He's quiet for several ticks of the clock. "I can't believe it's really you. I can't believe you're coming home."

"Psh, like you could get rid of me that easily."

I can't see his smile through the phone, but I can feel it just as sure as I can feel my own heart beating.

"Thank God. Things are awfully boring around here without you keeping us on our toes."

"Whatever, you'll be rolling your eyes at me in no time once I'm back." A grin finally lights my face and warms my heart. This feels good. Normal. I could use a big fat dose of normal.

"Let's hope so. I wouldn't want it any other way."

"Love you, Oran. See you soon."

"Love you, too. Be safe until then."

"Always."

The call ends, its bolstering effects infusing me with renewed energy and optimism. Things may not be ideal, but I get to see my family soon. That's the best gift I could receive.

Food and a shower are a close second and third. I set down the phone and dive into the white paper bag full of caloric goodness. However, things quickly sour. Turns out when you eat fast food after three weeks of meat and veggies, your stomach decides she's a little diva and can't tolerate such filth.

A burger and fries never tasted so good or sat so heavy in my gut.

I need to shower. That will make everything better.

I get the water started and strip out of my clothes. We should have thought ahead and bought something to wear while we were out, but it's too late for that. Hopefully, I can get housekeeping to wash them because there's no way in hell I'm putting them back on until they've been thoroughly scrubbed, and even then, only because I have no other choice. Every stitch of fabric at my feet is going in the garbage the second I'm home. Along with a match and some gasoline.

I'm about to step into the shower when I lock eyes with myself in the mirror. I was too mortified to look at the mirror in the hospital bathroom, knowing all the people around me were having to smell me. The mental image made it all worse, so I avoided looking, but I'm alone now, and I take in the shocking sight before me.

I knew I'd lost weight, but I'm shocked at the gaunt face staring back at me. This confirms it. I *did* switch bodies with someone. It's the only explanation because I don't recognize my own reflection.

I take in the image of me from the waist up, then try to shut it out of my mind. I'm about to shower, and nothing is going to ruin that.

I inhale a deep steamy breath of air and smile as I step in.

There's nothing quite like an orgasm, but if there was, it would be the feel of hot water pelting your body after three weeks with only a cold, wet rag for bathing.

Oh. My. Fucking. God.

That's the only way I know how to describe it. There are no other words.

I rotate every so often to let the water scour my front, then my back, and so on. Then I scrub. Every square inch of skin gets lathered in hibiscus perfection. Twice.

I shave my overgrown body hair, thanks to a disposable razor from housekeeping when we checked in, then I stand in the shower so long that I wonder if it's possible for a hotel to run out of hot water. If so, I have to be pushing that limit. I have zero guilt. I figure I'm using my three weeks' worth of showers in one.

When I finally turn off the spray and dry off, it's only because I'm dead on my feet exhausted. I go right to the bed after brushing my teeth and start to slide under the mounds of puffy linens when I see the burner phone on my night-stand. I told Renzo I'd bring it back to him and completely forgot about it.

I stare at the phone. He might need to talk to his people about getting us home. I need to get it back to him.

My gaze warily turns back to the bathroom, where I left my putrid clothes piled. There's no way. I can't possibly make myself put those rank, filthy rags back on.

Hell.

I yank the quilted duvet off the bed and wrap it around me as securely as I can without letting it drag on the floor, then I grab the phone and head to Renzo's room.

37

Kenzo

THE CREATURE COMFORTS THAT SHOULD THRILL ME HARDLY register. I have a full belly in a cozy hotel room and am clean and shaven for the first time in weeks. I should be savoring every gluttonous second, but instead, I feel numb inside. I sit on the edge of the cushy bed wrapped in a clean towel and feel nothing except disdain at the thought of sleeping alone.

That was my favorite part about our time at the cabin. No matter how irritated we were with one another during the day, I knew she'd still be wrapped in my arms come bedtime. And not because we needed the heat. We both found comfort in that physical connection and the security of knowing it was there to bolster us at the end of every day.

I miss it so much that I consider going next door and

insisting Shae give me another chance. But now that reality is setting in, I realize that I don't know what to say to her. As adamant as I was that things would magically work out, I don't truly have a solution. How can I go ask for her trust without being certain I can hold up my end of the bargain?

I don't have the answer except for one obvious option. One that would upend my life as I know it—that would crumble the legacy my father worked so hard to pass along and cast me into unknown waters. I'm shocked that I've even allowed the idea to materialize, but the fact that I have tells me how much Shae means to me.

It also tells me I've been an absolute jackass because I'd inadvertently put Shae in the position to make this same sort of decision without the slightest bit of empathy for what she was facing. My refusal to recognize the complexity of the matter hoisted an enormous burden on her shoulders. I know the weight of it because I'm testing its load as I sit and contemplate what it would be like to step down as boss so that I can be with Shae.

I was raised for the role. It's all I've worked toward, and I know despite the challenges, I'll lead the family with intelligence and honor. Would I be willing to give that up for the chance at love?

I would have to be certain of my choice and the lack of other plausible options.

I wouldn't want to harbor resentment toward Shae for my own choices, so I won't rush into a decision. I'll take whatever time I need until I'm confident in my path. Until I'm certain my actions won't hurt her again.

With that, I pull back the covers and am about to toss my towel to the floor when a knock sounds at my door.

Shae.

I'm on my feet in a flash, then open the door so quickly she takes a shocked step backward.

"Oh, hey … um … I forgot to bring this back to you." She hands me the phone, but her eyes have trouble finding mine. I don't rush her. I'm too busy lapping up the feel of her gaze raking over me.

She's wrapped in the duvet from her room with only her head peeking out like a little rabbit popping up from a snowbank. She looks so damn innocent and pure. Almost angelic. I think of the wars men have fought in the name of heaven, and now I know why. There's nothing I wouldn't do for the woman in front of me.

"Thanks. You have everything you need? I scheduled housekeeping to grab our clothes in the morning to be washed."

"Oh, that's good. I was thinking of calling as well."

"Yeah, we should have grabbed clothes," I admit, clearly stalling. "Anything else you need until then?"

"No, no. I think I'm good. I'll probably sleep for ages. I'm tired enough."

"Same, yeah."

"Okay, well. I guess I'll get to it." She flashes a thin smile, her gaze snagging one last sweep of my chest.

"Sleep well, Shae," I say gently.

She peers over her shoulder and nods before scurrying back to her room.

I may not have her in my arms when I sleep, but seeing her one more time before bed eases some of the tension in my chest. I toss my towel aside and turn out the light.

The next thing I know, housekeeping knocks on the door, and I have fifteen missed texts and six missed calls. Looks like Gino passed my number down the family phone tree because half of the Moretti organization has reached out to me. There are also several messages for Shae, which I greedily use as an excuse to see her.

I arrange for breakfast to be brought to our rooms while Shae returns her messages, then set about returning my own calls. Our laundered clothes are brought up midday, not long before my uncle informs me that a private jet will arrive at a local landing strip to pick us up. It's time to go home.

The hotel manager gets ahold of good ole Jean for us, and we're whisked away in our silver Dodge chariot for our much-anticipated return. Little is said on the way. I spend the entire twenty-minute drive debating whether Shae's silence is a good thing or a bad thing. Or not a thing at all. It's natural to be introspective in a time like this, regardless of the conflict between us. Yet I can't escape the feeling that it's related to me. Guess that's no surprise when I've already shown how self-centered I can be.

The plane is already on the ground when we arrive, though it's yet to shut off its engines. I have to laugh when the door opens and Noemi's head pops out. She's grinning like a clown and trying to wave while her husband Conner attempts to shove her back inside. He takes good care of my little cousin. I respect the hell out of that.

I'm not at all surprised to see her because not only is she my family, but she's become good friends with Shae, who is Conner's cousin. If Shae and I were to get married, I'm not entirely sure which side of the church Noemi would occupy —the bride's or the groom's. She's deeply entrenched in both our families.

Conner finally gets his wife to relent once we return her wave from the tarmac. She stays behind while Conner and my uncle Gino join us.

"A part of me still expected this whole thing to be a sick hoax or a trap," Gino calls out as he approaches, weary relief creasing the corners of his eyes more than normal. He wraps me in a bear hug—a term that now has a totally new meaning to me—then Conner grips my hand in a hearty shake.

"Damn good to see you," he offers, but his attention is drawn to the grinning woman behind me. Shae pushes past me and flings herself at Conner. He tosses his head back on a laugh and gives her a spin.

"Shit, little cousin. You gave us a scare."

"I will *definitely* do my best not to do it again. Once in a lifetime was enough." As she pulls away, our stares snag on one another.

I tell her with my eyes that it will never be enough.

I know she gets my message from the pink darkening in her cheeks.

I told myself to think through my options clearly, but every instinct I have insists Shae Byrne is mine. It's as simple as that. What is there to debate when my soul has already decided?

An overwhelming wave of relief sweeps over me.

Yes. Shae is mine—that's not up for debate. The only thing left to decide is how we move forward.

The newfound certainty eases my worry over parting with her. Because if Shae is mine, it's only a matter of time before we're together again. I just have to figure out how.

38

Shae

Half of New York stands on the tarmac when we land back home. From the looks of it, both our families came out in full force.

Catholic families of Irish or Italian descent don't play around when it comes to taking advantage of the child tax credit. Easily a hundred people are cheering and holding up signs when we exit the plane as if we've competed in the Olympics and have returned draped in gold medals.

I would have eaten up the attention a month ago. Devoured it like Thanksgiving dinner. I'm excited and touched that so many people came out, but I also feel an odd heaviness weighing me down. Even smiling takes effort. All I can think about is how long this will take before I'm allowed to go home and crawl into bed. I'm not sure why. I don't necessarily feel like sleeping. All I want is to be alone. In the dark.

Holy crap—am I depressed?

How? Why would I be depressed now that I'm finally home? Things are leaving off on a rough note with Renzo, but surely, that's not enough to drag me so far down. I don't think I've ever been legitimately depressed in my life. Usually, if I'm feeling upset, I go to the gym and spar with someone or beat the hell out of the heavy bag, and I'm right as rain in no time. When I think of the gym now, it has zero appeal. The opposite, if I'm honest. It sounds like way too much effort.

Yeah, something's not right.

Get through the next hour, then you can decompress and figure out where your head is at.

We are instantly absorbed into the crowd, smothered with hugs and happy tears. The unexpected bonus of looking like a skeletal version of myself was how quickly I was urged to go home and rest. Before long, I was ushered into the passenger seat of Oran's car. His fiancée, Lina, insisted on taking the back seat. He starts our drive by grumbling about how Noemi bullied their way onto the plane. I find this amusing because Noemi is no bully; my brother just didn't have the balls to tell her no.

He gives me a new phone synced to my old number, which is incredibly thoughtful. The last thing I want to do is go phone shopping. Or any kind of shopping, for that matter.

"You can drop me up front," I tell him when he nears my building. Parking isn't exactly easy to come by, and I'm beyond ready to be alone.

"I think I should make sure you get up there safely."

I level him with a murderous stare. "Oran Byrne, I may

look like shit, but it's still me. Don't go treating me any differently because of this. Renzo was kidnapped too, and I doubt his family feels the need to walk him to his door." This was exactly what I'd feared. I have to nip it in the bud before it can take root, though having the discussion with Lina listening in the back isn't ideal.

Oran scowls as he parks in the drop-off zone in front of my building. "Yeah, I know. I'll do my best," he mutters. His concession comes rather easily, and I can't help but think that has something to do with his headstrong wife sitting two feet away. I mentally retract my initial hesitancy about her presence.

My expression softens with a gentle smile. "Thank you. For everything." I give him a hug, and he squeezes me within an inch of my life.

"Anytime, Shae butter. And I *will* be calling tomorrow to check on you. Deal with it."

"I suppose I can manage a call," I tease, then tell Lina goodbye and step from the car.

Time to make the last leg of my journey home.

Only, it's not home that I return to because my apartment's been ransacked. Everything is disheveled and tossed about.

I walk inside vigilantly, going quietly to the kitchen, where I keep a gun hidden under the sink. I walk room to room and verify that the place is empty, then I take in the mess. My TV is still in place. So are smaller electronics like my iPad charging on the desk. Even my jewelry is all present, though it's been obviously riffled through.

I don't understand. Who could have done this, and what would they possibly be looking for?

The whole thing feels like yet another boulder on my

back. My legs threaten to give out from the weight. I can't deal with this. It's too much.

I don't even have the energy to worry about my safety. All I can manage is to crawl into bed and pretend the world doesn't exist.

39

Kenzo

GINO AND I TALK BUSINESS ONCE WE'RE IN THE CAR HEADED TO my place. He assumed control in my absence, and it sounds like everything went relatively smoothly. He's a well-respected capo in our organization. His authority wouldn't be questioned. In fact, some probably thought he was better suited for the job.

My father told me when he first promoted me to under-boss that he'd offered the position to Gino first, and my uncle had respectfully declined. He would have accepted if it had only meant being underboss, but the role is essentially training to become boss, and Gino was adamant he didn't want that sort of spotlight. With four kids and a wife he adores, he felt the position came with too much risk.

Despite his reservations, he assumed the role in my absence to protect me because he knew anyone else who stepped in would be reluctant to hand over control when I returned. It's an incredibly honorable sacrifice he made, even if only temporary. And it makes me wonder if having walked that path for a few weeks might have changed his perspective. If it was needed, would he accept the role now on a more permanent basis? The possibility gives me plenty to consider.

Being back in my apartment eases some of my physical tension, but my emotions are as tumultuous as ever. My mood is somber and introspective. I don't watch television or play music. I don't particularly want to distract myself from my brooding thoughts. Instead, I pour a glass of wine and watch the sun set over Manhattan outside my windows.

Exhaustion hits hard as darkness falls and the wine soaks in. I'm in bed before nine o'clock, and it's even worse than sleeping at the hotel. At least then I knew Shae was one wall away. Here in the city, she could be anywhere.

♠

"THE ONLY WORKING camera recorded a truck driving past, but we couldn't see the plates or who was in it," Gino tells me the next day when we sit down to talk more in-depth. "It was a safe assumption that it was involved in your disappearance because there's not much traffic over there, but we had nothing else to go on. It was a dead end."

"We were afraid of that." I lean further back in my desk chair and sip from my coffee. "Like we told you on the plane back here, we suspect they're Albanian. The Irish have some sort of beef with them."

"Well, they fuckin' have beef with us now, too." He snarls.

"Yeah, but I'm not starting a war unless I know for sure. I

think I can figure out what airstrip we were taken to. They were established in that hangar, which should mean there's rental records at the very least. And if needed, I can try to find the crash site. With the right equipment, we could get inside." It wouldn't be pretty, but it would be worth it if I could get some names. One way or another, I *will* find those bastards.

"That could take a while," Gino points out.

"I know, and I'm not going to lose my head going after them, but I need to give it a shot." Not just for me but for Shae. This feels like one of the few things I can do to help in my campaign to win her back. Two birds with one stone.

"You're the boss and the one who was taken. You tell us what you want to do, and we'll make it happen."

"Let's see what I can learn from here first, then determine if we want to head north."

He nods and drinks from his steaming mug. I use the opportunity to introduce the delicate subject of leadership in the family.

"I want to talk to you about something I was mulling over last night."

"Yeah, sure. What is it?"

"Dad told me that you didn't want to be the face of the organization, but that was back when I was promoted to underboss. A good amount of time has gone by since then. Kids are a little older. And you've had the opportunity to test the position for a few weeks. I was wondering if your opinion has changed any."

He studies me, his lips thinning. "Why would you ask me a question like that? You think I might betray you like Fausto did your father?"

"No! That wasn't it at all." I don't want to go into detail

about everything, but it seems I'll have to. "I had a lot of time to think while I was out there."

"You don't want to be boss?"

"It's not that either. Shae and I went through a lot together—"

"Ohhh." His head tips back in understanding. "Okay, now I'm starting to get it. You fell for the Irish spitfire. That's a tricky one." Leave it to Gino to call it like it is.

"No shit." I run my hands through my hair. The motion makes me think of Shae washing my hair. It's never-ending. Every-fucking-thing makes me think of her. She's everywhere around me except beside me, where she belongs. "She doesn't want to give up her role in the Byrne business, and I wouldn't want her to. Not when she loves it so much."

"But you'd consider stepping down for her?"

The audacity in his tone raises my defenses. "I don't know what I'd consider," I snap.

Gino waves a hand at me. "I shouldn't be so critical. My family was the whole reason I didn't want the job. Your issue is essentially the same, though the job is already yours."

"Except for the past three weeks, when you filled those shoes rather admirably." I level him with a pointed stare.

He considers me, staring intently as indiscernible thoughts pass behind his eyes. "Alright, look. I'll give it some thought, but I won't promise you anything."

"No reason to promise when I haven't officially asked," I offer softly with a smirk.

"Good, we'll both think about it. And in the meantime, let's see if we can't find the fuckers who did this."

Amen.

40

Shae

I FEEL MARGINALLY BETTER WHEN I WAKE THE FOLLOWING morning, though dealing with a call to Mari and cleaning up after the break-in quickly zaps my newfound energy. I can't fathom why someone would ransack my place but not take anything. What were they looking for? Could it have been a warning? From whom?

As far as the kidnappers know, we died in the plane crash, but no other culprits come to mind. I told my cousins that we suspect the Albanians but can't be sure. They weren't able to learn anything while we were gone. All they knew was that we'd disappeared with the guns. That was it.

I have to figure out who was behind all of this—the kidnapping and my break-in—for my own peace of mind and because it would be a perfect distraction from thoughts of a certain bullheaded Italian. But first, I have more immediate matters to deal with.

My place is nearly returned to order when Mari buzzes the intercom to come up. She insisted on coming over when I called to let her know I was back. I have to deal with her at some point. Might as well get it over with.

She flies at me the second I open the door, hugging me like her life depends upon it. "I can't believe you're here. I was so worried." Her words are saturated with emotion, so raw and dripping with heartache that I'm speechless.

My muscles crawl with the need to pry myself free, but that would be cruel. She obviously took my disappearance much harder than I expected. She not only noticed my absence but that I was ghosting her, then figuring out I'd been abducted when she went to the gym to confront me. While I hadn't introduced her to my family, she knew the gym where I spent most of my time. A bunch of my cousins box there as well. Conner told me on the plane ride home that a woman had come around asking questions. I knew it had to be Mari.

"Are you okay? They said you'd been taken. How did you get away? What happened?"

I realize that maybe the truth is the best way to go. The whole truth—I think it might ease the sting of me ending things.

"It's complicated, but the thing you need to know first is my family business isn't exactly legitimate."

"Your self-defense classes?" she asks in confusion.

"No, I don't even teach classes. I help with demonstrations sometimes at the gym where I train. My family owns a number of businesses. In particular, I help with security at a club called Bastion."

"I've never heard of it." Her arms cross over her chest.

"I wouldn't expect you to. It's a well-to-do social club."

She shakes her head. "I don't understand. Why didn't you tell me? And what does that have anything to do with you being abducted?"

"That's just one aspect of our business. I can't go into the others, but they put us in contact with some unsavory individuals. People with vendettas and no moral compass. In this case, someone tried to steal something from us. I happened to show up in the process and complicate things, so they took me and the man I was with."

"What do you mean the man you were with?" she blurts.

The question catches me off guard. I'm telling her about being kidnapped, and she's focused on who I was with?

"He's a business associate, Mari. I had a scheduled meeting with him."

She nods, sufficiently chastened.

"The thing is, my life isn't what you think. I'm not the person you think."

Before I can continue, she launches into another aggressive hug. "I don't care about any of that. I'm just so grateful to have you back. I've felt awful this whole time."

"Why would you feel bad? None of this is your fault."

"No, but I thought some pretty awful things about you at first."

"You couldn't have known," I offer gently while trying to keep a professional tone to my voice. This is *not* going how I'd hoped. I'm not sure how to say goodbye when her emotions are already raw and exposed.

She pulls away and nods, her teary eyes cast to the floor. "Still … when I thought maybe I'd lost you, it changed everything. I'm just so relieved you're back." She sniffles and gives me a sad smile.

"It's definitely good to be home," I say vaguely. "It's been a lot to process, though, so I'm going to need some time…"

"Oh, of course. I understand. You do what you need to do, and I'll be here to offer any support you need."

My smile is a grimace in disguise. "Thanks, Mari."

Awkwardness rolls through the room like a heavy fog off the bay.

"Okay, I guess I'll head out and let you rest." She gives me one last hug and a tentative kiss that wraps a barbed wire of guilt around my heart.

Mari is going to be a bigger issue than I'd hoped. I hate to hurt her, but it's inevitable. I'm not interested in seeing her anymore. And I'll tell her. Soon. Just not today. Not only would it drain me dry, but ending things the day I get back seems needlessly hurtful. I'll put some space between us, let our emotions recover, then gently part ways.

It's a plan, and having a plan is reassuring. I only wish I knew how to handle the other person in my life. Renzo is giving me space. That's what I wanted, so why do I feel so despondent? Why does my heart feel as empty as my bed? It's so damn big and cold. When I slip beneath the covers that night, I wonder how I ever found the damn thing comfortable.

I search my phone and am able to find an app that plays hours and hours of uninterrupted background soundscapes, including one of a crackling fire. It doesn't sound quite like the cabin stove, but it's close enough. When I close my eyes, I can almost imagine I'm back there. It's soothing, but I still can't fight off the chill at my back. I try not to think about what I'm doing when I lie on my side and wad up my duvet like a wall behind me. It's not radiating heat, and it doesn't hold me close, but it's enough to finally help me find some comfort.

I wonder if I'll ever readjust back to my old normal. To a time when my heart didn't ache every damn minute. I know I will, eventually. Probably.

God, I hope so because I hate the way I feel. Like someone stole the North Star from the sky, and I no longer have a direction. I feel untethered, which is unfathomable because I have an incredible family and a job I love. Surely, three weeks with someone can't negate all that.

It's the last thing I remember thinking before something wakes me in the night. Quiet footsteps here in my room. I lie perfectly still except for my right hand, which slides under my pillow to grip my Glock. No one gets the drop on me. This bastard's about to find out the hard way in three … two … one…

"Relax, Chaos. It's me."

"Renzo?" My heartbeat was swift but steady at the thought of an intruder. Now, it dips and swirls like a paper airplane running out of steam. "What are you doing here in the middle of the night?" I replace the safety on my gun and sit up.

"Getting some damn sleep," he grumbles.

I hear clothes rustling. "Are you … undressing?" I gape at him in the dark.

"I'm going to bed."

"Well, you almost got yourself killed instead."

"You wouldn't shoot me."

"Maybe not, if I knew it was you. Hard to know that when you break into someone's house."

"About that. Why the hell don't you have an alarm system?"

"Don't need one. Light sleeper. And speaking of, you can't sleep at your place?"

"No. I can't," he grumbles. "And judging by the sound of

a crackling fire in here, you're having trouble sleeping, too." He crawls into my bed, forcing me to scoot over.

"You can't just—"

"I can, and I am," he cuts me off distractedly as he fumbles with the covers. "What the hell did you do to your quilt?"

"It's a duvet," I say petulantly, avoiding his question. I don't want to admit to myself that I'd used my bedding to pretend he was here with me, let alone tell him what I'd done.

"It's chaos, but I suppose I should have expected that," he mutters before snagging me by the waist and pulling my back flush against his front.

"Let's get some sleep. I'm exhausted."

I open my mouth to argue, then close it when his masculine scent invades my lungs and scrambles my thoughts. His body wash is divine, but beneath that is an earthy scent that's all his own. A scent that lent me comfort for three weeks straight.

As the sounds of a fire fill my ears, and the warmth of Renzo's body melts every last ounce of tension from my coiled muscles, I can't think of a single reason to send him away. It's only sleep, after all. For one night. And I *was* having trouble sleeping on my own. I might as well take advantage and get some rest.

I sleep so soundly that I almost feel like I didn't sleep at all when morning comes and I wake to light streaming into my bedroom. A contented grin spreads across my face until I roll over and find the bed empty.

41

Kenzo

I SPEND TWO HOURS TOSSING AND TURNING BEFORE GIVING IN and driving to Shae's place. Then I do the same thing the next three nights in a row, giving in a little sooner each time like an addict needing a fix. Maybe if I gave it time, I'd adjust to sleeping without her, but I don't want to. And any resolve I might have had washed away the second I heard those fake crackling flames in her bedroom. She was using the soundtrack to take herself back there. That tells me all I need to know.

She hasn't written me off yet. She may be upset, but if she truly hated me for what I did, she wouldn't find comfort in reminders of our time together.

The discovery reassures me, but I still make sure to leave

her place before she wakes because I know I need to give her space. We both have shit to figure out, but I also know I can't come up with solutions unless I get some damn sleep, which doesn't come unless Shae is snug in my arms.

When I slip into her apartment on the fourth night, I smell remnants of a vanilla-scented perfume on her. It's not her scent. Too sweet. Then it hits me. "You still seeing that woman?" I ask, trying to stay calm but coming across as eerily unhinged.

"That isn't any of your business, Renzo," she answers quietly.

"I still want to know." Logic tells me she's right, but every primal instinct I have is frothing at the mouth when I think of her with anyone else.

"Look, here's the deal. She and I were only ever friends with benefits," she accentuates pointedly, "that has nothing to do with you or your nightly visits. In fact—" She sits up in the bed. "We can't keep doing this, Ren."

Normally, I love hearing her call me that, but it grates on my nerves this time because it isn't an endearment. She's placating me with a token of affection to ease the sting.

Am I making a fool of myself? I've felt so confident her feelings align with mine. That down beneath the hurt, she's equally as lost for me as I am for her.

But I could've been wrong.

Maybe I've seen what I wanted to see. Maybe the best thing for both of us is some time apart, no matter how maddening. If she has time to feel my loss, that could open her mind to taking me back. Maybe it's hurt talking. I'm not sure, but I suddenly feel the need to escape.

"You know what? You're right. We can't keep doing this." I get up and start putting my clothes back on.

"I'm sorry." The choked words are no more than a whisp of air in the darkness.

I still, weary resignation settling like a weighted cape over my shoulders. I pick up the rest of my things without putting them on and lean over, placing a kiss on her forehead so full of reverence and remorse that I feel her body shudder beneath me.

"Nothing to be sorry about. Sometimes things simply aren't meant to be." With the echo of truth ringing in my ears, I walk away from Shae Byrne and half of my heart because love doesn't follow the rules.

Love is chaos.

Unpredictable and transformative.

I love Shae, but sometimes not even love is enough.

42

Shae

He left, and I cried myself to sleep with his words wearing ruts in my mind as they circle round and round.

Sometimes things simply aren't meant to be.

The following morning, I sit in bed with my knees pulled to my chest and think.

Sometimes things simply aren't meant to be.

What does that even mean? Who decides what's meant and not meant? The more I think about it, the more it sounds like a cop-out. Like something a person says when they're tired of trying. I've never given credence to fate before, so why would I now?

I stare at myself in the mirror, my eyes locked on my necklace.

I met Devlin a month after I started hanging out with Mari. He and I were forces of nature that were cataclysmic when we collided. The magnetism was unreal, but our time together was short. He was in the States for less than a week before he had to return to Ireland. As much as I was drawn to him, I couldn't fathom leaving my family and everything I knew to be with him in Dublin. He felt the same about staying in New York. We parted ways, but the pendant was a reminder of the time we shared. A reminder of what a true connection felt like.

I saw Mari the same day he gave me the necklace and knew in my gut that she and I would only ever be friends with benefits. I wasn't stimulated by her the way Devlin captivated me. Having her around helped ease the disappointment of him leaving. I figured it wouldn't hurt anything to keep seeing her, then time drew on without me putting any real thought into the situation.

I put Devlin on a pedestal and doubted I would ever meet another person like him. I made the unconscious decision not to even try. Why bother when people outside my line of work reject the lifestyle, and those in the business are either family, rival, or foe. It seemed easier to keep my expectations low.

While I haven't met anyone like Devlin, what I did find was someone who made me realize how wrong I've been. What I felt for Devlin wasn't as compelling as I thought. How could it be when I never truly considered finding a way to be with him?

Leaving my family wasn't an option. But with Renzo … I can't shake the feeling that he's worth it. I don't even know what *it* is except a risk of change—the leap of faith that I'll find my footing again.

Am I willing to jump without any safety nets if it means being with him?

That is a choice. My choice.

It has nothing to do with what is *meant to be.*

If I don't fix things with him, I can't blame fate. A relationship with him, no matter the difficulties or rewards, would be a choice.

How many times am I willing to find someone incredible and allow challenges to become excuses?

Renzo is here in the city. I wouldn't have to move away from my family to be with him. And after everything we went through together, Renzo and I are family, too. All I need to do is decide if I'm willing to forgive him. That is the only question that matters because the rest will work itself out if we're committed. He'd said as much, but I couldn't see it then. I'm not sure why except that I knew it would be hard, but these days without Renzo have been miserable.

So I'm back to making a choice. I have to pick my hard—find a way to be with Renzo or find a way to survive without him.

He was willing to put both our lives on hold to be with me. He risked everything. It could have gone horribly wrong, and I don't like that he kept such a huge secret from me, but I can't deny his commitment.

Love makes people do crazy things. Like forgive one another.

The leaden cloak I've worn around my shoulders for days drops to the floor. I feel like I could float right off my bed, and that tells me all I need to know. I'm working in the right direction, but I have to set things straight with my family before I say anything to Renzo and risk hurting him.

I give myself until the end of the month—two weeks—to make arrangements and ensure I have no doubts. I'll see him at Oran's wedding, so I have to have a solution worked out by then.

My big brother deserves his happily ever after more than anyone after learning his first wife betrayed our entire family. That was the reason Devlin had paid our family a visit. His family over in Dublin had learned we had an informant in the family. Someone who had worked with the Albanians and stolen a shipment of guns. Guns we'd acquired with help from Devlin's family.

Oran was absolutely wrecked when he learned what his wife had done. I was so worried about him because he became so closed off and bitter. Then he met Lina, and his life completely turned around. He's a great example of someone who made the choice to open their heart and make room for love. He could have told himself a relationship with Lina wasn't meant to be. He would have been justified, considering the challenges they had to overcome. But he didn't, and now they're deliriously happy together.

If he can do it, so can I.

It's been my motto my entire life, where my brother is concerned. Seems like an appropriate time to revive the sentiment.

The next day, I take the first step on my new path by calling Mari and telling her that I can't see her anymore. She tries to reassure me that she won't pressure me, but I'm quick to assure her that it's over. I know I've done the right thing when I end the call and feel practically buoyant.

Next, I set up a meeting with Conner. We sit in his office at Bastion, and I tell him all about the situation with Renzo. As expected, he's exceptionally understanding. His wife is Renzo's Italian cousin, so I figured he'd be the least likely to be concerned about a relationship between me and Renzo. If anyone will balk, it'll be Oran. He still might harbor trust issues where outsiders are concerned.

"I don't have a problem with it, but others might."

Conner's face is lined with concern. He's worried I'm going to end up hurt.

"Oh, I know. I doubt the Italians will accept Renzo being with a woman who still works for another organization. If that's the case, and I still want to be with Renzo, I'll have to consider making a change."

Air whooshes past Conner's parted lips, his brows drawn tightly together. "You're serious."

"I am." I offer a weak smile.

"I never thought I'd see the day you found someone who meant more to you than the business."

I open my mouth to argue, but he cuts me off.

"That's not a slight—you don't need to get defensive. I feel the same about Noemi. I'm just sorry you're actually having to make that choice. But if I were in your shoes, I'd do the same. Some things are too valuable to give up."

"Thanks, Conner," I force past the emotion swelling in my chest. "I thought you'd understand, and that's why I came to you first."

"Hey, if it means I don't have to worry about you stealing my wife from me, I'm all for it." His playful jab about my friendship with Noemi reminds me there's something else I need to tell him.

"I'm glad you brought that up—"

"It was a joke, Shae."

"No, I know. It reminded me to tell you that my apartment was broken into while I was gone."

Conner's spine goes ramrod straight. "What the fuck, Shae. Why didn't you say something earlier?"

"I had a lot on my mind," I shoot back at him.

"I'll see if I can get security footage from the building cameras."

My instinct is to tell him I can do it, but something holds me back. "Thanks, I'd appreciate that."

Conner stares at me with a tinge of awe. "These past three weeks have changed you, haven't they?" His question is sincere. Almost gentle.

"I think more than anything, Renzo has changed me," I admit softly. "Hopefully for the better."

He grins. "Surely, you couldn't get any worse."

And that's why I love Conner. He speaks my language. When things get heavy, humor is always a good option.

"For you, I could try." I shoot him a wide grin as I stand. He gets to his feet and pulls me into a big hug.

"Don't do me any favors." He pulls back and winks. "Now, go on. I have shit to do."

"Need anything from me?"

"Not at the moment. Wait, I take that back. Go eat a burger. You're too skinny."

"Yes, sir." I salute as I leave the office feeling more energized than I have in days.

As I near my home, I see Mari outside my building. She's pacing. The likelihood of her being upset outside my place and it not having to do with me is unfathomably low. I have to wonder if she's more upset about me ending things than she let on.

Memories of her flashes of jealousy pop into my head. She was incredibly emotional about my return, considering she'd thought for weeks that I was ghosting her. I knew she was more invested in the relationship than I was, but could it be worse than that? Could Mari have ransacked my apartment?

Maybe, if she thought I had abandoned her for someone else. She could have gone looking for proof of an affair. It seems a little absurd, but it makes sense. I don't have any better explanation for the break-in, and her behavior now is definitely odd.

I consider walking over to confront her, but she takes off before I can get close enough. I'm not up for a chase. If she comes around, I'll see what I can find out. Otherwise, I have bigger fish to fry than a dejected ex. And who knows, I could be completely off base, though I find that unlikely.

43

Kenzo

I'VE SPENT THE PAST THREE EVENINGS TRYING TO IDENTIFY THE airfield where we were taken. After scouring pictures online for hours, I've come to the conclusion that Canadian airfields all look the same. If only there were more pictures of supply closets in airplane hangars. Oddly enough, that doesn't seem to be a popular feature to advertise. Go figure.

We only saw a quick look at the area where the airstrip was located when we walked from the hangar to the plane. Most everything was covered in snow, however, so that hasn't helped much. I'm having to fall back on deductive reasoning instead.

I've been able to roughly pinpoint where the cabin is approximately sixty miles northeast of L'Ascencion. The crash site couldn't have been much more than a couple of miles from there, and we were in the air for no more than thirty minutes before we crashed. With an average airspeed of 200 mph, that gives me a one-hundred-mile radius of possibilities with those on the southern side of that circle significantly more likely than the northern side. This would be incredibly helpful if rural Canada didn't have a ridiculous number of small privately run airstrips.

Taking all things into consideration, I've zoned in on three that I believe are the most likely candidates. The only way to confirm beyond that is to go in person and see them with my own eyes.

Maybe it's a waste of time to chase down answers like that. Some might say what's done is done, but that's not who I am. I need to know who was responsible. And I want everyone in the city to hear how I hunted down every last one of them.

The minute a family goes soft and allows something as personal as a boss to be taken hostage, that's the beginning of the end. It reeks of weakness. Vulnerability.

I refuse to allow it.

Even if I'm not at the helm when this is over, I won't be known as the man who led the Moretti family to ruin.

"I need to leave town for a few days," I tell Gino over dinner. "Not exactly sure how long it'll take, but I'll be in touch."

"You find something?"

I shrug and pat my napkin to my lips. "Maybe. Hopefully. Either way, I have to try." And no one else can do it for me. If I can find the airfield where we were kept, I know in my gut it will lead to useful information. And once I pinpoint who was responsible, I'll rip their fucking throats out. No one pulls that shit with the Morettis and gets away with it.

Gino nods approvingly. "I'm here to help on this end however you need me." He leans back and takes a sip of wine. "I've been thinking about what we discussed. If you really want me to take over, I'll do it, but I don't want you rushing into any decisions. You get this done first and see how you feel after. The rest can wait."

It can wait, but it won't change anything. I'll still want Shae, and she'll still be a Byrne.

I keep my thoughts to myself and simply nod.

"How many guys you planning to take with you?"

"I thought I'd take Ettore and have him bring four of his most trusted soldiers with him."

"What about your brother? Tommaso is nearly twenty now. He could use the experience."

Irritation quickly sours my mood. Gino isn't wrong, and I value his opinion, but my brother's situation is complicated. "This mission is too important to take any unneeded risks. We'll be going into their territory. I need to feel 100 percent confident in every man at my back."

"Fair enough. Just remember that he'll never get there if you don't give him a chance."

Gino knows as well as anyone that Tommaso's mind doesn't work quite like the rest of ours. It's created problems every time we try to bring him into the fold. Communication with him is a challenge at best. The most frustrating part is that the guy is a fucking genius. He's so damn smart but somehow can't understand the simplest instructions. I don't understand, and this isn't the time for practicing tolerance. I have enough on my plate as it is, so dealing with Tommaso right now isn't an option. I don't even want to discuss it.

"Speaking of kids, how's your brood?"

He smirks. "Quieter now that Pip is out of the house."

"That good or bad?"

"Hell, I don't know." He shakes his head and laughs.

We spend the rest of dinner on lighter topics, catching up on family drama and sports news. I lost my father earlier than I should have, but I count myself lucky to have an uncle like Gino to help fill those shoes. The load I carry on my shoulders is infinitely more tolerable with him around.

Two days later, six of us board a private jet and set out for Canada, unsure what we'll encounter. We're so loaded down with equipment and supplies that the pilot informs us we'll have to fuel up at each stop. I don't give a fuck. You better believe I'm taking an arsenal of guns, a satellite phone, emergency equipment, and a week's worth of provisions.

I saw the odd glances some of the guys sent my way but ignored them. They can give me a hard time after they've spent three weeks in a cabin hunting for their own food. Until then, they can keep their fucking mouths shut.

The first stop proves to be a dud. We don't have to leave the plane for me to know it's not the airstrip I'm looking for. A brand-new water tower stands across the runway from the hangars. It wasn't on the Google Map satellite photos, or I could have saved us the trouble. We fuel up and set out for our next stop.

As soon as we touch ground at the second stop, I know I've found my airstrip.

44

Shae

WHO IS NANA BYRNE? SHE'S AN EIGHTY-FIVE-YEAR-OLD grandma who relies on a walker to get around yet somehow still pulls the invisible strings that guide my family.

She's my idol.

I like to think we're kindred spirits.

If she'd been born in modern times, she would run this family outright. Nana is tough as nails, savvy, and loyal without fault. She's also funny as hell and can drink anyone under the table. Who wouldn't idolize the woman?

It's no surprise I find myself at her house. I can't imagine making any major life decision without talking it through with her first. I value her opinions as much as anyone, if not more so. That's probably why it's taken me a full week to make it over here. I'm not worried about her reaction, per se, but I don't want to disappoint her.

"You know, I was worried, of course. But not like I would have been if it was any of the others." She waves a gnarled finger at me, her eyes glinting with intelligence. "I knew my Shae would find a way home. I says to the others, until I see a body, my girl's not dead. And here ye are, whole and hearty and lovely as ever."

Nana never fails to make me smile, and today is no exception. I adore this woman.

"I'm sorry it took me so long to come by since getting back."

"Go way outta that." She waves off my apology. "You're a busy woman. I knew you'd be by when you could. Now, tell me. What's being done to catch the bastards who took ye?"

"We've been doing what we can, but there wasn't much to go on. Hopefully, we'll have a breakthrough soon. I'm definitely not giving up."

"Damn straight." Nana's eyes squint until I don't know how she can see out of them. "A Byrne never forgets."

I give her a beaming grin. "How've you been while I was away?"

"Can't complain. I'm still here."

I laugh and shake my head at her. "That's setting the bar awfully low."

"I can't reach so high these days. Best to be reasonable with my expectations." She winks. "Enough about me. I want to hear about the Italian you were stuck with for three weeks. Was he good looking?"

My jaw hits the floor. "Nana! He's Italian Mafia. I distinctly remember hearing you say that the Italians don't know their asses from their elbows."

"True, but the term Italian stallion exists for a reason, and while I never got to test the truth behind it doesn't mean you can't. For science. Wouldn't mean you'd have to marry the man." Her shrewd eyes hold me captive, scanning for tells. She reminds me of a human version of that fingerprint-matching software you see on TV shows where thousands of records are processed in seconds before a perfect match pops onto the screen. Nana dissects every tiny nuance and somehow deduces what's under the surface with eerie accuracy.

When she mentions not having to marry the man, she sees something in me that sets off her inner alarms. Within seconds, the savant puzzle solver has the entire picture, her eyes softening in the corners.

"Shae, lass. You've fallen for the man, haven't ye?"

Hiding anything from Nana is pointless. I nod and tamp down the tingles that burn the backs of my eyes.

"I don't know what to do, Nana," I admit in a whisper.

"Do about what? Does he not feel the same?"

"He's definitely crazy about me." Crazy being the key term.

"Well, that's good."

"It is?"

"For you, of course it is. You've too much life in you to settle for anything less."

I hadn't truly thought about that perspective. She's not wrong. "The problem is he's the boss of their family. He can't be with a woman who works in another organization."

She nods sagely, her thin, lined lips pursing together. "Loyalties would always be in question."

"Yeah, and I wouldn't want to ask him to step down, but I also feel like it's always women asked to set aside their lives for the sake of a man. That's not fair, nor do I want to be that woman willing to give up everything for a man."

"Shae, darlin'." She cocks her head to the side. "Tell me yer not making life choices based on other people's situations."

"No, but—"

Her brows jump to her gray hairline as she stares at me pointedly.

"I mean … women are always the ones asked to give up their livelihoods to be mothers and let men run everything."

"And I take it you see that as a negative."

"I guess it's not if that's what the woman wants as well."

"And this man of yours, do you think he expects you to sit at home and raise babies?"

"No."

"Do you think he or your family would respect you any less if you weren't working at Bastion?"

"No."

"Then it sounds like an exciting new opportunity to forge your own path if you ask me. You aren't other women, Shae Byrne. You look at you and your circumstances to make the decision. Nothing else. What do *you* want?"

My voice is as frail as a butterfly's wings when I answer because it's the first time I've even admitted to myself aloud what my heart has been telling me all along. "I want to find a way to make it work."

"Then ye have yer answer, darlin'." Nana's eyes are almost lost in the creases from her smile.

I cross from my chair at the kitchen table and wrap her in a grateful hug. "You're the best, Nana."

"Don't you forget it, love."

I laugh and sniffle, my emotions getting the better of me. "How about I put on a kettle? We can wake up Paddy and have him join us for tea and biscuits."

"Excellent idea." She gives a single nod, then lists in her

chair toward the living room. "Ach, Paddy, ye old fart," she yells with more volume than should be possible. "Come and join us for a cuppa."

My grandfather, Paddy, was snoozing in his recliner when I'd come over. Seconds later, he's standing in the doorway, rubbing his eyes.

"Jaysus, woman. What's with all the yelling?" He puts his glasses on, then beams when he sees me. "Shae, darlin'. When did you get here?"

Nana shakes her head and mutters, "Daft geezer."

I fight back a giggle and shoot up a silent thanks to the heavens for the best grandparents ever.

♦

FIVE MORE DAYS pass before I muster the courage to talk to my brother. Conner and Nana were one thing. Oran is another beast entirely, in part because of his unique perspectives but also because of my childhood admiration of him. It's easy to say I shouldn't care what anyone else thinks of my decisions. It's a lot harder to put that sentiment into action. I will always care what Oran thinks of me, even when I act like I don't.

Therefore, when I sit down with him in his living room, I'm extremely careful about the words I choose as I explain my situation. By the time I finish, his forehead is lined in confusion.

"Wait, you're telling me ... you have feelings for Renzo?"

"Yeah..." I draw out hesitantly. "Is that so hard to believe?"

"Conner told me about the insane tension between you and Renzo on the plane ride. And at the airport back home, you left without giving Renzo a second glance. Guess I assumed you were upset with him."

I was upset, but I'm not willing to explain why. Oran would go ballistic if he knew Renzo had kept me in that cabin longer than necessary. It's proof in my mind of where my priorities lie because I'd rather protect Renzo than tell my brother the truth.

"I was dealing with a lot of complicated emotions. Plus, I was worried how things might change with you guys when I got back."

"Change? In what way?"

"Like when you wanted to walk me to my apartment. I didn't want you to revert to being overprotective and keep me from doing my part."

Oran takes a deep breath. "I'm not gonna lie. The thought had occurred to me, but I dismissed it as soon as it formed because I know you."

"You know I'd never let that happen."

"I know you can take care of yourself," he quietly says the words that speak to my soul.

"Thanks, O." I have to clear my throat to recover my voice. "The thing is, as it turns out, I think I'll be the one taking myself out of the game."

"What's that supposed to mean?"

"It means, I love Renzo, and I want to be with him. I know the score. I can't have a foot in both worlds—the Irish and Italian. He's the Moretti boss. If I want to be with him, I have to be all in. No more Byrne family business."

"But you love your job. You've fought tooth and nail to be one of the toughest bastards in our family."

I grin at that, though it's tinged with sadness. "I appreciate that more than you can know. I do love working with all of you, but as it turns out, I love Renzo more."

His face splits in a smile that's pure delight. "Well, fuck me sideways. I never thought I'd see the day."

"That I'd settle down?"

"That you'd value anything over that badass image of yours," he ribs me in full big brother mode. He's got that same cocky glint in his eyes he used to get when he was giving me hell as a kid. I love it. That was our dynamic, and getting a taste of the old days fills my heart with warmth.

"At some point, I was going to start making you guys look bad. I figure better to retire before it comes to that."

He yanks the pillow off the sofa next to him and flings it right at my head. I deflect it, of course, giving into a fit of laughter.

"Make us look bad," he grumbles playfully. "Fat fucking chance."

I flash him a feisty grin as I retrieve the pillow and put it back in its proper place. "Everything ready for the wedding next week?"

"I assume so. I've been putting together a surprise honeymoon."

"Exciting! Where to?"

"It's a surprise, loose lips. I'm not telling you."

"I do *not* have loose lips," I shoot back with exaggerated audacity.

"Regardless, I'm not telling you," he says smugly. "But that reminds me. Did you know Renzo's in Canada searching airstrips?"

I shoot to my feet, all levity instantly incinerated. "Are you serious? Why didn't anyone tell me?" My reaction is so visceral that I surprise myself with the intensity of my emotions. What if he finds them? What if they outnumber Renzo's crew and hurt him? A thousand questions amp up my fear and anxiety, rushing at me like a swarm of angry wasps.

"I didn't talk to him myself," Oran says in his defense.

"Gino, his uncle, got in touch with Conner. Said Renzo had found the hangar. It was rented under the name Kola, but that didn't mean anything to either of us aside from confirming our suspicions that they were Albanian."

My heart loses its footing during a dead sprint and ends up slamming against my ribs.

Kola. It can't be a coincidence.

"What is it?" he demands, his spine stiffening.

God, please tell me I'm wrong. Please don't let this whole thing be my fault.

"The name might mean something to me, but I need to look into it. I'll get back with you." I don't want to say anything more unless I have definitive proof.

"You do anything that needs backup, you call me."

"If it gets to that, I will. I'm hoping to get an explanation about something before I cause an unnecessary stir." I minimize my concerns to Oran, but the more I think about it, the more certain I am that I've been blind. Coincidences like that don't happen out of nowhere. Not in my world.

I leave his place and rush home to my computer. I pull up the provider I use for background checks and enter the name Mari Cola along with her birthdate and anything else I know about her, which actually isn't all that much.

Zero matches.

Fuck.

♦

I SPEND the rest of the evening doing as much internet research as possible and decide to go by her place the next morning when I know she'll be at work. I don't have a key, but that sort of thing has never stopped me before. I let myself inside and take in the surroundings with new eyes.

She keeps everything surprisingly neat for a creative personality. Not evidence of anything, but something of interest. I carefully look through her drawers and closet. The place is small, so it doesn't take long. I don't find anything noteworthy. Not a single suspicious tidbit anywhere.

Could I be wrong? Kola and Cola are so similar that I can't discount the possibility she's connected. I'm going to have to talk to her in person.

I get out my phone.

Me: Hey, any chance we can get together and talk?

Mari: I had to pop out of town. We can get together when I get back next week.

Ugh, next week. I hate to wait that long, but I don't want to alarm her. If she is behind the gun theft, the last thing I want to do is tip her off that we're onto her. And if she's not a part of this, I don't want to fuck with her emotions and let her think I'm taking her back when I'm not.

Me: K, the 4th work? We could meet for coffee.

Mari: that works

Mari: I'm glad you reached out. I've missed you.

God, I hate this.

Me: Same. Looking forward to seeing you.

♦

IF THE BEST thing about short hair is not hindering me in a fight, a close second is how easy it is to do. No matter if I'm going to a wedding or grabbing lunch with friends, my routine is essentially the same. One look. No fuss.

No fancy updos for me today, but I do take a bit more time on my makeup. Oran and Lina are getting married, and Renzo will be there. I'm going to tell him how I feel. I took the two weeks I'd promised myself to think it through, and I'm sure of my decision. I want to be with him.

I'm so eager to finally see him again that my palms sweat while I get ready. I'm dressed and pacing my living room a full two hours before I need to start the trek from the city out to Staten Island for the wedding. That's when the text comes in.

Mari: Hey, I was able to get back early. Want to meet up?

This is perfect! I can talk to her then go to the wedding with answers.

Me: Yeah, Brew House in ten?

Mari: Can we make it an hour?

I can't imagine our visit will last more than an hour, which is when I need to leave for the wedding. It'll be cutting things close, but it's doable. I'm desperate for answers. I'd rather use this time to talk to her than let it linger a minute longer.

Me: Works for me, see you then.

She hearts my text, setting our date. All I need to do is change dresses to something that will conceal a gun, and I'm good to go.

45

Kenzo

I wouldn't have rushed back from Canada for the wedding if it weren't for Shae. Oran seems like a decent guy, but his wedding didn't trump my need for answers. Shae, on the other hand, trumps everything.

I haven't seen her in weeks. The wait has been killing me while also being exactly what I needed. I know what I want without a doubt. Tonight, I tell Shae that she's mine. And as an added bonus, I've returned from Canada with information.

I show up early at the gardens where the wedding is being held and spend the next half hour scouring arrivals for short dark hair and mountains of sass. I know she'll be here. It's her brother's wedding, after all.

I had hoped to get her alone before the ceremony, but as time ticks down, I know that isn't going to happen. I should have anticipated she might be in the wedding party. I tamp down my impatience and wait for the telltale music change to signal the bride's arrival. A teenage girl walks down the aisle —someone I've never met before—and then the bride makes her walk with an old woman at her side. That's it. No customary parade showing off the bride's extensive tribe of girlfriends. Interesting. And disappointing. Where the fuck is Shae?

By the time the ceremony is over and I can get access to one of the Byrnes, we've moved to the reception site in a nearby tent with my temper perched on a knife's edge. I've been so distracted that I've hardly given two thoughts to Sante. I brought him with me to see his sister, Noemi. I wish I hadn't. The kid thinks I haven't noticed he's been sipping from a flask. I see him, but I don't have the capacity to care at the moment. The second I get a chance to snag Conner, I pull him aside and ask about Shae.

"She texted earlier saying she got caught up at a meeting, and I haven't had a chance to look at my phone since." He pulls out the device. "Yeah, she texted thirty minutes ago and said she's following a time-sensitive lead."

"You're not worried something's wrong? She missed her brother's wedding."

Conner levels me with a stare that says, *really*? He types out a text, then chuckles at the response before showing me the screen.

Conner: proof of life

She answers with a picture of her hand flipping the bird.

"She's fine. You know Shae."

I do, but that doesn't make me feel better. Her missing the wedding doesn't sit right. I know she'd want me to trust her, however, so I dig deep and ignore the skin-crawling feeling of needing to do something. I don't eat or dance. I sit in a chair and watch the crowd. I must be putting off quite the vibe because no one interrupts my brooding. My eyes cut to the tent entrance every so often, desperately hoping to see Shae nonchalantly walk through as though nothing is amiss. Instead, I happen to spot Sante having words with the bride. I'm instantly on my feet.

"Everything okay here?" I ask, eyeing the way Sante has inserted himself between Lina and her young bridesmaid.

"This one's been spiking my sister's punch," Lina clips angrily.

Sante raises his hands innocently. "It's just a tiny bit of vodka. No need to make a big deal."

Jesus Christ.

I'm so fucking furious that I'm not sure I trust myself. "Can't fuckin' take you anywhere," I spit at him. I don't care if he wants to make an ass of himself getting drunk at a wedding, but spiking a teenage girl's drink is next fucking level wrong.

"You mean you don't ever want me to have any fun."

My hand is around his throat in half a second, lifting him nearly off the ground with the force of my fury. "What have I told you about disrespecting me?"

He grabs at my wrist, wheezing as he tries to talk. "*Just … a little … fun.*"

"No," I snarl at him. "You're embarrassing our entire family, and now we're leaving." I drop him, though I'm nowhere near done with him. "Lina, Oran, I'll make sure this is handled appropriately. You have my apologies," I say to the bride and her groom, who has since joined our little party.

Oran reaches his hand around Lina for me to shake. "We're glad you could make it."

I give a nod in appreciation of his understanding and usher Sante toward the door before I beat the shit out of him in front of everyone. He stumbles to keep up with me once we're outside. I've had enough bullshit for one night. It's time to drop Sante with Gino until I can deal with him later and go find Shae. I've gone far too long without a little chaos in my life. I'm done waiting.

46

Shae

"How have you been?" I ask Mari once we're both seated with our coffees.

"Not great, honestly."

"Yeah, it's been a rough couple of months for me, too. I think the whole kidnapping thing got to me more than I realized." I read from my mental script, playing the part of distraught victim.

When thinking about how to handle this meeting, I decided to try deception first. Mari was eager to see me when I got back from Canada. She was genuinely upset when I broke up with her. Either she's one hell of an actress with balls of steel or things aren't what they seem. Going in soft and seeing what I can learn felt like the best tactic. If I'm getting nowhere using that angle, I'll pivot.

"I can't imagine. It had to have been terrifying."

"Oddly enough, I wasn't as worried at first as I was later. The men whose robbery we interrupted were clearly just as surprised by us as we were by them. I kept thinking they'd take what they came for and leave us behind. Even when we were at that airplane hangar in Canada, I didn't see how killing us served any purpose. The fear really kicked in when our plane crashed. That next week was pretty awful."

She reaches across the table and squeezes my hand. "I was so worried when you disappeared."

"My cousin said you came looking for me at the gym."

"I was desperate to know what had happened. You're not the type to ignore people, so I knew something was wrong."

"You were right to worry." I inject a touch of frailty into my smile. "I was in a lot of trouble. I think it didn't fully set in until I got home, and then it all felt like too much. I've needed some time to process everything."

"That's understandable. How has your family been since you got back? They keeping a close eye on you?"

Mari may not have known about the criminal element of my family while we were together, but I'd complained to her about my cousins treating me with kid gloves and not letting me be a part of their boys' club.

"They've actually been pretty great. No hovering or locking me away in a cage." I pause to redirect things. "About them, I'm a little surprised you were willing to meet up now that you know the truth about what I do and have seen how dangerous it can be. I figured that would probably scare you off."

Her gaze drops to the coffee cup in her hands. "It's not

ideal, but I know you, and you're not a monster. You protect people, not hurt them."

"I handle security, but that doesn't make me a saint. I hurt people if I have to," I say softly.

"Only when you have to—that's a big caveat," she urges. "You're a good person, Shae. I know you are. And I'm willing to wait for you to sort things out if it means having a chance with you."

I can't find a single suspicious thread to pull in any of her responses. I debate confronting her directly with questions about her name and the lack of an online identity but decide to try one more avenue.

"That's very generous of you. I appreciate how understanding you've been, even getting together on short notice. I'd like to keep talking, but I actually have a family wedding to get to."

"Ah, I wondered if there was a special occasion. You look stunning."

"Thank you." I stand from my chair, and she follows suit. "No big date or anything like that, in case you were wondering." I give her a wink.

Her answering smile is radiant.

"Can I have a hug before I go?" I ask hesitantly.

"Of course." She opens her arms, and I wrap her in an embrace, making sure to snake my hand stealthfully into her open boho tote purse.

My plan is to take her wallet and see what I might find, but when my hand unexpectedly connects with the distinct feel of a passport booklet, I nab that instead. It's too unusual to ignore. Who carries a passport around in their purse?

She said she'd been out of town, but it still seems strange. Plus, I know she doesn't drive, so she probably doesn't have a driver's license in her wallet. This is my best bet for getting information.

I slide the booklet up the sleeve of my jacket and squeeze her arms affectionately as I pull away. "It really is great to see you. Maybe we can do lunch this week?"

Happiness shines in her eyes. "Yeah, I'd love that. Definitely."

"I'll give you a text tomorrow."

We give one last goodbye and part ways from the coffee shop, going in opposite directions. I force myself to wait until I'm a full city block away before I slip into an alley and examine my find. It's a US passport, the edges worn from regular activity as though she keeps it in her purse often. Inside, I find her photo and the name Marsela Kola, not Mari Cola.

Such a small distinction, but it makes all the difference in the world because the Italian girl I thought I knew is actually Albanian.

It can't be a coincidence.

No matter how convincing she may have been, Mari is somehow linked to the men who took us and that airstrip in Quebec. I flip through the pages and see multiple stamps for Canada. None for Albania, but that doesn't mean anything. I consider myself Irish American, but I've never actually been to Ireland.

The woman I screwed for six *fucking* months is a fraud. She fed her family information about our guns that she somehow skimmed from me. I was the source. Everything that happened was because of me.

Renzo was right. It was all my fault.

My rage and frustration consume me with such ferocity that I struggle to breathe.

I try so fucking hard to prove myself worthy of the Byrne

name and the respect it deserves. I strive every single day to show that women are equally as capable as men, especially in criminal pursuits where violence, strength, and bravery are essential to success. And I didn't even abide by my own lessons. I never considered Mari to be a threat because she's a woman.

What a fucking hypocrite I've been.

And blind. So fucking blind.

Now, I have to go to my family—to Renzo and his family —and tell them that it was all my fault. I inadvertently leaked the information that almost got us killed. Am I supposed to do that at my brother's wedding? Because there's no way I can go and pretend to be fine. They'll know something's wrong and demand the truth.

I'd rather miss his wedding than have my shame broadcast to the entire family at the event. I'm not proud of how I feel, but it is what it is.

Now, I have an inkling of how Oran must have felt when he learned his wife was responsible for the betrayal that led to our dad's death. I thought he'd taken it hard at the time, but now I see the incredible fortitude he must have had to keep from falling apart.

The guilt and shame. It's sickening.

I literally have to choke back my self-disgust as it rises in the back of my throat. I definitely can't go to the wedding. Not now. I consider going after Mari right now and force her to confess everything. The intensity of my need to follow her is what stops me. I'm a little scared of what I might do to her. I shouldn't be. She probably doesn't deserve my grace, but I decide not to act while I'm still overcome with such extreme emotions.

Instead, I start to walk with no destination in mind. I just walk.

I'm embarrassed and ashamed and so fucking furious with myself and with her. The emotions claw at my heels, spurring me on faster while tear-filled eyes blur my vision and slow me down—pushed and pulled by opposing forces that keep me perpetually frustrated. My life is no different. I have to be tough but sensitive. Cautious yet bold. And above all, flawless.

As a woman in a man's world, I am absolutely not allowed to show weakness because it will be weaponized and used against me without fail.

I do my best every day not to let the double standards get to me. I know my worth. I also know that not everyone will see it. Little setbacks rarely faze me.

This is different. A crack in the foundation I've stood upon for years. I start to wonder if stepping down wouldn't be best for my family, whether I do it for Renzo or not. My confidence is so profoundly shaken that I don't know what to think. I don't know how to process it, so I do the only thing I can and move forward.

I walk for what feels like ages, though I don't know for sure because I refuse to look at my phone. I walk until the sky is dark, and my feet take me home of their own volition.

I numbly jab the elevator call button when I reach the lobby of my building. The light dings, announcing its arrival. I lean forward, my weight shifted in anticipation of escaping upstairs, only the universe isn't done toying with me yet. When the doors open, Renzo Donati stands on the other side.

My lungs seize tight on a wheezing gasp as though I've been sucker punched. "What are you doing here?" I blurt, my panicked brain unable to properly process as my skittering heart forgets how to beat.

Renzo's entire face goes dark, each sculpted edge

suddenly razor sharp. "What the fuck is going on? Where have you been?"

"You should go. This isn't a good time." I shake my head and inch backward.

Quick as a striking viper, he clasps my hand and tugs me into the elevator car.

"Renzo, please. I'll call you tomorrow. I just need some space right now."

"You can beg all you want. I'm not going anywhere except up to your place, where you're going to tell me exactly what the fuck is going on."

Like a wounded animal backed into a corner, I wrench my wrist from his grip and back away to the opposite wall of the elevator. "You have no right to demand anything from me." I sound like I'm possessed, hissing at him for seemingly no reason, but I can't stop myself.

Maybe I am possessed. Maybe that's what he's been trying to tell me all along.

Renzo refuses to give an inch, closing the gap between us and forcing my gaze to his with a hand cupping my jaw. "Good thing I don't give a fuck about rights. I take what I want, and I'm done waiting."

His lips slam down on mine, a sensual assault that makes my battered heart weep. With joy. With devastation. His kiss breaks me down to nothing and builds me back up, but underneath it all, I'm still the same flawed little girl I've always been.

I'm the first to pull back, tears finally cascading down my cheeks. "You want the truth. I'll tell you." My voice is tone-less. As empty as my heart feels. "The guns, the kidnapping, it was all my fault. You were right to blame me." As the elevator doors open behind me, I spread my hands wide in supplication. "I am chaos."

47

Kenzo

I'M NOT SURE WHAT SHAE IS TALKING ABOUT, AND I DON'T CARE.
She's finally letting me in, and I intend to embed myself so
deep inside her that she forgets how to function without me.

I walk her backward until we're both out of the elevator,
then place my hands on either side of her face and lock eyes
with hers. I want to make sure she hears my words along
with the sincerity behind them.

"I know exactly who you are, and it turns out that chaos is
the best fucking thing to ever happen to me."

"You don't mean that." Her eyes squeeze shut. She wants
to shut me out, but that's not happening again. Ever.

"I do mean it, and I'll prove it to you." I take her hand and
tug her down the hall to her apartment door. "Open it." I'm

not having this conversation in a fucking hallway. I need privacy for what I have in mind.

Shae relents, and we step inside. She sets down her purse and takes off her jacket, avoiding my stare while I focus every ounce of unrelenting attention on her every movement.

"First, tell me what this is all about."

Her shoulders rise and fall on a long, even breath as she stands in the entry with her back to me. "It was my fault. I leaked the information that led to the robbery and us getting captured."

"Then I owe you a debt of gratitude," I tell her in an even tone.

Bemused, she looks over her shoulder, brows pinched and lips softly parted. "What?"

"If we hadn't been taken, if that plane hadn't crashed, we'd have never had those three weeks together. And those were the best three weeks of my goddamn life." I slowly circle her, loving how her body naturally follows mine.

"How can you possibly say that? We almost died."

"And I'd do it again in a heartbeat if it meant making you mine."

"You can't—" Her hand goes to her chest as if she's in pain, her eyes drifting shut. "You can't say things like that."

I take her face in my hands again and wait until her eyes meet mine. "I can say it if I mean it. And I mean every fucking word. You're mine, Shae Byrne, and I'm yours. We're a team. And I'm not going one more day without you by my side because you're already in my heart. My fucking *soul*. These weeks apart made it clear to me that you are the only thing that truly matters—without you, the rest is meaning-less. That's why I've made arrangements for my uncle Gino to take over the family."

"*What?*" she gasps, shaking her head in my hands. "No, Ren. You can't. Not for me."

A prideful energy vibrates through me like a full-body purr. "Say it again," I rasp.

She sighs. "I know I can't tell you what to do—"

"No." I cut her off. "My name. Say it like that again."

Her eyes soften. "Ren." The single syllable coming from her lips is a sunrise over calm waters. It soothes the turbulent soul and gives life meaning.

I shrug off my suit jacket and coax her arms up to lift her dress over her head and off. "You're going to say it again, but this time, you're going to moan it while I fuck you. No more running, Chaos. You're mine."

48

Shae

I've never been scared to believe someone. Either believe them or don't. But every word past Renzo's lips fills my heart with such profound happiness that I can't ward off a sliver of fear. I'm scared that if I grab hold with both hands only to discover it's an illusion, my shattered pieces will never fit back together.

This man has listened to my desires, witnessed my failures, and seen me living my deepest fears. In a short span of time, he's come to know me better than anyone. Not only does he want me but he's also willing to give up everything to have me.

I can hardly wrap my mind around it.

I thought I'd never want to belong to anyone, but with

Renzo at my side, I feel stronger, not weaker. Our connection builds us taller than we could stand alone. And when we fall, like I've done today, our bond is a safety net.

How could I have ever seen that sort of symbiosis as a weakness?

I'd already come to accept my feelings for Renzo. I love him. There's no denying that. But at this moment, I recognize our connection for the gift that it is, rather than a situation I have to sort through.

"I'm yours," I breathe in awe. "I love you, and I'm yours."

His chest expands as though the emotions within are too vast to be constrained. "You're goddamn right you're mine."

He kisses me.

I rip open his shirt. Buttons scatter to the wood floor.

He pays no mind, yanking off the shirt while I grapple with his belt and pants. Weeks of frustrated desire boils to a frenzy, making us mindless with need for one another. He kicks off the rest of his clothing. I'm expecting him to come at me with ravenous hunger, but he stills instead. I look down and realize what's caught his attention. He's staring at the gun in my thigh holster. I'd forgotten about it and am now wearing nothing but it, my bra, underwear, and a pair of ivory heels.

"Fuck, Shae. You're the sexiest thing I've ever seen." He nudges a finger under the elastic strap holding my tiny .22 caliber in place and slides his finger around to my inner thigh, his hand drifting up to cup my sex over my pink thong. "Do you have any idea how often I've fantasized about finally having your sweet pussy wrapped around my cock?"

His free hand tugs down my strapless bra, freeing my breasts to set atop the padded cups. He bends and fills his mouth with my breast while his hand slip beneath my silk panties to spread my arousal in slow strokes to my clit and back.

I lean against the wall, my eyes rolling back in my head.

He kisses lower until he's on his knees. "As sexy as this is, it has to go." He slides my thigh holster down my leg and off. "With our combined luck, one of us will end up shot."

I have to laugh because he's not wrong, but my smile quickly fades when he spreads my thighs apart and rips the bottom of my thong clean in half. The elastic waist is still on me, but the front and back hang loose like straps for a garter, leaving me bare. And this time, I'm truly bare—trimmed and shaved and ready to be eaten alive.

Renzo is up for the task. He begins to devour me, draping my legs over his back, then standing up with me seated on his shoulders. My back rests against the wall for support while his mouth is buried in my pussy as though he's eating the ripest, most delicious slice of watermelon he's ever tasted.

And the sounds he makes—I've never had anyone make me feel so damn sexy from moans of pure delight at pleasuring me. He's playing a role to get me to the finish line. He's legitimately loving every second, and that helps me relax and enjoy the feel of his incredible touch.

When one hand squeezes my ass cheek and the other twists one of my pierced nipples, I have to grab a handful of his hair to ground myself. The pleasure is overwhelming. All-consuming.

My legs begin to twitch and tremble. "*Ren*, I'm so close already. *Oh God.*" I don't know if it's his skill or the emotions or too long between orgasms, but this one barrels at me like a freight train. I feel the rumbling tingles of its arrival seconds before it careens into me.

Waves of electric pleasure short-circuit every nerve ending in my body until I am nothing but sensation. Pulsing, coursing, vibrant sensations from the crown of my head to the tips of my toes. And when the intoxicating storm starts to recede, I'm left feeling like I'm floating on a lake of serenity.

Renzo slowly lowers my feet back to the floor, but only long enough for him to swoop me back into his arms, bridal style. It's a good thing, too, because I'm not sure my quivering legs could have held me upright.

"That was so fucking phenomenal," I breathe into the crook of his neck.

"Silly girl, that was just the appetizer."

He takes me to the bedroom and lays me down, my head nearly hanging off the foot of the bed. When he stands over me and strokes his throbbing cock, I realize his intent and lick my lips.

"Fuck, do it again," he growls.

I slowly slide my tongue along my bottom lip. A shiver of anticipation wracks his body before he brings the head of his shaft to my lips. I open and flatten my tongue, welcoming his thick warmth into my mouth. I angle my head back further so I can take more of him in. When I moan, his core flexes as he presses himself all the way to the back of my throat. He doesn't stay there long, careful to make sure I have no problem breathing.

For several long minutes, he leisurely fucks my mouth. My hands squeeze and tease my breasts because it feels good but also because I know he likes it, and this is about him. I want him to feel every bit as incredible as he made me feel.

I suck and lick and moan and touch myself until he hisses and pulls away, his breaths coming in shallow, ragged puffs. He immediately joins me on the bed, aligning his body with mine.

"I didn't think it was possible, but that was even better

than I imagined." He kisses a path along my neck, his cock warm and deliciously hard against my upper thigh.

"Imagine it often, did you?" I tease.

"You have no fucking idea."

My humor dissipates as carnal hunger takes its place. "I might be more familiar than you'd expect." I wrap my arms behind his neck and my legs around his middle. "Fuck me, Ren. I need to feel you inside me."

He angles his hips so that his head is teasing at my entrance. "Didn't put a condom on."

"I'm not on birth control, but I just finished my period, so I don't think it's an issue." I know I should be more careful. I'm not ready for kids yet. But that's not the way it works with Renzo and me. Our love isn't careful; it's consuming. And I want to connect with him without anything between us.

Skin to skin.

Heart to heart.

Renzo starts to ease inside me. "Good, I want more than anything in this world to see my cum dripping from your cunt and know that you are unequivocally mine, so long as I live and breathe." His voice grows more strained as he surges deeper inside me.

I gasp and nod, holding him tighter. "Yes, I'm yours. Only yours."

That's his cue. He sinks all the way inside me … then again … and again … and again until he is pistoning his way deep into my soul. Each powerful thrust is so commanding, my body has no choice but to come alive with pleasure.

His body slaps at the perfect angle against my clit while stoking that secret bundle of nerves inside me. I don't have to chase anything because my orgasm stalks me like a ravenous panther. It's so intense, I can feel my core swelling and throbbing in preparation.

"*Ren … it's so good.*" My dazed words are breathy and tense with anticipation because this feels different from anything I've experienced before. "Oh God. *Ren, it's coming.*"

"You squeeze me so damn tight. Say my name, baby. Say my name when you come apart."

His voice is as ragged and strained as mine, and hearing that lights the final spark that detonates a bomb inside me. I start to cry his name, but it morphs into a scream of intense pleasure. My inner muscles spasm with such force I'm vaguely aware of what feels like liquid squirting past those muscles.

"*Fuck yes,*" Renzo says in a half hiss, half moan before his orgasm overtakes him. His body curves around mine as his core contracts. I cling to him, reveling in my waning pleasure and relishing the sight of him finding his own release.

We hold one another as we recover. And once we're both breathing evenly again, Renzo rises to his knees and stares raptly at my core as he slides his cock from inside me. It makes me remember the squirting from before. Is that what he's looking at? Is there a puddle beneath me?

I'm suddenly mortified. My knees try to angle inward.

His hands ease my legs back apart. "Told you I wanted to see my cum dripping out of you, and fuck is it perfect." He takes his thumb and smears the liquid in a circle around my opening. My inner muscles clench involuntarily, which squeezes out more.

Renzo groans, and it's the most heady, addictive sound I've ever heard. I think he might take pictures and hang them on the walls if he could.

"I thought you were looking at the bed. I think I might have made a mess. I'm sorry. That's never happened before."

The most self-satisfied smile I've ever seen creeps across his face. "That means I'm doing it right."

Somehow, that doesn't make me feel better.

"You don't look convinced."

"It's not that. I'm just worried I might do it again. The mattress—"

"Has a cover," he continues for me, lowering back down to lie at my side. "And I'll buy a goddamn truckload of sheets if we need them. Never felt anything sexier than you squirting all over my cock. Jesus *Christ*, my woman can fuck."

I can't help myself. I toss my head back into the pillow and laugh from deep in my belly. When the laughter subsides and I bring my gaze back to Renzo, his hooded stare fills me with warm summer picnics and cozy winter nights by the fire. He doesn't hold back an ounce of his adoration. He shows me everything he feels and gives me all that he is.

How could I ever consider refusing that sort of honesty and devotion? It's the greatest gift I've ever received, and I won't give it up for anything.

"You know, you're stuck with me now," I whisper to him, the tiniest hint of my insecurities resurfacing.

"Stuck implies a need to escape, and I don't ever want to be free of you."

"Okay," I breathe.

"Okay," he says back.

As simple as that, my heart is his. Signed, sealed, and delivered.

49

Kenzo

"You think anyone else noticed I wasn't there?" Shae asks lazily, her body entwined with mine now that we've showered and moved to the guest bed.

"I'd say it's a safe bet I wasn't the only one."

She sighs.

"What was the lead you were following?"

She takes a slow breath as if preparing to unload the news of a loved one's death. "It's kind of a long story, but when we got back from Quebec, my place had been ransacked."

I prop myself up on an elbow and stare incredulously. "And you're just telling me this now?"

Her hand presses against my chest, her face staying

serene. "Things were complicated, Renzo. I told my family, though. It wasn't like I kept it a secret."

I don't like it. My irritation is irrational, I know that, but I still don't like it. I lie on my back and try to convince my body to relax. "You figure out who it was?"

"I'm almost certain it was the woman I was seeing, though I didn't even suspect her until a few days ago."

"What made you think it was her?" I'm curious where this is going. I don't know anything about the woman, and I'm suddenly wishing I'd asked a few questions.

"Nothing tangible at first, but when I heard you'd gone to Canada and connected the airstrip to the name Kola, it seemed like too much of a coincidence."

This time, I sit all the way upright. "Are you telling me this woman is connected to the Albanians?"

"I discovered tonight that she *is* Albanian." Shae sits up with me, pulling the sheet around her. "I met up with her under the pretense of reconciling."

"Jesus, Shae. Did your family know you were meeting up with her?"

She glares at me, then continues as if I hadn't spoken. "Everything seemed kosher during our talk, but I nabbed her passport from her purse on a whim. She lied to me about her name. I knew her as Mari Cola."

"Italian," I note.

"Right. But her real name is Marsela Kola. Albanian. And the booklet was half full of stamps for Canada."

I roll off the bed and hold out my hand for her. "Come on. We're getting out of here."

She doesn't move at first as though she's debating whether to argue.

"Until we know exactly what's going on, even you have to admit that my place is safer. No reason to take chances." I'm able to keep my cool, but only because I know she'll never cooperate if I don't. What I actually want to do is rage at her for staying here when she knew it wasn't safe. And she still doesn't have a damn alarm. I bite my cheek to keep my thoughts to myself.

Shae gets up and follows me back to her bedroom where we left our clothes.

"Pack an overnight bag."

She peers at me shyly over her shoulder. "You're handling this better than I would have expected."

"How's that?" I ask distractedly, typing out a text on my phone while we're talking.

"You haven't yelled or threatened to put me in a safe house. A night at your place to sort things out is very reasonable."

"Glad you think so, but the sorting out's been done, and the overnight bag is to get you by until my guys move the rest of your stuff to my place tomorrow." I hold up my phone. "It's already been arranged."

She stares at me as though I've farted butterflies out of my ass. "What?"

"You can't move me into your place without even asking."

I decide to let it slide that she's told me yet again what I can't do and cross over to where she's standing, pull her even closer with my hand cuffed around her neck to place a gentle kiss on her nose.

"Shae Byrne…"

A kiss on her eyelid.

"Will you…"

A kiss on her other eyelid.

"*Please*…"

A kiss on her forehead.

"Fucking move in with me."

This time, my lips touch hers in a leisurely caress.

"Okay," she breathes. "See, was that so hard?"

I grin ear to ear because that's my Shae. Always with the last word. And I love her for it.

Instead of packing, however, she stands with her brows pinched.

"What is it?"

"How's this going to work, Renzo? I'm genuinely not okay letting you step down, but I'm also not the stay-at-home mom type either. There are our families and—"

I place my hand over her mouth, relieved when she doesn't bite me before I let my hand fall back down. "I've gone through all those thoughts as well, trust me. I know you better than to expect some '50s stereotype. And you know what I've come to realize?"

She shakes her head.

"So long as it's my cum running down your thighs and your lipstick on my cock, nothing else matters."

"Renzo, I had no idea you were such a romantic." Her teeth snag her bottom lip, fighting back a grin.

I spin her around and slap her ass. "Pack that damn bag so we can get home. I need to fuck you again."

Her gasp of outrage dies away as her eyes dilate with the promise of my words. "Yeah, okay. Time to get packing."

50

Shae

Waking up at Renzo's place feels surprisingly normal, considering I've never been here before last night. I suppose it's not so much the apartment that feels familiar as the man. I think I might feel at ease no matter where I am so long as he's there with me.

I don't even have to open my eyes to feel the effects. His pheromones are to me what catnip is to cats—a single tendril of his scent and my insides go all warm and gooey. I stretch out in the bed, relishing the feel of waking to such sublime contentedness.

"Never letting you out of my bed again," Renzo murmurs in a gravelly voice heavy with sleep as he pulls me closer with an arm lassoed around my waist.

The joy in my heart unfurls in a smile. "Never is awfully absolute. I might need to go to the bathroom or eat every now and then."

"Nope. Too risky."

I giggle and snuggle up closer to him. "What do you have planned today?"

"If you are absolutely sure you don't want me to step down, then I need to talk to my uncle and tell him that he doesn't have to take my place as boss. He'll be relieved, so that will be easy enough."

"I'm certain."

He nods. "After that, I should probably deal with my cousin Sante. He made some seriously poor life choices last night. That *conversation* won't be so pleasant."

"Noemi mentioned that he was having a hard time dealing with his dad's betrayal."

"That's putting it mildly," Renzo mutters. "What about you? You have plans today?"

"I suppose I'll start thinking about what I want to do with myself. I didn't get a chance to tell you last night, but I've already told my cousins I'm stepping down."

He lifts above me so he can see my face. "You sure about that? I don't want to be the reason you quit doing what you love."

I smile softly. "I've thought about it extensively over the past couple of weeks, and I'm positive. You're worth the change."

He kisses me ardently. "Fuck, I love you so much. And I promise you won't be bored. We're doing this together—not only going after those Albanian assholes but all of it. We're a team on all fronts. My role as boss included."

"You think your family will accept me? Trust might be an issue."

"It took you a handful of days to have me eating out of the palm of your hand. The others will be no different."

I like his optimism, but for once, I'm having trouble seeing it. "The other thing I need to do is check out the address on Mari's passport. It's not the same as her apartment."

"It wasn't familiar?"

"Nope."

"Well, that sounds like a perfect excuse to avoid dealing with my cousin. Let's get cleaned up, and we'll check out the place together."

My answering grin makes the Joker look demure. I'm definitely a little unhinged when it comes to Renzo, but I adore how happy it makes me to work alongside him and to know that he wants me right there with him. We *are* a team—a good one—and I'm so damn grateful to have him.

Two hours later, and we're standing outside the small apartment building housing the unit listed on Mari's passport. We investigated the address online and found it's listed in someone else's name. That's about the extent of what we learned, which meant it was time to do an in-person visit.

Renzo arranges for several of his men to meet us near the building. We decide on a direct approach of knocking on the front door with me taking the lead. Renzo joins me while the others are on standby down the hall. We're both armed, though we leave our weapons holstered as we wait for someone to answer my knock. It's an older building without an entry code, so anyone can get in. It's not that the buzzered entries are all that difficult to circumvent.

I knock again after no one answers. We wait another minute, then decide to go in. I take out my lock-picking kit and have the door open in thirty seconds flat.

"They need to upgrade to a better deadbolt," I say distractedly as the door swings open, and we peer inside. The place is small. Looks like a family home—maybe an older couple. It's not what I expected to find.

We do a careful sweep to make sure the place is empty before we start combing through its contents. The main bedroom has one of those old oak rolltop desks. Photos are stacked in piles and shoved in the open slots. It's overflowing with pictures, and most of them are of me.

"*Fuuuuck*," I say on a weary exhale.

"Jesus Christ. Who is this woman?"

"Hell if I know." I thought I knew, but clearly, I was horribly wrong.

Renzo flips through the stack of photos that's most front and center of the desk, pausing to show me one. It's me and Devlin hugging.

She was stalking me.

She knew I'd had a thing with him. She was glaring at the necklace because she knew damn well who'd given it to me.

My stomach makes a quick trip down to my toes and back.

Renzo doesn't ask about the photo. He simply keeps flipping until something else catches his attention, drawing a string of curses from him.

"What?" I crane my neck to see what he's looking at.

Photos of Conner. Several of them, with and without Noemi.

"This was last week when he was getting ready for the wedding." My words are paper thin, too shredded from shock to have any substance. She's still following me and my family. "I don't understand. Is she a stalker or a mole for the Albanians? What the fuck is going on here?"

He doesn't answer because he's equally as baffled. Instead, he flips to the next photo, which has my blood running ice cold. It's a close-up of Noemi, and someone has drawn a red X over her in fat red Sharpie.

"I don't like this, Ren," I whisper.

"Me either. Give Noemi a call and make sure she's okay."

I nod and pull out my phone with shaking hands. I select her in my favorites and wait while the phone goes unanswered. The second voicemail picks up. I end the call and dial Conner.

"Good to know you're alive," he says when he answers.

"Where's Noemi?" I demand.

"She and a few of the other ladies who were in town for the wedding went to brunch this morning, which you'd know if you'd made it to your brother's wedding last night."

"Where are they?"

He's quiet for a second. "Why? What's going on?" Wary concern sharpens his tone.

"I think Noemi might be in danger. There's not time to explain. Where are they having brunch?"

I have his full attention now. Conner gives me the name of the place, and we all race over. When we find the group, Noemi isn't with them.

"She saw a friend she hadn't seen in a while and said they were going to visit for a bit. Why, what's going on?" They all give us worried looks, but I don't have time to explain.

"This friend—did you see her?"

They nod.

"Brown hair and eyes, Romanesque features, very striking?"

"Yeah, that's her," one of them says warily. "Why? Who is she?"

"Motherfucker," Conner barks, slamming his fist on the table.

The entire restaurant quiets.

I look back at the ladies. "We don't have time to explain, but you guys should get home. We'll let you know when we have her back safely."

We don't wait for a reply, barreling back through the restaurant. The second we're outside, Conner starts pacing.

"Tell me you know where she is, Shae," he demands. *"Where the fuck is my wife?"*

Being responsible for the gun theft was bad enough. If something happens to Noemi because of me, I'll never forgive myself.

Think, Shae. Where would Mari take Noemi?

Not her apartment or the house. She shares a photography studio with two other people, so that's unlikely. Could she have gone to her rooftop? No other place comes to mind, and it makes sense. Whatever is going on is personal for her. She's likely to go somewhere familiar. Somewhere she knows I could find her.

"I think I know where they are."

51

Kenzo

Our plan makes sense. I understand it. I know that being where I am on an adjacent rooftop with a sniper will do Shae more good than if I were standing next to her. The logic isn't lost on me, yet I hate it so much my body vibrates with the need to go over there.

"How long will it take you to get set up?" I don't want to rush him, but I want to be ready. Shae and Conner will be on the roof any second. She was right. We spotted Noemi and Mari from our vantage point above her, being careful not to let ourselves be seen.

If it were up to me, I'd have our hired gun take the woman out as soon as his sights are aligned. Shae insisted we give her the chance to talk to Mari first. I get it, but again, I don't like it.

"One more minute," the man says evenly without taking his eyes from his task. He moves with a preternatural calm that baffles me. He's one of two marksmen used by our family when the situation calls for it, though this is the first time I've ever seen either of them in action. It would be far more fascinating if my cousin and the woman I love weren't both at risk of losing their lives.

As if on cue, Shae and Conner slowly step from the stairwell and onto the roof. Mari whirls around, clutching Noemi in front of her with a gun to my cousin's head.

This will be the ultimate test of my trust, and even I have no idea if I'll pass or fail.

52

Shae

THE MIND'S ABILITY TO PERPETUATE DENIAL IS MYSTIFYING. NO matter how improbable, I still held out hope that Mari wasn't responsible. That there'd been some horrible misunderstanding that had led us to the wrong conclusion. But when I step onto the roof and see her holding Noemi hostage, there's no denying the truth.

"*You*," she growls, jabbing the gun at my cousin. "It's *you*. You're the one." She looks terrible. Dark circles under her eyes and a frenetic energy so unlike the woman I thought I knew.

"Mari, this is my cousin, Conner. Do you know him?" My voice is infused with calm. I would bet my life that she has feelings for me, and if I show her compassion, I'm hoping to get through to her. I want to find out what the hell is going on and do my best to resolve it without anyone getting hurt.

Mari's chin quivers, her face contorting in hatred. "I know he's the one who killed my twin brother. For *nothing*. He showed up in a rage at my parents' house looking for information, desperate to hurt someone. My brother was the only person at the house."

So that's what this is? Revenge? She used me to get close to my family, then … stole our guns? It still doesn't make sense.

I look at Conner, trying to sort it out.

His eyes narrow. "I remember the night you're talking about—it wasn't that long ago. Earlier that day, we'd been in a car chase when your people tried to kill my wife." He nods at Noemi. "I remember that day well, and I never killed anyone at that house."

"No," Mari agrees. "You punched him so hard that he fell back and hit his head—"

"He was never even unconscious."

"*It didn't matter*," she screams, then calms herself before continuing. "Two days later, he collapsed, dying instantly of an aneurysm from that head injury. You. Killed. Him."

Fuck, this is so much more complicated than I imagined.

I can understand why she's upset, but the chances of that sort of thing happening are so incredibly slim. Conner may have punched the guy, but his death was an accident. A horrible, tragic accident.

When I look into Mari's vengeful stare, I know she'll never see it that way. To her, Conner will always be the man who stole her brother from her. But that doesn't explain going out with me for six months and breaking into my place. Why not go after Conner from the beginning?

My thoughts fly at me a million miles a minute as I try to

process everything in real time while simultaneously trying to figure out how to defuse the situation.

"If that's the case, I'm sorry," Conner offers, the strain of his forced calm evident in his stilted tone. "But I had no way of knowing that would happen."

Mari's face twists with disgust. "No, but it's okay to go around beating up people because you're upset?"

Conner's jaw flexes as his hands lift placatingly. "You're right. I was wrong. But Noemi isn't a part of this. Please, let her go. You want someone, take me. I'm the one who killed your brother."

I take a slow step forward. Conner's hand locks around my wrist to keep me in place, but I shoot him a look that demands he trust me. When he reluctantly lets go, I continue with carefully measured steps toward Mari. We watch one another intently. I look for signs she may lash out, while she makes sure to keep Noemi between us.

"That's how this started, but it's not the whole story, is it?" I ask gently.

Tears run down her cheeks. The way her head lists longingly to the side when she looks at me makes my heart ache for her. She's so much more damaged than I ever realized. I thought of her as feminine and dainty when the reality is, Mari is a fragile glass flower wrought with cracks.

"I was just supposed to use you," she whispers. "But then … you had to go and make me fall for you. You were different from your family. I told myself you were innocent of any of it. I tried so hard to be exactly what you wanted so that you'd want me back, but you didn't." Her face twists with disgust. "You wore the necklace that man gave you when you were only with him for a *week*, yet after all the time we've spent together, I still mean *nothing* to you."

Her eyes drop to my neck where the pendant still rests.

I'm not even sure why I'm still wearing it after all I've been through with Renzo except that I've had too many other things on my mind.

I take the necklace in my fist and yank it free from my neck, breaking the chain. "This was a gift, but it doesn't hold the significance you may think. Not anymore." I let the object fall to the gritty rooftop surface. I can't tell her I love her, but I can reassure her that she's wrong if she thinks I loved Devlin.

"Maybe not, but only because he left you. I was *there* for you. I protected you. No matter how much I wanted your cousin dead, I didn't kill him because I didn't want to hurt you like that. Passing information about your family to my uncle was my gift to you. A way to punish them without hurting you." Her eyes fill with more tears. "You were never supposed to be involved. I never meant to hurt you."

"Things don't always work out how we plan. I get that."

"All I wanted was for you to want me," she whispers. "When I came by your place after everything got fouled up, I'd wanted to be near you. To find some shred of evidence that you felt for me what I felt for you." The words are thin and raspy, forced past a throat tight with emotion. She's drowning in pain, and I almost feel bad until I watch every ounce of that emotional storm evaporate like spring rain on a hot city street. The change turns my stomach because the person standing before me now is almost unrecognizable with such hatred in her gaze.

"There was nothing. Not a single memento of me anywhere in your apartment. I started to accept that it was best you were gone, but then suddenly you were back. I was so relieved you were alive, all my hope reignited. Then days later, I faced devastation when you broke things off and took it all away, only to call and pretend you wanted me back. You were toying with me like a cat with a string." Her voice is thin, almost distant, as though stuck in the nightmare of her emotions. "You made me think maybe we actually had a chance, but that was never the case, was it? I felt so fucking bad about what happened that I even understood why you broke things off. I'd been ready to forgive you for pushing me away, but when I saw that my passport was gone, I knew every minute of it had been a lie. All you wanted was information. That's when I knew it was really over. All of it. And if I was ever going to get justice, I needed to act."

I want to find a way to talk her down, but she's past that. The pain of her past has warped her mind such that logic and reason no longer resonate. No amount of negotiating will talk her down from this ledge. She's going to hurt the people I love if I don't stop her. I can sense it with every fiber of my being, and it breaks my heart.

"I'm so sorry, Mari. For everything."

Her eyes fill with rage, and her lip peels back in a vicious snarl. "No, you don't get to be sorry!" she screams.

But I don't engage her. This conversation is over.

I raise my right arm—the signal Renzo's been watching for. Not two seconds later, there's a thwack sound, and Mari crashes to the ground, the soundwave of a gunshot following close after.

Conner and Noemi fly at one another. Relief sucks the air from my lungs, making my head spin.

I look in the direction of the neighboring rooftop as Renzo rises to his feet. Right where I knew he'd be, which is why I'd needed to walk toward Mari and have our conversation. I'd needed to be certain she couldn't be saved but also ensure his man had a clean shot. She did exactly as I'd hoped and aligned herself with his sights so Noemi wasn't at risk.

I kiss my fingertips and send him my love and gratitude. His right hand lifts to his chest, coming to rest over his heart.

It dawns on me that without Mari, I wouldn't have Renzo. In that one regard, I owe her a debt of gratitude. And besides that, we were inadvertently responsible for her brother's death and her mental collapse. She was a casualty of a world she was too fragile to inhabit. As much as I wanted to hate her when I learned the truth, I can only summon pity now.

"We need to make sure she's buried next to her brother," I say to Conner when I walk back to him and Noemi.

"It's safer to have the cleaners come and make her disappear."

"I know, but it would mean a lot to me if we could find a way for her to be reunited with him."

He studies me, then nods. "Let's get out of here."

Noemi leaves her husband's side and envelops me in a crushing hug. "Thank you, Shae. You were absolutely incredible." When she pulls back, pride and respect shine through puffy red eyes.

"I second that," Conner says softly from behind her. "I owe you, Shae."

"Rest assured, I won't let you forget it." I manage to keep a perfectly straight face. Just barely.

A lazy grin creeps across his face until even his eyes are smiling. "Wouldn't be our Shae if you did."

"Damn straight. Now let's get out of here. I'm exhausted."

53

Kenzo

It takes what feels like forever for the three of them to reach the street. I know Shae is fine, but I can't stop my skin from crawling with the need to be near her. To have her safely within reach.

When they finally join me on the sidewalk, I first give my cousin a kiss on her forehead. "You did so good, Em. So brave. I'm proud of you."

"Thank you, Renzo." Her eyes shine with love.

Conner extends his hand for a shake. "Seems we owe you again."

"Not this time," I correct him. "This one was personal for me, too." I pull Shae to my side and feel my heart rate finally settle.

"You know," Conner says, "if she tried leaving us for anyone else, I'm not sure I'd let her go."

"As if you could stop me." Shae scoffs under her breath.

I'm glad they're keeping things light, but that brings up a point I need to make. "I hope you know that I would never ask her to quit doing what she loves. I told her I'd step down, but she insists that she be the one to make a change."

Conner stares at me as though he's piecing together a puzzle. "I'm not sure if I should respect you for making that offer or question your safety when she has no outlet for all that energy."

Images flash in my mind of all the creative ways I could make use of her energy. I can't hold back a wolfish grin. "Shae won't get bored, trust me."

She smacks my chest. "That's enough—you two are talking about me like I'm not standing right here. *Jesus.* Conner," she barks. "You get Noemi home. We'll wait here for the cleanup crew to arrive."

His smirk fades before he gives us a nod and leads his wife to their car.

I pull Shae in for a hug, holding her snug against my body. "I don't know what you said out there, but you were incredible to watch. Terrifying but also incredible. The way you stayed calm and talked to her. I could tell you were doing everything you could to save her, but when that didn't work, you made sure we had the best shot possible."

"*You* were terrified?" she balks. "I was scared shitless, but I had to keep cool so I could save the people I love."

I kiss her long and deep, savoring her taste. When we come apart, I trail a finger over the red line around her neck where she pulled off her necklace. "Did she give you the necklace?"

"No, someone else. Someone she was jealous of."

I'm so damn curious who gave it to her and whether I have reason to be jealous, but I don't want to sound insecure, so I keep quiet. Thankfully, Shae anticipates my curiosity and explains.

"I met a man about a month after I started seeing Mari. He was only in the country for a week, but that was all it took for me to be swept away."

This couldn't have been that long ago, and I'm suddenly questioning whether I really want to hear this story. With no way to back out, however, I force myself to listen.

"The pendant was a memento—a keepsake of the one that got away. I didn't realize then, but you helped me learn that being together is a choice. Even if it doesn't seem like a relationship is an option, there's always a choice. *Not meant to be* is a choice. He may have been memorable, but neither of us was willing to sacrifice anything to be together. That was a choice, and it meant he was never the one who got away. He was just a man who made me happy for a week. A man who helped me recognize what the right one truly felt like. Because when it's right, making a change doesn't feel like a sacrifice anymore. It feels like the freedom to be together."

"Fuck, I love you." I have to kiss her again. I'd do more than that if we weren't in public. For now, I settle for a toe-curling, intoxicating kiss that leaves us both breathless.

"Love you, too, Ren. Forever and always."

Epilogue

Three Weeks Later

Renzo

"THE PROBLEM IS THEY'RE DISORGANIZED," I EXPLAIN TO GINO. "The Albanians are at war among themselves, and the people associated with Mari's family are fringe at best. Identifying them hasn't been easy, so I've hired help."

"A PI or a contract?"

"Neither. There's a new agency in town that handles private security and investigative matters. Name's Viper Industries. I heard about them through the Genoveses. Guy who runs it is ex-cartel."

"I didn't think anyone was ex-cartel and still breathing."

"Me either, but from what I hear, this guy's the real deal. I met with him last week, so we'll see. I'm not letting this go until I at least get the four who took us."

Gino nods sagely. "I think you're right to push the issue. We don't need the problem spreading."

"Exactly." I start to stand from my desk chair when Gino raises a hand in a silent request to give him a moment.

"I think all of that sounds good, Renzo, but I'm concerned about your plan to send Sante off to Italy. He's already been through so much. We may be trying to help, but to him, it might look like yet another family member abandoning him."

I sink back into my chair, the weight of my worries making the mechanism groan. "I get it, Gino, I do. But I can't let him continue down the path he's headed. Between the booze and reckless behavior, it's like the kid's got a death wish."

He releases a weary breath. "I suppose you're right. He's my nephew, same as you, and I don't want to hurt him. Hopefully, time with the Donati cousins will give him a new perspective."

My lips thin, knowing where this is headed. "He's not staying with the Donatis. When I called to make the arrangements, Dad's cousin Francesco told me he'd recently been diagnosed with a brain tumor and is undergoing surgery soon. He can't take on a project like Sante right now. And I'm not familiar enough with any other individuals on that side of the family to ask for this sort of favor."

"So where's he going?" My uncle's tone is grim. He already knows the answer to his question.

"Lazaro Malgeri." My mother's cousin … in Sicily.

"Jesus, Renzo. The Sicilians are *ruthless*. They're a whole other breed."

"Don't you think I know that?" I bark back at him. "What other fucking option do I have? The kid is going to get himself killed here. And there's no point in arguing about it. I put him on a plane this morning. He either learns to swim or he drowns."

Gino glowers, but before he can say anything, Tommaso whirls into the room. His normally impassive eyes are spitting fire, his lip curved in a snarl.

"I begged you not to send him away. You told me this would be best for him, but I heard you just now. Drowning? That doesn't sound like what's best. You *lied*."

"It's not a lie." I'm back on my feet. "This is what's best for him. You want him to be tortured to death by the Russians? Because that's what would have happened if I hadn't stepped in. This is the only way I know to try to save him."

"And what about me?" He spreads his arms wide. "Having Sante here was the first time I felt like I had a friend. Someone who accepted me for who I am, and you stole that from me."

I can't win no matter what I do.

"Fuck, Tommy," I say on an exasperated breath. "I don't know what to tell you except that if you feel so hell-bent on staying together, go with him."

"You want me to go?" he asks in a hollow voice.

"No, I want you not to be pissed at me. Look, we can discuss this later, okay? We can figure out times you can visit or something, but for right now, I have somewhere to be." I have another thirty minutes before I technically need to leave, but I have to get away from this conversation.

I love running this family in so many ways. It's challenging and different every single day—I'm never bored. But dealing with bickering and personal problems, I could do without. I'm running a business, not a daycare. I know that's all part of the leadership gig, and it's not a problem most of the time, but it's more than I want to deal with today. Fortunately, I'm headed to see the one person I can count on to brighten my day rather than darken it.

Shae

"REMIND me what we're doing here?" Renzo peers up at the brownstone home where I told him to meet me while I punch in the code on the lock box to get access.

"I was talking with my real estate agent while we were doing paperwork for the contract on my apartment. I told her how we'd spent some time in Canada and how we'd both enjoyed certain aspects of a … *cozier* mountain-style home. She got excited and showed me pictures of this new listing she had, and I got a great vibe from it, so I asked if I could bring you over. She'd normally come with, but I really wanted to look at it with you alone." I gnaw on my bottom lip, my eyes doing a quick sweep of the entry. "I know we hadn't even talked about buying a place, but it spoke to me. It just felt like … *us*."

"I like what I see. Let's look at the rest."

We do a sweep of the main level, pausing in the front living room. I watch Renzo almost as much as I take in the space. The historic brownstone is a single-family home on a quiet street with mature trees lining the sidewalk. The previous owners did a phenomenal job honoring the home's history while modernizing with wide-plank wood floors and contemporary design elements incorporating a wealth of natural materials.

"I love the look and feel, but this is my absolute favorite

part." I lean my arm on the reclaimed wood beam that serves as a fireplace mantel. "*Ten* wood-burning fireplaces. All of them functional. How cool is that?" I ask excitedly, curious if Renzo will feel the same draw to the place as I do.

He slowly strolls over, his eyes locked on the iron grate staged with fresh wood. "It's incredibly cool," he finally says, amusement creasing the corners of his eyes.

"I know it's not a fancy high-rise—"

Renzo cups my face in his hands, smiling warmly. "Shae, it's perfect."

"Really?" Giddy anticipation raises my voice an octave. "We can go upstairs and see the rest. There's two more floors and even a fully finished basement with a gym."

"I'd like to look around, but I think I'm already sold. You're right. It does feel like us. Like home."

I'm so excited that I launch myself at him, hugging him with my arms wrapped tightly around his neck. "I'm so glad you feel it too because I sort of already made an offer." I pull back and give him a crooked smile. "I'd say I'm sorry, but that would be a lie."

Rolls of laughter rock his body. "Why am I not surprised?"

"Well, if that doesn't surprise you, I have one more thing for you that might." Nerves swell in my stomach and send a rush of tingles to my palms. I take a small step back and breathe in through my nose, out through my mouth. "Renzo Donati, in a short span of time, you have become the center of my world. You challenge and support me in ways that bring out the best in me, and I want nothing more than to do the same for you. You're my person. I love you with my whole heart and want to spend every day of forever tackling life together."

I pull a black titanium ring out of my pocket and drop to one knee. Renzo is so still, I'm not sure he's even breathing, and a flood of emotions passes behind his eyes. I try not to overanalyze his reaction because I'm trying to do this right, and if I worry about what he's going to say, I'll fuck it all up.

"You know I don't do anything by half measure. If we're a team, you're my ride or die for life, and I want the world to know. So … Renzo Agosto Donati, will you do me the honor of agreeing to be my husband?" Each word is more strained than the one before as emotion threatens to overcome me.

Renzo coaxes me to my feet, then gently plucks the ring from my hand, studying it like he's never seen a ring before. It makes me nervous.

"It's more of a wedding band than an engagement ring," I blurt. "But there doesn't seem to be such a thing as an engagement ring for a man, so that limited my options. If you're not crazy about it, we can exchange it. You don't even have to say yes, obviously. I know we haven't talked about it at all yet." I'm babbling. I know it, but I can't stop myself. I need him to say something and put me out of my misery.

He holds the ring between his thumb and finger, his smoldering stare finding mine. "This is the most touching, humbling gesture anyone has ever done for me. And coming from you, I'm speechless." He slides the ring on his finger, then cups my face like he does when he's at his most earnest. "I would be the proudest man on earth to be your husband. As you know, I've been calling you my wife since the first week we met."

"Awfully presumptive of you, but considering the circumstances, I'll let it slide." I beam at him, smiling like a golden retriever with a new tennis ball.

His eyes go soft with adoration before he kisses one

eyelid, then the other. "I love you, Shae. I live and breathe for you and can think of nothing better than to spend my life being Mr. Shae Byrne."

We come together in a kiss. My heart feels full enough to burst in a confetti explosion of sunshine and rainbows. I wouldn't even be sorry if it did because this love I feel for Ren is worth whatever price.

When we draw apart, I'm reminded of a gentle wave slowly receding from a sandy beach. Our connection is as unrelenting as the sea and its shore. Sometimes the waves may be turbulent, and others placid, but we will always find ourselves coming back together, one way or another.

"Neither of us are quick to put stock in fate, but today feels like an exception." Renzo reaches into his pocket and pulls out a small black velvet drawstring bag. "It just so happens that I picked up something for you on my way over here." He dangles the bag for me to take.

I'm so incredibly curious, and when I hold the item and feel what's inside, I'm even more curious because it's easy to identify. It seems like such an odd choice of gift. I open the pull strings and slide the small pocketknife onto my palm, recognition slamming into me. "It's the knife from the plane," I breathe in awe. The same white pocketknife I used to help us escape from the Albanians.

"Turn it over."

I do and see that a single word has been engraved into the metal handle.

Chaos.

"I found it in the wreckage and had to keep it. I like to think it's a fitting representation of my faith in you and a reminder of all we've been through together."

I had the same knife secretly stashed in my pocket the first time I asked him to trust me. And he did.

I'm stunned. I knew he'd found the plane crash because he came back with the names and information on the dead men inside, which we've been using to track down the others. I'd completely forgotten about the knife.

"Ren, this is so incredibly thoughtful." I love it so much. I'm not sure if I want to keep it with me and use it or frame it so I never lose it. "Thank you," I force past the emotion tightening my throat.

"Anytime, beautiful. Now, are we going to have a look upstairs or go straight to the jewelry store?"

"Jewelry store?" I ask, confused.

"The world needs to know you're mine, which means *you* need a ring."

I shake my head and laugh. "Impatient much?"

"Only when it comes to making you mine." The heat in his eyes darkens them to a dusky shade of midnight.

Warmth coils in my belly, then unfurls outward to my fingers and toes. "Maybe we take a quick trip upstairs before we go. You know … to have a look around … while we have the place to ourselves."

"We'd be negligent not to." He takes a step, forcing me back toward the stairs.

"I'm glad we agree," I respond distractedly, mesmerized by the grace of his movements.

"Shae?" he prompts in a velvety caress.

"Yes?"

"Move your ass before I take you here on the steps."

"Oh!" I gasp when my heels bump against the first stair.

Renzo is quick to steady me. I peer up at him to say thanks and am rendered speechless by the savage lust I see in his eyes. So predatorial. So primal.

He leans in close to my ear and whispers one single word. "*Run.*"

He doesn't have to tell me twice.

I whip around and bolt up the stairs, squealing in delight. I hear him close on my heels and know I'm the luckiest woman in the world.

Bonus Epilogue

Four Years Later

Shae

"I can't believe you talked me into this." I'm staring at the zipper of my leather skirt as if I can intimidate the damn thing into zipping the rest of the way shut. Considering I'm a full six months pregnant, the fact that I'm only now growing out of my clothes is a win, but it's still annoying.

My husband, the bastard, has the audacity to smirk at me. "As if anyone could talk you into anything you didn't want to do. *You* are just as guilty as I am, and you know it."

"Only because you're so damn cute." I glower at him with

enough playfulness that he knows I'm not serious. "If it hadn't been so tempting to see what a Renzo Junior would look like, I never would have entertained the idea."

He takes one measured step after another, hands casually resting in his pants pockets. I don't turn to face him. Instead, I watch him in our full-length closet mirror until he's standing right behind me. My heart pounds a little more forcefully at his approach, even after three years of marriage. I can't imagine ever being immune to that predatorial heat when it burns in his gaze.

"And what if Renzo Junior ends up being Shae Junior?" he asks huskily as his arms wrap around me so that his hands can cup the soft swell of my lower belly. His thumbs gently stroke my skin in a way that sends my heart and my hormones into overdrive.

"Then I guess we'll have to try again." My voice is a breathy shadow of its former self. Ever since the second trimester started and the sickness ended, the tiniest whiff of Renzo's cologne or the graze of his hand makes me feral with the need to mount him. I'm worse than a cat in heat.

Renzo couldn't be happier.

No matter how much I want to give him a hard time, I need him to give it to me hard even more, and he knows it. His lips tease the curve of my ear.

"Hands on the mirror," he orders in a dark rasp.

I press my hands to the cold surface. Renzo's hands trail down to the bottom of my offending red leather skirt and lift it over my hips. He grips me firmly and presses his hard cock into the crease of my ass. A wanton moan rolls past my lips.

"I don't have time to play, baby. I need you to give it to me."

He tsks as his hands slide back up my body and cup my swollen breasts. "I may have to keep you pregnant all the time, between that greedy pussy of yours and these incredible tits of yours."

"That's not … funny." My words hitch when he pulls the cups of my bra down and grazes his fingers over my nipples. They're so damn sensitive, he's had to learn to be extra gentle. And the piercings are gone. They were fun, but I never planned to keep them forever. Making a change is worth it for the right reasons. And no matter how much I joke, this little one means everything to me.

"My girl's too needy to play, is that it?"

I whimper as his hand drifts lower, dipping a finger beneath my panties and stroking my slit.

He inhales sharply through his teeth. "So fucking wet for me."

"Swear to God, Ren. You don't fuck me soon, I'll get out my vibrator."

His deep chuckle resonates from his chest to mine, driving me half mad. "I'd love to see you try."

Just when I think I might throw the ultimate tantrum, I hear the slide of the zipper on his pants.

Thank *Christ.*

I lean forward, pressing my ass out and arching my back. Renzo slides my panties to the side and plunges all the way inside me in one possessive thrust. My eyes roll back, lids drifting shut in blissful relief.

"This what you needed?" He pulls out an inch or so, then slowly glides back in. Once. Twice. Three times. He's teasing me. And I know with my man that the only way I'm going to get what I want when he's in a mood like this is if I beg. Lucky for me, Renzo's cock is the one and only thing on this planet I'm not too proud to beg for.

"Please, Ren. *Please,* give me more. I need it so bad." I press back, only to get a warning slap on my ass.

"Behave, Chaos, or you'll never get to dinner on time."

Fuck dinner. I want to come.

That's not true. I'm excited for this girls' night out, but damn, do these hormones make me crazy.

I clench my inner muscles tight and try to be good. Renzo groans when I squeeze him, his hands clasping my hips tighter. That's when I smile because I know it's coming.

I look up in the mirror and meet his ravenous stare with enough challenge to fray his control. He knows I'm testing him, but he's too far gone to hold back. Renzo slams into me, pistoning again and again at the perfect angle to melt my insides.

"Eyes ... on me," he demands when the pleasure starts to overwhelm me, and my eyes try to drift shut.

I do as he says, keeping that invisible connection intact. My lips part. My body sizzles. I'm so damn close, but I need something more, and he knows it.

"Touch that pretty pink clit of yours," he tells me through labored breaths. "Soak my cock with your cum."

He doesn't have to tell me twice.

I roll my fingers over my clit, the bundle of nerves primed and ready like kindling waiting for the smallest spark. My body ignites in release. Electric flames lighting my insides brighter than Times Square on New Year's Eve. Wave after wave of liquid pleasure takes over my bloodstream until I float away on the stuff.

"*Fuck,*" Renzo roars when my release triggers his. He pulses inside me, guiding his body into mine with slow, deliberate movements to savor the intense pleasure of his orgasm.

After a minute, he slides out of me, but I don't move from my position. I know my husband by now, and nothing makes him happier than watching his cum run down my thighs. I grin to myself, squeezing those muscles and internally preening when I hear his prideful hum of satisfaction.

"*Now* you can go to dinner," he murmurs distractedly.

I peer over my shoulder with a playful smirk. "Nice try, big guy." Men and their need to mark their territory. I'll never understand it.

He fights back a grin before bringing a warm wet rag back and gently cleaning up our mess. I'm already behind schedule, so there's no time for a shower. This will have to do.

"By the way, Ettore texted to ask if you'll be at the teamsters meeting next week." I snag a pair of stretchy jeggings from a drawer. They're not fancy, but they fit.

"Why the hell did he text you instead of me?"

Amusement tugs at the corners of my lips. It took a solid year to win over his men, including a number of physical fights in which I had to kick a few of their asses. But when they finally accepted that Renzo and I were a team, and that I wasn't going anywhere, they realized I was a hell of a lot more fun to work with than my husband. Another three years down the road, and every damn one of them would lay down their lives for me. I'm an acquired taste, like an aged whiskey. It burns at first, but once you get used to it, you realize there's nothing finer.

"He likes me better," I explain with exaggerated sympathy, brows knitted together as I shrug helplessly.

Renzo narrows his eyes to angry slits, playing along. "Just make sure they don't like you *too* much. You're mine."

I cross over to him and rise on my toes to give him a quick kiss on the lips. "I'm pretty sure that's well established, but I'll make sure to be annoying enough to keep them from falling at my feet."

My husband grunts, then smacks me on the ass. "Finish getting ready. I'll text Ettore."

◊

Renzo drives me to the restaurant where I'm meeting my friends. We're also family, for the most part. My sister-in-law Lina is bringing her sister Amelie, and Pippa's younger sister Aria is joining us. The other ladies are all my cousin's wives —not blood, but they might as well be.

We've become incredibly close-knit, especially since everyone started having babies. I'm not sure what's in the water, but it's potent. And a little scary. Noemi had twin boys three months ago, and her cousin Pippa is pregnant with twin girls. Their mothers were twins, so it runs in the Donati family. I have no clue how that stuff works. What I do know is they need to keep that shit to themselves. One kid at a time is plenty for me.

As expected, I'm late arriving, not by much, but enough that the rest of the ladies are already seated at the table. I'm met by a sea of smiling faces and warm greetings. That is, everyone except Pip, who gapes at me with her mouth open.

"You cannot be serious," she blurts as I take my seat at the table.

"I'm usually not, but what am I not serious about this time?" I ask, grinning.

"You are six months pregnant, and you're not even showing!"

I sit a little taller. "Actually, it took me five tries tonight to find something that still fit, thank you very much."

Pip places her palms on the table and slowly rises to her feet, unveiling her enormous belly. The entire table is silent for a beat before bursting into riotous laughter, me included.

"So not fair," Pip grumbles, dropping back into her seat.

"Oh … my God, Pip," I say through peals of laughter. "You're right, that's not fair."

"I'm only two months ahead of you!"

"With *twins*!" I remind her. "And if it's any consolation, I've had killer heartburn. I have to prop myself upright at night."

Her playful outrage melts with the hint of a smile. "I don't want you to feel bad, but yeah, that kinda makes me feel better."

I stick out my tongue, and we're all laughing again, Pip included.

"Noemi," I call to get her attention. "How are you holding up? How are the boys?" I know they've had a lot of help, but she's still been exhausted. This is the first time since she's had the twins that we've been able to get together as a group.

"They're doing amazing, and I think we're finally settling into a routine. It changes almost daily, but it's still sort of a routine. Sort of." Uncertainty lines her forehead, making us laugh.

"I can't even imagine what you've gone through." Twins, plus their three-year-old little girl who needs attention, too. It makes me tired just thinking about it.

"It would be absolutely exhausting if it weren't for Conner and all of you. The meals. Taking Luna out and giving her loads of love and attention. It's all been so incredibly helpful."

"That's what we're here for," Lina offers. "You reach out anytime you need us."

Stormy raises her water glass. "Hear, hear. I'll drink to that."

We all laugh and raise our glasses, the majority of which only contain water because most of us are either pregnant or breastfeeding. Lina, Amelie, and Aria are the only ones indulging in wine. I know that I could have a glass, but I don't feel the need. These ladies are plenty of fun without booze.

"Sweet baby Jesus," Aria breathes. "Do not look all at once, but there is one *fine* looking man at the bar."

Pip's eyes round. "That suit with those tats. Good God. I can't see his face from here, but I'm not sure I need to."

Noemi and I have our backs to the bar, so we both take sweeping glances over our shoulders as if merely appreciating the ambiance. We are comedically indiscreet in our efforts, making the whole table double over in stifled laughter.

"You single girls should definitely get a piece of that," Noemi whisper-shouts to Aria and Amelie.

"I'll thank you to stop corrupting my innocent little sister with such filthy suggestions," Pippa jokes in her best matronly tone.

A catlike grin stretches lazily across Aria's face. "I'd tell you to corrupt away, but that ship has sailed."

Pip gapes at her in mock horror. As everyone's laughing, I notice Amelie is being surprisingly quiet. And in fact, she looks rather pale.

"Amelie, you okay?" I ask quietly.

"Yeah." She nods and smiles, but it's not at all convincing. "Just a little tired."

"*Y'all, he's staring right at us,*" Stormy hisses in her adorable Southern drawl. "And he *is* beautiful but a little scary, too."

All attempts at discretion are abandoned, and those of us on my side of the table turn to take in the tattooed god behind us. Like Renzo, his tats tease up from beneath his shirt collar, but his ink also covers the backs of his hands, which I see as he lifts a glass of amber liquid to his full lips and drinks, eyes locked on our table.

Not our table. He's got only one person in his sights.

I turn back around to look at Amelie, who is now ghostly white.

"Holy shit," Noemi breathes beside me.

"Right?" Pippa chirps. "He looks like the best kind of trouble."

"Pip, do you seriously not recognize him?" Noemi shoots at her cousin, her voice losing all levity.

Everyone at the table quiets, turning somberly back to the man at the bar.

When Noemi speaks, her voice is a breath of heartbreak and hope. "That's my brother. Sante's finally come home."

Thank you so much for reading the *Craving Chaos*! While this was technically the last novel in *The Byrne Brothers* series, you'll see more of the characters you love in the spin-off series, *The Moretti Men*, which you can read more about below.

Devil's Thirst (The Moretti Men #1)
Amelie falls hard for a new neighbor with a secret identity … and a deadly obsession to claim her.

♦

Curious about Conner & Noemi?
Silent Vows **(*The Byrne Brothers* #1)**
Missed the first *Byrne Brothers* novel? In *Silent Vows*, Conner
chose his arranged marriage bride because she was mute,
thinking he wouldn't ever have to talk to her. But when he
learns Noemi was silent to protect herself from an abusive
father, he becomes obsessed with his new wife and vengeance
on her behalf.

♦

Stay in touch!!!
Make sure to join my newsletter and be the first to hear about
new releases, sales, and other exciting book news!
Head to www.jillramsower.com or scan the code below.

ACKNOWLEDGMENTS

As I mentioned in the dedication, this book wouldn't exist if it weren't for my readers who rallied for Shae. Thank you for inspiring me to come up with what has been one of my absolute favorite stories to write. Once the story formed in my head, it practically wrote itself. That is the *best* feeling!

My partner in crime, Sarah, is always the next crucial piece of any book. In most cases, I am grateful for every bit of feedback she gives me, though I couldn't get on-board with her bearologist suggestion this go-around. At least now I can say that technically the word bearologist did make it into the book, per her insistence. You're welcome.

Chris, Patricia, and Megan—your beta feedback is the cherry on top. Thank you!! I am so fortunate to have a team of incredible people helping me polish and promote my books.

I'd also like to thank authors like Tracey Garvis Graves who wrote *On the Island*—an incredible forbidden love story about two people stranded on an island together. Stories like hers and so many others gave me a passion for the trope. The intensity and desperation that bond two people to a point of no return. I can't get enough!

ABOUT THE AUTHOR

Jill Ramsower is a life-long Texan—born in Houston, raised in Austin, and currently residing in West Texas. She attended Baylor University and subsequently Baylor Law School to obtain her BA and JD degrees. She spent the next fourteen years practicing law and raising her three children until one fateful day, she strayed from the well-trod path she had been walking and sat down to write a book. An addict with a pen, she set to writing like a woman possessed and discovered that telling stories is her passion in life.

Social Media & Website

Release Day Alerts, Sneak Peak, and Newsletter
To be the first to know about upcoming releases, please join
Jill's Newsletter. (No spam or frequent pointless emails.)

Official Website: www.jillramsower.com
Jill's Facebook Page: www.facebook.com/jillramsowerauthor
Reader Group: Jill's Ravenous Readers
Follow Jill on Instagram: @jillramsowerauthor
Follow Jill on TikTok: @JillRamsowerauthor

Made in United States
North Haven, CT
17 February 2025

65883200R00205